the

Colors

of

Rain

a novel by
Abigail Hayven

CONTENTS

For the ones with a story but without a voice.

euismod lacinia at quis risus sed vulputate odio. Sed
euismod lacinia at quis. Ut tellus elementum
ricies lacus sed turpis tincidunt id aliquet
assa ultricies mi quis. Magna fermen-
llus. Eget sit amet tellus cras
vitae et leo duis ut diam
aculis eu non diam phasel-
Cursus sit amet dictum

llamcorper sit amet
per feugiat nibh
g elit duis tris-
mauris nunc
la fames ac
h mauris.
At

gray

fear; confusion; worry

EVAN

> "Crying is all right in its way while it lasts. But you have to stop sooner or later, and then you still have to decide what to do."
>
> C.S. Lewis, *The Silver Chair*

I THINK OUR STORY begins the day I threw Dickens' masterpiece, *A Tale of Two Cities*, at my bedroom wall. I can't tell you how much I hated that book that day. It wasn't Dickens' fault. It was definitely mine. But it turned out to be the best mistake I ever made.

I stared at the book lying discombobulated on my floor, spine bent awkwardly and pages creased in such a way that they'd never be the same again. Dad would've had a panic attack at such mistreatment of one of his beloved tales.

I ran my fingers through my hair, still matted with sweat and dirt from the garden. I needed a shower. I needed to read. I needed to fix our family. I needed to be someone Dad would be proud of. And more than anything, I needed a stupid story idea that I could write ten thousand words about.

You're confused, I guess. I'll lay a little groundwork.

Ava was a pistol. Mom and I could hardly stand it anymore. We were all grieving, but her grief turned to bitter anger and we were the victims. Not to compare, but I took my grief outside and grew a late summer garden out of it. Mom took to decorating the new house, making it a home. Ava shot looks that could cut skin and draw blood, gave us the silent treatment, and turned every anthill of a problem into a mountain.

"You ought to take up knitting or something," I quipped at her one day. She responded by slamming her bedroom door in my face. Maybe it was a bad idea after all. She might have stabbed someone with her knitting needles.

But as determined as she was to be miserable, I was just as determined to be the glue that held us together. I had promised that I would. In an attempt to keep that promise, I convinced Mom that what we needed was a new beginning—to run after the one dream we'd had as a family. It was Dad's dream first, and somehow, he inspired us to chase it too. He had a way of doing that—making anything seem like an exciting adventure. Once he was gone, making it happen seemed like the right thing to do, and Mom agreed.

Our quest for a new beginning landed us in Ivy Hollow, an unbelievably small town in the mountains of Virginia. Ava resented us for it. She hated being the new girl at school, and I'll give her that. Ivy Hollow kids grow up together and have friendships with roots as old as they are. Most of them are cousins. Basically, the schools are pretty clique-ish. I didn't exactly love my new school either, but I only had to endure it for one year. Ava was still in middle school.

The town itself was quaint and made smaller by an immaculate, mountainous view. It was everything you would imagine a small, country town to be like. Narrow roads going nowhere in particular. Shops four times my age with old-fashioned candy on one side of the store and garden rakes on the other. Made-to-order fried apple hand pies that would change your life could be found at the only gas station for fifteen miles.

As incredible as the hand pies were, Ivy Hollow High School seemed to be the whole town's pride and joy—especially the football team. It was totally unique to anything I'd ever experienced before, and it made my Chicago education seem mass-produced and sterile by comparison. The teachers were parents to the kids who went there, or they were close friends with whoever the parents were, which meant no funny business and created a close knit community that I'd never known before. Being called "sugar" and "darlin'" by my teachers definitely took some getting used to, along with all the deep southern accents and phrases that sometimes sounded like another language. It was different but not spectacular.

Except for one thing. One *girl*. Rain Brooks. She was a spectacular kind of different in the strangest sort of way.

On my first day of school, as I twiddled my thumbs and mentally assured myself that I wasn't nervous, she drifted across the classroom and claimed the desk next to mine. Her presence was ghost-like, the way she went unnoticed by the other students, instantly finding a place as close to the back of the room as possible, which is exactly where I wanted to be, too. Her eyes met mine for half a second as she passed by my desk until my gaze darted to the flash of color on her hand which gripped her backpack strap for dear life. She turned her back to me before I could make sense of what I'd seen.

I kept my attention toward the front of the class but listened as she plopped her bag down and slid into the creaking, wooden desk chair. My fidgeting turned into curiosity and I couldn't keep my eyes from sweeping over her as quickly as possible. The back of her left hand was painted. The image was of a stack of old books, and it spread from her knuckles to down past her wrist in pastel colors. The detail was incredible. I could almost feel their texture just by looking at them. But I looked too long, and I felt the blood rush to my face when our eyes met again. I darted my attention to the front of the class. From the corner of my eye, I saw Rain shimmy her denim jacket sleeve over her wrist to provide her artwork a little more coverage from the apparently unwanted attention.

Roll call began, and her name was called third. Rain Brooks. It stuck out like a sore thumb in contrast to the Hannahs, Rachels, and Abbys. But the uniqueness of her name seemed to match her character, considering her hand was painted and she dressed differently than the other girls. She wore a forest green T-shirt under her denim jacket tucked into a floral skirt which just hit her knees. Different colored paints stained her white sneakers, but I thought maybe I noticed a few tiny doodles of stars hidden in there, too.

"Here," she said when her name was called, raising her right arm. That's when I saw it. Her right hand didn't exist.

Each day after, I waited for her to sit next to me and would attempt to peek at what sort of masterpiece she'd have on her wrist that day. She started acknowledging me with a smile as she sat down and would turn her arm toward me for a few seconds to let me get a look. Midnight skies, flower fields, and vibrant patterns continually blew me away. I wondered how she painted it when she didn't have a right hand.

At lunch, she usually sat alone at a table toward the back, and for the life of me, I couldn't muster up the courage to sit with her. I walked into the cafeteria each day determined to but chickened out each time. So I sat at the opposite end of the room and watched her, telling myself tomorrow would be the day.

Usually, she had her face buried in a book. A Tale of Two Cities, to be exact, which I should have been reading too since it was required in our novel studies class. But what little bit I had read put me to sleep. Not to mention, it was one of Dad's favorite books. I'm not sure what made me neglect it more—being bored by it or being reminded of him every time I opened it.

A week into the new school year, I failed my first pop quiz on what I should have already read but still hadn't. I went home, determined to catch up. That was the night Mom finally snapped.

"I've had it, Ava!" I heard her yell from downstairs.

I huffed and stood from my desk chair; I had just sat down to try and squeeze in a few chapters before dinner. At my bedroom door, my hand resting on the knob, I waited. Mom was a generally quiet and laid-back person—always able to keep a level head even when the world around her crumbled to pieces. I saw it firsthand during Dad's cancer journey. Even in the midst of all of that, she never had outbursts like this.

"You shouldn't have moved me out here, then!" Ava yelled back. "You knew I didn't want to come."

"There are more people in this family than you. This is what's best for all of us."

I could almost feel Ava rolling her eyes. "Yeah, Dad dies so we up and leave everyone else in our lives to top it all off. It sucks here! We're in the middle of nowhere!"

"We all wanted this, including you. What happened?"

"*Dad* wanted this. This was supposed to be for him so he could quit his job and be with us more. What good is that now?"

"You'll meet new friends, and you'll love it here." Mom's voice wavered slightly. She was backing down.

My grip on the door handle tightened, ready to intervene if she needed me. I hoped she didn't need me. I was tired of feeling needed. And I hated myself for being so weak.

"I hate it here. I'll always hate it here. Dad wouldn't have made me go. If I didn't want to, he'd have stayed. I wish you'd died instead."

The following silence was louder than their yelling combined.

I exhaled, finally twisting the knob. When I reached the bottom of the stairs, Mom's eyes were filling with tears, but she was trying to remain strong. Ava appeared relentless, but I could tell she was on the verge of breaking down.

I put myself in the line of fire, sliding between their face-off to confront Ava. "Do you not hear yourself? How selfish you sound?"

Green eyes that matched mine refused to meet my questioning stare. Ava crossed her arms over her chest and darted her head to look at the wall like she didn't have an ounce of patience for this.

I shook my head and raked my fingers through my hair in an exasperated motion. "The world doesn't revolve around Ava Lawson. We don't all stay in stuffy Chicago because you say so. Mom doesn't die and Dad lives because it works better for your social life."

Ava's gaze finally met mine in challenge. "You're only saying that because you get your stupid garden and that's what you always wanted. I'm the only one who loses. It's not fair, and you know it."

It's true that in Chicago I had tomato plants and herbs basking in my bedroom window. Watering them was a mess, as I'm sure you can imagine. It took some creativity and a lot of plastic storage tubs, but year after year I did it, waiting for the day I could run my fingers through some real soil instead of having dirt stuck in my carpet and somehow making its way into my sheets at night. Ivy Hollow gave me that with our little yellow farmhouse perched on a hill, and all the earth I could dream of managing by myself to cultivate and bring a harvest from. But all the tomato plants in the world couldn't replace what I'd lost. My garden just kept me from losing my mind over what I would never get back.

"You're wrong," I said, slipping my fists into my hoodie pocket and lowering my voice. "We've all lost something, and we're all just doing our best to rebuild. Why don't you grow up and help us? Quit fighting it."

Ava didn't respond. She turned on her heel and stormed upstairs.

I waited until I heard the slam of her door before I released my last angry sigh and turned to Mom who had her hand covering her face.

9

"Were we wrong?" she asked in a whisper. "Should we have left everything behind for this?"

I looked back at the stairs where Ava had just made her dramatic exit. Dad handled her so much better. He was always getting through to her in a way I couldn't, no matter what I did. He held us together without even seeming to try.

I attempted to give Mom a reassuring smile. "I think it'll just take time to see the reward."

She looked as hopeless as I felt, the way she fixed her gaze on the floor and brought her arms tightly around herself. "I hope you're right."

I didn't get caught up on my reading that night. Or the night after that. Everything seemed to take top priority over Dickens, whether it was warranted or not. Looking back, though, my negligence was just the first of a series of events that made up a story even greater than Dickens'. At least in my humble opinion.

The plot began to escalate one day after school. When driving through the historic part of Ivy Hollow, I saw Rain secure a bicycle against a light pole and then walk into one of the shops. She had ridden her bike there. In the rain.

I passed her by in my truck, tapping my finger on the steering wheel, trying to decide what to do with the urge to follow her. Raindrops pecked at my windshield, and I could tell by the hostile clouds ahead that I wouldn't be able to kill time in my garden when I got home. In an attempt to keep out of the house just a little longer, I made a loop through town and decided to try out the antique store she'd walked into—for non-creepy reasons of course. I'd been wanting to go in since we moved to Ivy Hollow anyway.

I parked my truck across the street and jogged over with my head down to block the rain from my eyes. The smell of time wafted over me when I pushed my way through the door—dust, old wood, and paper. An elderly man with bright blue eyes and a half smile greeted me as he organized shelves of trinkets, but I didn't see Rain anywhere.

I made my way slowly around the store, looking at the different displays. Some things were more than twice my age and would likely outlive me. It made me wonder how many owners they'd gone through. How many photos of mortal beings had slid in and out of the tarnishing gold frames? How many bundles of mail had been brought in from the mailbox and laid on the old desk? How many homes had displayed and relied on the grandfather clock as it ticked through its allotted time before it finally ran out and was sent away to start a new life?

I shook my head to clear it as I set down a silver letter opener. Dad's death had me thinking about weird things like the fragility of time.

Most antique stores I'd been to were messy, and shopping was hard work, but this one was organized and tasteful. A wall full of paintings caught my eye, and I made my way over to look at them. One depicted the mountains and an incredible, dazzling sunset. Another was a desk with a book and a candle, placed in front of an open window where a gloomy rain fell. None of them were realistic; all of them were done in abstract strokes. It wasn't wild, yet it wasn't tame. It wasn't messy, but it definitely wasn't neat. It was complicated and incredible. They sort of reminded me of something you'd see in an illustrated children's book but with much more detail. I would have recognized the art style

11

anywhere by that point, but as if to confirm my suspicion, the initials "RB" were at the bottom, left-hand corner of each one.

"Your coffee's done," I heard a voice say, and I turned to see Rain walk out of a back room, carrying a mug to the old man. Her damp hair was now pulled up into a lively bun on top of her head, and she had new clothes on. Her eyes met mine, and she smiled politely.

I nodded my head at her and returned my gaze to the art. A moment later, she was by my side.

"Can I help you find anything specific?" Her eyes looked sheepishly from me to the paintings.

I fought the urge to smile at her slight southern twang. While the accents took getting used to, they intrigued me. It added a little bit of extra personality to the town. Rain's accent was more faint but still there.

I pointed to the gallery wall. "Did you paint these?"

Her eyes stayed fixed on the art, refusing to meet mine, as her cheeks tinted a light shade of pink. "I did," she said and pushed the black-framed glasses higher on her nose.

I admired again the swirl of colors, the blending, and the character of every piece. Each scene could have been studied for hours to truly appreciate the immense detail she'd put into them. "They're incredible," I told her.

Rain tensed up and rubbed her right forearm with her palm, which made me look over the art on her hand again. Earlier that day it had Big Ben with a night sky surrounding it, displayed from her wrist to her fingertips. Now it was pretty much smeared off. Only a few constellations remained. I wondered how she could stand it. To put so much work into a masterpiece, knowing that by the end of the day it would be gone forever.

"So... you never answered my question," she said quickly, seeming anxious to turn my attention away from her art. "Are you looking for something specific?"

I slipped my hands into my front pockets and shrugged my shoulders. "Oh, no. I'm just killing time." Killing time. Filling silence. Staying busy. I felt like that's all I ever did anymore.

"Killing time," Rain repeated, but in a voice that sounded like a soft lament. "That's a shame. We don't get enough as it is, you know." Her lips were gathered to one corner in a sad sort of smirk.

My mouth hung open slightly waiting for my brain to come with any sort of response at all. It was such an odd thing to say, but it hit me deep. She sure had a way of digging up emotions and memories and throwing them in my face.

Rain gave a knowing smile, like she could see that her words had evoked something in me. It made me feel eerie. "Well, just let me know if you end up needing me," she said, using the stub of her handless arm to push a stray curl away from her eye.

I blinked a few times as she walked off and shook my head for the second time, trying to clear my mind. Normally, conversations with antique store employees didn't have that sort of effect on me.

A few minutes later, Rain had a ladder out and was filling the wall's bookshelves with old volumes. I couldn't help but watch as she climbed with her one hand, a stack of books in the bend of her other arm. I was afraid she'd fall, but it seemed effortless to her. That is, until one of the books tumbled from her arm and hit the wood floor with a hollow sort of thud that echoed invasively through the otherwise silent antique shop. I immediately walked over to grab it.

"*Great Expectations*—also by our good friend Dickens," she said, watching me bend down to grab it for her.

I must have visibly cringed because her eyes squinted curiously as I handed the book up to her.

"How do you like *A Tale of Two Cities* so far?"

I rubbed the back of my neck, feeling my face go warm. "I've hardly read any of it to be honest. I'm pretty behind."

Rain shuddered with disbelief and excitement—the most animated I'd ever seen her. "But it's so good! Just wait 'til you read the end." A flicker of pride wandered across her expression. "This is my second time reading it."

I smirked, unable to keep from reacting to her obvious thrill. How it came from dusty old books like the ones cramming the shelf in front of us, I would never understand. "I'm not sure I'll be able to get through it once, let alone twice. Reading has never really been my thing."

Rain slid the book onto the shelf gingerly, as if she wanted to show it affection with her touch. She and Dad would've gotten along well. "How much you miss."

I pointed to the smudging scene on the back of her hand in a desperate attempt to rid myself of the thoughts of Dad that she seemed to constantly stir up. "How do you decide what you'll paint?"

I held my breath and watched cautiously as she released her grip on the ladder and leaned her weight on it to stay steady. She brought her hand close to her face to look it over, making me think she must be near blind to need to look so closely at something to see it clearly. I respected her immense eye for detail even more if that was the case.

"Different things inspire me," she said. "Sometimes it's what I have planned that day, or the weather, or emotions, or what I'm reading. Stuff like that."

I leaned my shoulder against the bookshelves and crossed my arms over my chest, the old, rough wood picking at my T-shirt and poking my skin. "So what about Big Ben?"

"That would be from what I'm reading. Or *rereading*, I should say. *Peter Pan*. It's one of my favorites." Her finger ran across the volume spines until it landed on a copy of said book. Her gaze lifted and her expression lit up slightly, as if she were seeing something invisible to the rest of us, like fairies and pirates straight out of the story. "I think that if I were a book, I would be *Peter Pan*." The second funny thing she'd said that day.

I wasn't sure if I should chuckle or take it seriously. For a girl who loved to read so much, she sure was hard to read herself. I couldn't figure her out, and maybe that's why she interested me so much. Rain wasn't what I'd call eccentric. She blended in and stood out all at the same time. She was like the poetry Dad used to read at the dinner table sometimes—a small amount of words with a lot of power behind them.

"Why is that?" I asked, trying to recall what little bit I remembered from the story of *Peter Pan*. Though all I knew about it came from the various movie adaptations I'd watched as a kid.

Rain shrugged and continued her work. "I don't know. I just think it matches me well. Or maybe I've read it so many times I've started to become like it. That happens, you know."

I definitely *didn't* know. "I'll take your word for it."

Rain slid the last book into its place on the shelf and climbed down the ladder. She stood in front of me, almost like she was sizing me up—challenging me. I hadn't noticed how short she was until then. The top of her head hardly reached my chin.

"You can learn to enjoy anything if you set your mind to it," she said.

"I'm not so sure about that."

She bent down to a cardboard box packed with books at the foot of the ladder, grabbing another arm full. "Well then, you have a *very* long and boring road ahead of you. A *Tale of Two Cities* is anything but short."

I snorted. "I've noticed."

Rain climbed back to the top before looking down to give a reassuring smile. "The end is worth it. I promise."

And that was the extent of my first conversation with Rain Brooks.

On the morning that I threw A *Tale of Two Cities* at my wall, Rain's hand was painted in a variety of bright colors. No shapes or patterns. Just colors exploding everywhere. It popped in contrast to her outfit which was a simple white T-shirt tucked into her ripped jeans with her usual sneakers. Her jeans were stained with paint. I was beginning to notice that everything she owned was stained with paint.

As she took her seat next to mine in homeroom, I leaned closer to her desk. "What's today's based on?"

"Emotion, I guess. Today's a good day, and I felt creative," she said, tucking that unruly strand of hair behind her ear again. "Are you caught up and ready for the quiz in novel studies today?"

My heart skipped a beat, and my hand flew to my forehead. I'd forgotten all about the quiz. Every three chapters, we were quizzed to see what we'd retained. This would be the fourth I'd failed.

Rain's face fell in what I could swear was disappointment in me. "I'll take that as a no."

A twang of guilt rose in my chest as a result, though I didn't understand why her opinion mattered to me so much. I wanted to defend myself, and I almost did. I could have told her about Ava and how she'd been stirring up disarray in our family since Dad's death. I could have told her it was his favorite book and I didn't care to pick it up just yet. But that would've been weird. So I turned to face the front of the class instead, hoping the day would fly by.

Later in novel studies class, the cliff notes I'd found online during lunch weren't enough to help me pass. Mrs. Jones made me stay late as a result.

I stood in front of her desk, feeling the stares of the other students burning my back. Mrs. Jones waited patiently for the class to empty before she made eye contact with me.

"We're not even two months into the school year and you're already falling behind, Mr. Lawson. You aren't even trying to read it, are you?" she asked, removing her cat-eyeglasses and setting them on her desk.

"No, ma'am," I admitted.

"Do you have a good excuse?"

I ran my fingers up and down the backpack straps hanging over my shoulders. Maybe I did. Maybe the fact that it was Dad's favorite would have sufficed, but I wouldn't play the grief card. I'd had enough people feeling sorry for me over the past few months. And besides, I still couldn't entirely convince myself, let alone her, that I wasn't avoiding it just because I was bored.

"I just haven't prioritized it, I guess."

She looked me over as if trying to decide what she'd do with me, bringing a finger to her fuchsia-tinted lips.

I liked Mrs. Jones. Actually, she was my favorite teacher. She was the sort of enthusiastic teacher you heard people talk about making an impact on their lives well into their adult years. And I could tell that, like Rain, she loved and respected the books she had us reading. She wanted us to enjoy them, too.

Mrs. Jones's face softened and she reclined in her chair, as if finally resolved. "Alright, Evan. I'm going to give you an opportunity to make up your grade. I'm giving you a writing assignment."

"Writing?" I said it too fast. Dread laced my voice, and I didn't even mask it a little. I hated writing even more than reading.

Mrs. Jones snickered at my obvious dislike of the project. "Yes, writing. I think if you had more respect for the talent of authors, you'd be more apt to prioritize their work."

I doubted it would produce the results she was looking for, but I didn't say so.

"I want you to tell a story. It can be fiction or nonfiction, but it needs to be at least ten thousand words."

My jaw must have nearly hit the floor. "Ten thousand?"

"Dickens wrote over one hundred thousand in a A *Tale of Two Cities*." A gloating smile formed in the corners of her mouth, like she was personally proud of his achievement.

I frowned. "He could've done a little less. It wouldn't have hurt my feelings any."

Mrs. Jones looked like she didn't want to chuckle, but she did and then waved it off. She laced her fingers together on her desk in front of her before getting serious again. "I'm giving you plenty of time to do it. Time to do it well, not time to procrastinate, mind you. You have until November."

I released a heavy sigh as I thought the task over. How in the world was I going to come up with a story to write that many words about? I knew figuring that out would be half the battle.

"And don't forget to catch up on your reading, too. Besides, you'll need all the inspiration you can get. The two most important steps to becoming a good writer are lots of reading and lots of practice."

As I walked the halls to my next class, eyes practically rolled into my head, the fire alarm went off, just to add to the excitement of my day.

I came to Ivy Hollow looking for a new beginning, but I hadn't known that I would have to build it from the debris of the life I'd had before. If I'm being honest with myself, I wanted to run from the problems, but they were still there. I still saw Dad between the lines of his favorite books and in the items at antique stores. I still had Mom and Ava's grief to try and mend, even with a new set of distractions. And I still had to be a kid, keeping up with school when I felt ready to leave it behind and become the man my dad wanted me to be.

And that brings us to the real beginning of our story, because that's why I threw A Tale of Two Cities at my bedroom wall that night.

R A I N

> "I believe the nicest and sweetest
> days are not those on which anything
> very splendid or wonderful or
> exciting happens but just those that
> bring simple little pleasures,
> following one another softly, like
> pearls slipping off a string."
>
> L.M. Montgomery, *Anne of Avonlea*

JO ONCE TOLD ME when I was very young that we all live out a story but only some of us are born with one. She was wrong. I think we're all born with one. Some just happen to have a plot twist very early on, like mine.

It's a story I've known all my life. It's hard not to ask questions when you have one less hand than everyone else. And while it seems unique to those around me, it has never been a shock to me. I never gasped upon hearing it told. I never experienced a revelation of pieces coming together. It just was.

But that isn't to say it never hurt. It isn't to say I never cried myself to sleep over it or spent days battling the negative thoughts that waged war on my joy and threatened to make my life miserable.

It was also never a secret. Not until Jordan came. And trusting Evan to write my story meant risking it all.

But we're getting ahead of ourselves.

I heaved a sigh of relief when the fire alarm went off during math class. I hated math class. It was only a drill, of course, and the deafening squeal of the siren was a welcome interruption.

As our class stood and formed a line to exit the building, Evan was just making his way into the classroom. I'd heard Mrs. Jones tell him to stay after class, and I could only assume it meant that his efforts to cram over lunch were in vain. It was only fair, but I still felt sorry for him. He dropped his bag by his desk with an air of drama that I couldn't help but snicker at once my back was turned to him.

We were the first class to make it to the parking lot and were directed to sit in the schoolyard grass while we waited for everyone to evacuate. I chose a spot decently far off from the others. Jo says I have a magnet somewhere inside me that draws me to solitude no matter where I am. It isn't necessarily the solitude that draws me in though—it's the view. I like being able to scan the room and take in the action without having to be a part of it. It's far more enjoyable to be on the outside looking in than on the inside being observed.

Evan followed me absently, like he wasn't even thinking about it. I wondered if he had a magnet inside, too.

"I take it that you and Dickens aren't on good terms," I said, trying to make conversation as he plopped down beside me.

He leaned his weight on his arms behind him and lifted his head to let the sun hit his face. "You could say that."

Across the schoolyard I saw Thomas evacuating with his class and being directed where to wait. He settled his wheelchair and waved at me when our eyes met. I waved back with a smile. "I can't imagine Mrs. Jones being too hard on you."

In my peripheral vision, I saw Evan whip his head toward me, and I turned to face him again. His expression seemed to say, "Wanna bet?"

"She gave me a writing assignment to make up my grade," he mumbled. "I have to tell a *ten-thousand* word story."

My eyes enlarged. "Ten-thousand?" I picked a few blades of grass and rubbed them between my fingers. I'd known Mrs. Jones most of my life, and it was she and Mr. Clark who were sole-ly responsible for my book addiction. She always gave me the best book suggestions when I was a kid—stories I would devour quicker than she could recommend them. She knew what she was doing. She was showing Evan the beauty of storytelling, whether he realized it or not.

I offered a sympathetic smile in his direction, though he'd hardly made eye contact with me at all since sitting down. "I know I ought to feel sorry for you, but I honestly think it's brilliant of her."

Evan didn't respond but followed my example of picking grass. His movements were quicker and more rigid than mine. The still-blaring fire alarm likely wasn't helping to calm him either.

"What will you write about?" I asked.

A heavy sigh from deep in his chest left his lips. Such drama. "Deciding that will be the hardest part," he said.

If it had been me, I'd have probably had a hard time stopping at ten-thousand words. I always thought that maybe one day I'd write a book, but I hated typing. It took forever with just one hand, and it always made it cramp up. So I typically stuck to shorter things like an occasional poem. But mostly, I preferred sitting at the feet of the masters—like Dickens, Austen, Barrie, Lewis, and Montgomery—and hearing the tales they'd composed in a much better fashion than I could have. When I got my creative itch, I couldn't keep from picking up a paintbrush, and it left little time for me to pick up a pen.

I crossed my legs in front of me and leaned forward. "But it's also the funnest part. You can create another world, a plot, amazing characters—"

The closest thing to a smile that I'd seen since we'd sat down tugged at his lips. I felt my cheeks go red. I was pretty sure he was trying not to laugh at me. "I think I'll be keeping it simple. It definitely won't be fiction. I can't create something out of thin air."

It was my turn to smirk. I couldn't help it. "You're right," I gloated, not bothering to constrain the pride in my voice, "authors like Dickens must be pretty talented to be able to accomplish something like that."

The glare Evan cast through squinted eyes told me he wasn't amused. "It isn't that I don't respect their work, I just don't enjoy it."

I shook my head hopelessly. I never understood or sympathized with those who disliked reading. Written words were practically my lifeblood; stories gave my heart its rhythm, while colors gave my world its meaning.

But Evan was new to Ivy Hollow, and something about him provoked pity in me, though I couldn't quite pinpoint what. I laid down my prejudice and surrendered myself to doing the right thing. "Well, if I can help in any way," I told him, "I'll gladly do it. I can give you some books to help inspire you."

He responded with a sarcastic chuckle. "I think I already have enough reading to keep me busy."

The fire alarm turned off, sending a welcome quiet over the schoolyard, and that was the end of my conversation with Evan.

Walking back to class, I wondered what exactly it was about him that grabbed my attention. Ever since the beginning of the school year, he had made an effort to talk to me. I didn't mind, but I also didn't exactly care to encourage it either. I'd never been a social butterfly when it came to school. I had my people—Jo, Mr. Clark, Thomas, and even Mrs. Jones from time to time—and they were more than enough for me. But there was something about Evan. Something genuine and kind that drew me in. And I felt bad for him. No one liked being new. I didn't have the heart to brush him off.

I didn't know much about him and his family, except for the gossip and hearsay I'd heard around town. The fact that he, his mom, and sister had moved here from Chicago was all agreed upon, but everyone in town seemed to have a different explanation as to why. Jenny who worked at the diner had told me his parents divorced and that his mom wanted to get far away. Mr. Calvin at the grocery store had said his dad was in the military and they decided to settle here. Mr. Clark heard from someone else that Evan's dad was in prison. But I didn't take any of it as truth. Two things grow fast in Ivy Hollow—our corn crop and rumors.

At work after school, I told Mr. Clark all about Evan's project. He agreed with Mrs. Jones and I, of course.

"It'll be hard for him though." I stood in the front window, working to rearrange the display. "Especially since he isn't a reader."

Mr. Clark blew the dust off an old book and squinted behind his glasses to see the title. "If I were him, I think I'd become a reader."

"I tried to suggest that."

His eyes lifted to meet mine with a look of doubt. "You might need to help him, Rain."

"I don't think he wants my help, but I did offer." I pulled a rag from my pocket and began scrubbing vigorously at a streak on the front window. How it managed to get so grimy I didn't understand.

Mr. Clark had been working slowly through the new inventory he'd picked up at an estate sale that morning, but he stopped to rest in his worn wingback chair off to the right of me. He lowered himself down into the chair slowly; he was getting a little slower with each day, and watching him from the corner of my eye sent a pang through my chest.

"It makes me think of something I read this morning," he said, reaching over to the nearby end table to grab his coffee mug.

I stopped my scrubbing to glare at him over my shoulder. "You didn't read *Frankenstein* without me, did you?"

Mr. Clark waved an aged, quivering hand in front of his face as he sipped his coffee. He swallowed and gave a satisfied sigh as he set the mug back down. "No, no. I've started reading *War and Peace* again."

Content with his answer, I went back to scrubbing. "Oh, really? And what did you read this morning that comes to mind?"

I thought about the first time I read through *War and Peace* for myself at ten years old. That had been quite a volume to tackle. It was one of the very few books whose movie adaptation I liked better. Audrey Hepburn playing the role of Natasha was pure perfection.

Mr. Clark cleared his throat before reciting the quote. "'Nothing is so necessary for a young man as the company of intelligent women.'"

My scrubbing came to a halt again as I repeated the quote to myself in my head. "Hm. That is a thought," I said. "Do you think it's true?" I turned and watched a smile lift his wrinkled cheeks.

"I can't speak for every man, but I can speak for myself." He removed his glasses and began rubbing the smudges away with his green-and-blue plaid shirt. "Bonnie was very intelligent. She made me want to act smart, knowing good and well I was a young fool. So I'd say she was very good for me—Lord knows, the very best thing for me."

I couldn't help but smile, too. Even after four years of being separated by death, he was still so in love with Mrs. Clark. But then, Bonnie Clark was one who could never be forgotten by anyone who had met her.

"Well, there must be a little truth to it, then," I said.

Once the glaring streaks in the front window had been dealt with, I turned my attention to the display. I liked to change the window display out often, especially with the seasons. It was September, and it was at that beautiful point where summer lingers and fall approaches, and they collide into a kiss. You can feel the heat of summer but smell the breeze of fall. Summer memories linger like a dream, but autumn lures you in with that wistful desire for change and something new.

Maybe you don't know the feeling. Anyway, it inspired me to change out the window display.

The centerpiece of my display was the beautiful, refurbished 1950's typewriter that we'd just gotten in. It was sleek black with a shine you could almost see your reflection in. It was another product of Thomas's handiwork, and this time, he'd truly outdone himself.

I set it up in the window on a roll-top desk, next to a vintage teacup and a candlestick close by. I decorated the top of the desk with a few vintage books and a set of gold swan bookends from the '70s. It felt cozy and creative and—to me—like the epitome of autumn.

That evening, Jo got off work early and brought dinner to the shop for Mr. Clark and I. "The window looks wonderful, Rain," she said as she walked into the store. "You'll have all those items sold before we get to thoroughly enjoy your work."

I walked over to the door to flip the sign to the CLOSED side. "That would mean I've done my job well."

My favorite time of the workday was closing time. If Mr. Clark and I closed the store together, we would usually sit sipping tea and coffee while I read aloud. We were reading *Frankenstein*.

Mr. Clark had always been like a grandfather to me and the closest thing to a father figure that I ever had. And I can't complain one bit. He and Mrs. Clark had been right beside Jo and I all my life. They babysat me while Jo worked, watched me take my first steps, came to every birthday party, and were always there to walk me through whatever it was I faced. They couldn't have been more like family if we'd shared blood.

That evening, Mr. Clark and I sat in our wingback chairs while Jo sat at my feet. We all enjoyed burgers and milkshakes from Shirley's—the local diner—and watched the sun set outside the store window. Red, yellow, and orange covered the canvas of the sky and seeped into the store as Jo told us stories from her day at the hospital, Mr. Clark made us laugh, and I took it all in.

It was mundane, sure. But it was perfect.

This was my family. This was my life. And I didn't want it ever to change.

A week from the day of the fire drill, Evan stopped by the antique store again. "Killing precious time or is there something I can help you with?" I asked as I swept the floors.

He gave me a smug look, sliding his hands into the back pockets of his jeans. He wore a green shirt that matched his eyes and square-toed leather boots. He matched the look of our town, and I wondered if he was trying to fit in or if he dressed that way in Chicago, too.

"Actually, there are two things you can help me with."

I leaned my broom on the wall and slipped my hand into the pocket of my sweater. "Oh, really?"

"First, I was wondering if I could get a closer look at the typewriter in your window."

My eyebrows lifted. I was surprised, considering he didn't care a whit about reading or writing. "You planning on writing a story or something?" I teased.

"Yeah, something like that."

I led him to the front and retrieved the typewriter off the desk to set it down on a nearby wooden trunk. I watched as he leaned over it, studying and admiring it. Even more surprising was that he knew what he was looking at. He lifted the ribbon cover and played with the insides, examining the ribbon and checking to see if any of the keys were stuck or bent.

After a few minutes of looking it over, he glanced back at me and smiled in response to my curious expression. "If my dad were alive, I would have bought it for him," he said. His Adam's apple rose and fell, and he kept an uneasy smile on his lips, like he was trying to act indifferent to the words he'd just said.

So that was the story. His dad had died.

"He used to drag me through antique stores all the time just to look at them. I couldn't have cared less about them then." Evan lifted a finger to scratch the side of his face as he blinked a few times. "He never found one that worked well enough to justify the price. Does this one work? It looks to be in great shape."

I brushed some imaginary dust off the back of the typewriter and tried to think of a way to move the conversation along, seeing he was uncomfortable. "It was just refurbished, and I've tested it myself. Actually, the guy who fixed it goes to school with us. He's younger than us, but maybe you've seen him. Thomas Helms. He's in a wheelchair and almost always wears some kind of nerdy movie T-shirt."

A look of recollection lit up his face. "Yeah, I've seen him." Evan's eyes didn't leave the typewriter. He must have been weighing the pros and cons of the purchase in his mind. "I don't know why I want it. I'll never use it."

But I knew why. It was a sentimental thing for him. Oftentimes, the things in an antique store are. They hold pieces of the past that we don't want to forget, even though we don't need them. After all, there are far more efficient tools and items now, but we like to hang on to those little time capsules sometimes. Too often, though, we can't seem to justify the price of sentiment the way we can practicality. It's sad, really.

"I bet Mrs. Jones would give you extra credit for typing your story on a typewriter," I said, trying to add practicality to justify the sentiment.

Evan's eyes met mine. "That's the other thing I came to ask you about." He seemed grateful to leave behind the topic of the typewriter and the memories it triggered, and I had a feeling I wouldn't be selling it that day, despite my stellar window display. "I wondered if maybe you could give me some ideas. I've spent all week trying to think of something worth writing so many words about, and I've got nothing to show for it."

I turned to the long wall of books stretching the length of the store. Countless titles of inspiring stories filled those shelves. I made my way over to them, and Evan followed. "What sort of stories interest you?" I asked. "Since you don't read books, think movies, news headlines—things like that."

Evan was silent a moment. His deep green eyes lifted to the top shelf absently as he thought. I took in their color and decided I would mix paint and create his shade that night.

"Realistic stories," he said finally. "Or at least a story that makes me believe it's possible."

I climbed the ladder and began thumbing over the spines of various fictional adventures. My attention shifted to my right, and I gripped the shelf to pull my weight and the ladder over to the biographies—stories of war heroes, missionaries, royalty, holocaust survivors, and everything in between. "Okay, so write about someone you know. Write the life story of a family member or even your own story." I looked down over my shoulder at him. "Write about coming to Ivy Hollow."

Evan snickered. "It wouldn't be very interesting."

"It could be. We all have a story. A good storyteller can make any person a compelling character and any mundane plot worth reading. Not because the person isn't already compelling or the events aren't already worth investing in, but because they're talented enough to pen the things we often aren't able to translate. They get into our heads and then preserve the things we don't have the courage or ability to fully express."

Evan stared at me with a combination of confusion and surprise.

I became fidgety, and my hand gathered the loose hair at my neck to create a ponytail. Playing with my hair was a nervous tick of mine. At least that's what Jo said. A dead giveaway of my plaguing insecurity.

The empty silence killing me, I tried another approach. "I guess what I'm trying to say is that a good storyteller is able to show us the value of the mundane."

Evan's lips curved into a smirk, and my face warmed. I must have sounded ridiculous. But then his eyes were searching mine, and I imagined I saw a longing in his gaze, like he didn't quite understand me but wanted to.

I internally rolled my eyes at myself and climbed down the ladder. It was a ridiculous thought. I sounded crazy, and his smirk was an attempt not to laugh.

Evan grabbed a random book from the shelf directly in front of him and began fanning the pages. It made me notice his hands. They were calloused and scratched from some form of hard work.

"I just know that I'm not that kind of a storyteller. Heck, I'm not a storyteller at all. I need something to work with."

"What you're looking for is a significant plot twist," I said. "If you ask someone the right questions, you'll realize we all have a plot twist. Even you."

Evan closed the book and put it back on the shelf in the wrong place.

I cringed, fighting the urge to fix it. I'd put it back later.

"Well, I think you've gathered my plot twist already, and I just got through living it. I can't say I care to write about it now."

I bit my lip, wishing I hadn't suggested it. I didn't blame him. I knew better than anyone what it meant to face a messy past, and dissecting it wasn't for the weak. It took me years to finally be at peace with my own. Years of questions I knew might never be answered. Years of pain I had to keep from controlling my outlook on life.

Almost like he was reading my thoughts, Evan smirked again. "What about you? What's your plot twist?"

I didn't care for the twisting feeling in my stomach as the conversation shifted. I shrugged a shoulder and walked across the room to grab my broom again. My hand shook a little.

"My plot twist is complicated," I said and looked up from my task long enough to the spark of curiosity gleaming in Evan's eye.

"Complicated makes for a good story."

I chuckled dryly. He had no idea. "Writing my story would be biting off more than you care to chew."

"Try me." Evan stepped forward to grab my attention, and his eyes both challenged and begged me at the same time.

I wasn't intimidated. I felt invited. I shook my head, trying to shake the feeling, too.

Evan grabbed the boom handle. He was smiling suspiciously. "Is it a secret?"

Either his smile was contagious or my nerves were getting the better of me—probably both—but I couldn't help but smile back. "Not really," I said, pulling the broom away and crossing the room as I swept. I wasn't being at all thorough, just nervously pushing dust around. "Most people around here know at least a big part of it. I'm adopted for starters, and my birth story isn't exactly traditional." With a town as small as Ivy Hollow, there weren't many secrets. Plenty of people knew mine and Jo's situation, and it wasn't a big deal.

Evan seemed to be thinking through the different scenarios that could make up my secret. "An adoption story sounds interesting," he said. He was dead serious.

I froze my task and blinked at him a few times. "Do you honestly want to write about me?"

He had no way of knowing, but my adoption story wasn't for the faint of heart. It had its good parts for sure, but it wasn't exactly a well-rounded, heart-warming tale.

Evan's lips bent downward into a thoughtful frown. "Maybe. Why not? I haven't found anything better. I feel like the story of the local artist who shows up to school with a masterpiece painted on her hand each day would be worth writing."

I searched his eyes, wondering if he was making fun of me, but he seemed completely genuine.

I wondered if I could somehow share parts of the story without giving away the whole truth. Evan would have a decent topic, and I could keep my privacy. But I wasn't sure how I could only tell most of it. After all, the greatest plot twist was the part I wanted to hide most.

"I'll think about it," I finally said. "I'll let you know soon."

"I knew you'd have a story for me. I didn't realize it was yours, but I knew you'd have something."

I turned away from him and busied myself sweeping again. "Well, I haven't promised anything yet. I'd keep brainstorming if I were you, just in case."

"You think on it, and I'll think on the typewriter. No obligations either way."

"Deal," I said.

After he left, I swept the rest of the store, thinking about the idea of sitting down and spilling my entire life story to him. It made me uneasy. I hated talking about myself, and an entire paper about me didn't sound fun. But only Mrs. Jones would be reading it, and she already knew the whole story anyway. What could it hurt?

But so much can change in just one day.

The next day, my story became a secret. Because that's when Jordan came to Ivy Hollow.

JORDAN

"Nothing is so painful to
the human mind as great
and sudden change."

Mary Shelley, _Frankenstein_

MOM WAS HAVING ANOTHER one of her _moments_. She'd had a lot of them that week. Well, really since the divorce, but that week had been especially bad. All three of us were on edge with new jobs, schools, state, and town, so I guess I couldn't blame her much.

I could hear her downstairs on the phone with Aunt Cassidy.

"What the heck was I thinking, Cass? We're all going to be miserable here."

Pause.

"Maya's fine, but she's always been my outgoing one. Jordan is too quiet to say she hates it, but I can tell she does."

Another pause.

"I know, I know. New beginnings. But there's *nothing* here. I feel like I'm trying to create a new life for them out of absolutely nothing! Out of thin air. Thin, dusty country air!"

I was lying on my bed, staring at the popcorn ceiling while I listened. I twirled my fingers absently through my stick-straight hair, avoiding the feeling of helplessness that had plagued me since Mom and Dad first told us about the divorce. I'd wanted to fix the problem. I was the family peacemaker and problem solver—I always had been. But this time, there was nothing I could do.

Without even realizing it, my hands traveled to my abdomen in response to the sick, nervous feeling growing in my stomach. I tried to be helpful on the really bad days, but most of the time I just felt like I was in the way. I decided doing anything at all was better than listening to another venting session while my anxiety built up inside of me like a storm, so I rolled off my bed and made my way downstairs. As I passed Mom's bedroom door, I tried to block out the noise of her conversation with my own reassuring thoughts.

She'll be fine. We'll get through this.

I ended up in Mom's office that was separated from the living room by two glass doors, which I shut behind me. Mom had complained all week about how she couldn't think for all the clutter piled up in here, so I thought that maybe getting it organized would help. She worked from home except for two days a week when she went into her new townhouse office. She's a realtor, and she heard that people were looking to move out of big cities and into places like Ivy Hollow to escape the fast-paced hustle and bustle. After the divorce, she said, "What the heck," and moved us out here.

If you ask me, moving to Ivy Hollow was more like a decision to stop living altogether more than it was to start living slower.

One by one, I organized the drawers of her desk, finding places for her pens, printer paper, files, and stationary. I enjoyed organizing. It gave me an outlet to feel in control, I think. I couldn't control the move, I couldn't control Dad's decision to leave us, I couldn't control my own emotions, but I could decide that pens, pencils, and paper clips went into the top drawer, and that the sticky notes were in order by color according to the rainbow.

I used the turquoise, polka-dot scissors from Mom's desk to slice through the tape of another cardboard moving box. When I opened it, I realized it was misplaced. Inside were mine and Maya's baby books, and those belonged in the attic.

My face fell and the anxious feeling in my stomach started up again. The attic was like a museum full of items that told the story of the life we had before. Mom's wedding dress was up there and dozens of framed family photos. And the board games we used to play every Friday night with Dad. Now I went to add a new exhibit to the collection.

The entrance to the attic was just in front of my bedroom door, and a musty smell greeted me as I pulled the hatch. Nose crinkled, I climbed the ladder awkwardly with the box tucked in the bend of my arm. I paused at the top to listen before I made the final commitment to enter.

When we first moved in, Mom said she didn't doubt this old house had a ghost or two, and while I wasn't the superstitious type, I figured it couldn't hurt to be a little cautious. Mom swears she's encountered three haunted houses in her fourteen years of being a realtor and said this house was just the sort she expected to have a ghost. I had rolled my eyes at her when she'd suggested it, but I still listened at night for any unexplainable sounds, and I still paused before finally entering the attic.

I used my cell phone flashlight to help me find the single, dim lightbulb over head, then tossed the box down among all of the various other items we'd shoved up there since the move. I don't know why, but I lifted the lid to look through it one more time. As I did, I couldn't help but ask myself, "How?" How could two people who had once been so in love call it quits forever? They built a life and a family together. Wasn't that worth fighting for?

My baby book was on top; Maya's was under it. A little white shoebox was under hers. I recognized the box because it had a sketch of the shoes on the side—the pair that both Maya and I wore at our baby dedications. We never went to church except on Easter with Grandma and Papa, but Grandma had insisted that both Maya and I be dedicated, and she bought me a white lacy dress and little satin shoes to wear for the occasion. A few years later, Maya wore it, too.

But when I slid the cardboard lid off the box, the shoes weren't there. All that laid there was a tiny hospital bracelet and a small diary covered in sequins.

The bracelet was incredibly small. I hadn't been around many babies, but it felt unrealistically tiny in my fingers. I peered to look for mine or Maya's birthdate, but I didn't find either. My mother's name was on there with her maiden name, and the date was August 2nd, 1999. Two years before I was born.

My chest tightened, and my breathing became shallow as I considered what this meant. My mom had another baby before me.

"No way. This doesn't add up," I whispered, my hand planting on my forehead. I'd figured out a long time ago that Mom got pregnant with me before she and Dad were married. I was born just six short months after the wedding. But I'd never once thought or even gotten a clue that Mom had given birth to another baby before me.

How had I never known this? Why had Mom never mentioned it?

Questions piled one on top of another in my mind about who this baby was and who its father could have been. And what happened to it?

My hands shuddered as I observed the little bracelet again, and this time, I noticed the name of the hospital in a tiny, worn font.

Saint Mary's Mercy Hospital / Richmond, VA.

"Richmond," I said as the pieces tried to come together. The baby was born in Richmond, almost three hours from here. Where Aunt Cassidy lived.

A fresh wound of betrayal scarred my chest. It was just another reason to believe our family was broken from the beginning, and we never had a chance. I couldn't ask Mom about it. Not now. She'd kept it a secret for a reason, and now was definitely not the time to bring it up. Not with her anxiety and depression flaring like it was.

I would go on pretending she had nothing to hide in order to keep her afloat. Because that's what I did. Even when I was drowning, too.

I traced the plastic edge of the bracelet with my pointer finger, desperately trying to summon the answers to all my questions out of it. 1999. I started doing the math in my head.

Mom and Dad didn't meet until college, and Mom hadn't been to college yet when this baby was born. She was fresh out of high school. I knew that she took a few months break before going to college to stay in Richmond with Aunt Cass, and the pregnancy must have been why. Did Dad even know about this baby? Did my grandparents know?

My eyes dropped to the shoebox again. The bracelet couldn't be the only remaining witness to what had happened, and I remembered the little diary. I'd never seen it before, but it was definitely from the '90s. There was no question about that, thanks to the bright colored sequins. Inside was a letdown.

There were only a few doodles and names written in girlish fonts, but I could tell it was Mom's handwriting. Slid into the pages were different movie tickets, high school play programs, and a few Polaroid photos of Mom with friends. One of them had her sitting on the couch, a guy next to her, and his arm wrapped around her as they looked at each other with bright smiles. The photos also preserved the dark existence of low-waisted jeans.

A page that caught my eye had her name with a plus sign and then the name of a guy, surrounded by lots of hearts.

Reagan + Andy

I wondered if he was the guy in the photo and the dad of the baby, but Mom had a lot of boyfriends in high school, according to Aunt Cass.

I set the journal back in its box and practically collapsed on the attic floor with my knees to my chest. My life felt like it was coming undone at the seams all at once. First, my family fell apart, and now I'd uncovered what looked to be a dark secret. This whole life I'd once had—had it all been fake? Just a façade? I thought we were happy and normal and close. We loved each other, enjoyed each other, and trusted each other. And yet the fact that all of the pieces from our happy life laid scattered around me, and the fact that my mom had kept a huge secret from me my whole life... All of it had me asking if I'd been wrong. Had I been living a lie?

EVAN

> "It's been my experience that you can nearly always enjoy things if you make up your mind firmly that you will."
>
> L.M. Montgomery, *Anne of Green Gables*

I GAVE RAIN UNTIL Monday to think through helping me with the project. Ever since we first talked about it in the antique store, I got the feeling she was avoiding me. After close to a week of waiting, I decided it was time to clear things up.

I found her sitting by herself at lunch like she usually did, reading *Peter Pan*. Her eyes lifted slowly from the page when I sat across from her.

"I take it this seat is free," I said.

She nodded and reluctantly set her book down.

I cleared my throat and tried to find a way to break the ice. I didn't feel very welcome, despite her permission. "Did you have a good weekend?"

Rain turned her attention to her lunch in front of her, poking her fork at a piece of grilled chicken in her salad. Her eyes met mine briefly in an effort to keep things light, but it wasn't working very well. "Yeah, I'd say so. I painted a lot, and Jo was off work all weekend which is rare, so we did some hiking."

"Jo?" My mind immediately assumed a boyfriend, and I felt uneasy. My efforts to unzip my lunch bag came to a halt.

Rain gave an apologetic smile realizing she'd forgotten to explain. "She's my mom. She adopted me. But I've never called her mom." Of course she would call her mom by her first name. Rain became more odd with every conversation I had with her, but to her, it seemed so natural and normal.

I began unpacking my lunch from my bag—a sandwich featuring vegetables from my garden and potato chips. "So about that adoption story..." I prompted.

Rain eyed me sheepishly. Much more so than the other day when we first talked about it. It had been obvious she didn't love the idea of me writing about her, but today was different. There was a fear in her eyes that hadn't been there before. Something new was definitely holding her back.

She put her fork down and gripped her book on the table absently. "I'm not sure. I really don't think it would be any more interesting than writing your own story."

My own story. The one I was trying to avoid even more than A Tale of Two Cities.

I shook my head. "I don't think so."

It wasn't even all about avoiding unpacking my own past anymore. From everything I had already learned about Rain, and by the things she refused to say, I could tell there was a lot more to her story than she let on.

Rain looked at me doubtfully. "You don't even know anything about me. Not really."

"So tell me."

Crickets.

I smiled. "So it *is* a secret?"

Rain blushed and rolled her eyes. "No. Not really."

"Then what's the big deal?"

"It's complicated," she said through a sigh. "Besides, you're practically a stranger."

I wanted to retort—to remind her that she was the one who told me to pry into peoples' stories and ask them questions about their "plot twists," as she called it. But I didn't bring it up.

She pushed a stray piece of her brown hair behind her ear as she thought. That day, her hand was painted in dark blobs of gray, black, and dark blue. It reminded me of storm clouds.

"New question," I said.

She waited expectantly.

"What was the inspiration behind your hand today? Did Peter Pan have a rough go with the pirates, or is it you who's having a bad day?"

Rain gave a weary smile, like she was fighting hard to get it to appear. "Maybe both of us have had it rough lately. But Peter's story is coming to a close. I'll have it finished before the end of the day." She brought the book to her lap and looked over its worn cover.

"And your story has yet to be written," I said, raising an eyebrow dramatically.

She kept her focus downward.

When I first met her, she'd been so warm and open. She wasn't exactly what I'd call outgoing, but she never shied away from a conversation with me, and she always displayed little pieces of her personality in our conversations, the way that her hand did. I always walked away thinking she was a little more interesting than the last time I talked to her.

Now she was nothing like that. And it had come as suddenly as a storm cloud, like the ones painted on her hand and pointing to her mind. I couldn't figure out what had gotten to her.

I tossed my last potato chip in my mouth and wiped my hands on my jeans. "What happened to make you use those colors?"

Rain's eyes scanned the room, but they still wouldn't meet mine. "Black usually means fear. Gray is confusion. Dark blue can be pain."

"The colors have meanings?"

She lifted and dropped her shoulders bashfully. "They do to me. Actually, it's more like feelings have colors. It's how I communicate and express them in my art." She took the first bite of her salad and wiped something invisible from the side of her mouth with her napkin. "Think about it. You can draw an ocean and we'll know what it is, but the shades and colors you use will tell you if that ocean is angry and stormy, or wild and free, or enchanting and mesmerizing."

There it was. The odd little tidbit I would walk away with this time. I'd gotten it after all.

"You know, the more I talk to you, the more convinced I become that you would make an incredible main character," I said.

She didn't answer, and I released a surrendering sigh. I was going to need to find a new subject. I couldn't push her anymore; I couldn't ask her to do what I wasn't even willing to.

I didn't know what was most disappointing—having to find a new topic or not getting to hear Rain's secret.

Rain took a sip from her water bottle, then began spinning it in place on the table as she thought. "It isn't that I don't want to help you; I just don't know that I want the story to be mine," she said, like she was trying to convince herself that she couldn't trust me with whatever her secret was.

Our eyes met, and she must have seen the spark that had ignited in me as I couldn't help but hope that whatever part of her that wanted to help me would win the battle being fought in her mind.

Rain stopped spinning her bottle and began twisting a lock of her brown hair around her finger instead. "I know it sounds strange, but if you'd asked me to help you with it last year, I would have. But things have changed, and I just feel like it's a bad idea."

"Alright, alright." I gave in, but my curiosity was burning. What could have possibly changed to make her afraid so suddenly? It sure sounded like a plot twist to me. "I'll come up with something else. But if it sways you at all, you're the only person in this whole town that I know. I promise it will stay between us. Us and Mrs. Jones, of course."

"Mrs. Jones already knows," Rain said.

I smiled and swung my arms open. "Perfect! It's just me you have to take a chance on."

Her eyes looked desperate. I wasn't sure what they were desperate for though. Probably for me to leave her alone.

I tried to imagine her story for myself, and I studied her hand, expecting to find some hidden clues. Something intertwined in the dark blobs that might reveal a hint of the fight that was happening in her head. Then, I looked to her other hand—or where it should have been, I guess. Maybe that one was more telling of her backstory.

"How do you get the paint to stay on all day?" I asked.

"I have a water resistant face paint that I use to do it. It lasts for a little while but not all day," she said, but I could see her mind was still behind, thinking over whatever it was that was holding her back.

Rain rubbed the back of her neck with her stubbed arm. I wondered what it felt like to only have one hand. To make use of the stub. Did it hurt when you touched it?

Rain's eyes slowly lifted to meet mine. "You swear you would keep it between us?"

I grew hopeful. "I swear."

"You wouldn't tell a soul?"

"I'll take it to my grave."

She crossed her arms self-consciously over her chest, and she looked me up and down, like she was searching for something in me to believe in. "Fine. I'll do it. I don't know why, and I'm probably an idiot, but I will."

I exhaled and crossed my heart with a finger. "You can trust me, I swear."

"I hope so." Her complexion looked pale. How deep could this secret be? She picked up her book again and fanned the pages with her thumb. "I'm not going to tell you everything just yet. You're gonna have to earn my trust a little." The incoming of a challenge laced her voice.

"Okay," I agreed, wondering what I was about to get myself into.

She slid *Peter Pan* across the table. "You can start by reading this."

"Seriously?" I didn't bother to hide the dread.

"Yep. Consider it research. Pay attention to the writing style and notice the difference between Barrie and Dickens. Besides, like I said, if I were a book, I would be *Peter Pan*. If you're gonna write about me, you're gonna have to get into my head and learn the things I enjoy."

I began to retreat. By asking for Rain's help, I may have just turned this already hard project to nearly impossible. I got the feeling she'd attempt to have me write something comparable to A *Tale of Two Cities* itself. All I really wanted was a good idea and to get by with it. But I was desperate, and now I was on the edge of my seat about her.

"Yeah, I guess. But don't you wanna finish it first?" I asked, hoping to procrastinate a little, which is what got me writing this paper in the first place.

"I have two other copies at home."

Of course she did.

"Collecting different editions is part of the fun." Her lips perked into a smirk as she saw through my attempted procrastination.

I couldn't complain. Without her, I had no ideas whatsoever. If she wanted me to read it, I would. Even if I hated every second of it. Besides, it was a children's book. How bad could it be?

Rain's expression had relaxed slightly, and I could tell she was enjoying my pain. "Get started on that, and we'll regroup on Monday." She crumpled the paper bag her sandwich had been in, and I watched as her grip tightened around the paper until she set it down on the table.

"There's one more question I want to ask you about your hand painting, but I don't know if I should ask it," I said.

Rain smiled knowingly. "You want to know how I do it when I only have one hand."

I felt my face go warm, and I shrugged.

"You can ask. I don't care. I hold the paintbrush between my teeth."

My eyes widened as I tried to imagine her painting some of the detailed designs I'd seen on her hand. "Seriously? That's amazing."

Rain glanced over her work for herself. "Not really. Just different. You learned how to use two hands. I learned to use my hand, a stub where the other should be, and my teeth. I just adapted. Humans are good at adapting. The worst can happen to us, and then we're surprised at how little time it takes us to get on like it never did."

Adapting. That's what I was afraid of most. The pain I felt when Dad died was almost unbearable, but imagining a life where I was able to move on scared me. I didn't want to feel the pain, but I was afraid and ashamed to let it go.

"Now I'll ask *you* a hard question that I'm not sure I should ask," Rain said, almost as though she'd read my mind. I knew where the conversation was going before she said it.

My fingers tensed around the metal bench. "Well, it's only fair," I admitted.

"What happened to your dad? You don't have to talk about it if you don't want to."

"No, it's alright," I told her, but the dryness of my throat told me otherwise. "It was stomach cancer. He'd been fighting it for three years. He passed away in February."

Rain winced. "I'm so sorry."

Everyone said that. They meant it, of course, but grief is a strange thing. You don't want to pretend it never happened—you can't. You expect and want the support of others. But you also don't want people to bring it up. You don't want the sympathetic looks and the uncomfortable conversation. I don't believe there's a great way to approach grief.

I shrugged as nonchalantly as I could, but I know it came across as stiff and uncomfortable as I felt. "It's alright. We're learning to get by, I guess. I think the move will help."

"What in the world made you choose Ivy Hollow?"

She smiled a little, like she was trying to ease my nerves, but my neck and shoulders grew more tense the deeper she pried. Deeper into the wound.

"My dad. He'd always wanted to move out this way, buy a piece of property, and write from home. He was a journalist, but he wanted to be a novelist, and he wanted to do it while my sister and I were still home. My mom and I decided after he died to try and make at least part of the dream happen."

Rain leaned her arms on the table in front of her. "Well, I hope it gives you the new start you're looking for. Ivy Hollow is small, but it's beautiful, and you won't find a nicer group of folks anywhere else in the state."

"I've noticed, and I love it here so far," I said. "If only my sister was as taken with it. She's twelve with the attitude of a sixteen year old and going through a crisis right now over leaving her friends."

Just that morning, I'd had to rescue Mom again from another one of Ava's verbal lashings. I knew it was hard for Ava, and I was trying to understand. She and Dad had been close—maybe even closer than I'd been with him. But it was getting to be ridiculous, and I'd just about had it.

"Some people take longer to adapt to a new life than others," Rain said. "She's had a lot of change over the past few months. I can't say I handle change very well either." She chucked her ball of trash toward a trash can about ten feet away, and she scored.

I clapped slowly. "Pretty good for a girl. So you're an artist and you can shoot hoops with just that one hand?" I crumpled my own trash into a ball. I didn't dare throw it. I felt sure I could make it, but if I didn't... Well, it wasn't worth the risk.

In one swift motion, she pulled her hair into a ponytail, wrapping it in a green hair tie that she had on her wrist. "Didn't expect all that, huh?"

"Not at all."

"Alright, what about you?" she asked, resting the side of her face in her palm with her elbow leaning on the table. "You know all my pastimes. What are yours?"

"It's kinda opposite, huh? You know all about my family and little about me. I know a good bit about you, but your family seems to be a big secret."

She rolled her brown eyes behind her glasses. "Look, I agreed to tell you. Don't push it or I might change my mind."

"Okay, okay," I said, raising my palms in front of me defensively. "Well, I'm not as exciting as you. I can't paint with my mouth or anything cool like that. I like to garden. That's what I was most excited about when we moved here. I tried to grow a few plants in my room and on our back patio in Chicago, but that's all." I scanned the cafeteria, looking anywhere but at Rain. Gardening felt like a stupid hobby when I voiced it out loud.

"Well, you're in good company. We have lots of farmers in Ivy Hollow. What about gardening makes you love it so much?"

When I finally met Rain's gaze again, I could feel the look in her eyes encouraging me, as if she knew I was reluctant. It reminded me of how shy she seemed when I admired her work at the antique store. She knew what it was to be insecure about something she was passionate about.

"Uh, I don't know," I stuttered. "I guess it's the hard work and the satisfaction. There's a lot of hot, dirty, back-breaking work to it, and it sort of makes you feel alive. And then when you finally reap the harvest that you worked for... there's nothing more satisfying. It makes you proud."

"I believe it, and I'm glad you're able to finally do it. I'd love to see your garden someday." She grabbed her backpack off the bench beside her as she stood. The bell immediately rang. "But until then, I guess I'll see ya around."

"Yeah, I'll see ya," I said, and watched her walk off, her handless arm hanging at her right side.

The cafeteria around me began to buzz as kids left their tables and started making their way out. Once I was mostly alone, I picked up my ball of trash, aimed at the trash can, and made my shot.

I rolled my eyes as it hit the side of the can and dropped to the floor.

R A I N

"Some people seem to get
all sunshine, and some
all shadow..."

Louisa May Alcott, *Little Women*

"I WOULDN'T WORRY ABOUT it too much," Jo said, pulling the baked potatoes out of the oven.

I reached around her to flip the steaks on the stove. I was venting, and she was planting my feet on solid ground yet again. Jo was the Marilla Cuthbert to my Anne Shirley, always balancing my drama with logic. And I was the one who dared her to dream a little and not stay so firmly planted that she never took risks. We needed each other as much as we needed air to breathe.

Jo set her oven mitts down and assessed the potatoes with a slight wince before going on. They were nearly burnt, of course, because I was on dinner duty and she'd just come home from work to swoop in and help. I inevitably burnt everything.

"They live in the same town," she said. "It's gonna come to light eventually. You just need to brace yourself for it now. And besides, if you get to know Evan and decide he's not worth your time, you aren't obligated to go through with it."

I absently flipped the steaks again. They'd likely been flipped fifty times already. "Yeah, I guess."

"Is he cute?" Jo's back was to me, but she looked over her shoulder to watch my response.

I tensed but tried to distract her from it with a glare. "I dunno."

Her chin tilted downward, and her eyebrows raised. "Yes, you do."

"He's not *not* cute." I was blushing as I busied myself flipping the burnt-to-a-crisp steaks again. I didn't exactly know why I was blushing. I'd hardly paid much attention to Evan's appearance since I'd met him. Except for the color of his eyes, of course.

Jo swooped in to take the spatula from my hand and flipped the charred steaks onto a plate, saving them from further doom. "Right. I figured that had something to do with his persuasiveness."

I stepped to the side to let her finish the task and rolled my eyes. "I'm not that shallow."

There was something about Evan that was persuasive to me, but it wasn't his looks. There was something endearing about him. I think perhaps I was as curious about his story as he was about mine.

"Well, I wouldn't be mad if you invited him over one day after school to work on the project so I can meet him." Jo had a teasing look in her eye. "Can you at least tell me what he looks like?"

I thought about him, and mostly colors came to my mind. They always did. He was green, brown, and gold to me. But of course, that's not what Jo was asking.

"He has dark brown hair. Green eyes. He's tall."

"What's green again?"

"Creativity, growth, life…"

She nodded, looking pleased. "Ah. That sounds right up your alley."

I eyed her seriously. I felt bad for him. He was new, and the project definitely wouldn't be easy. Who else could he ask?

I pulled a stick of butter out of the refrigerator and set it beside Jo for her to add to the potatoes. "It'll take him every second leading up to November to get this done. So I *will* invite him over to work on it. Any chance you can be off Wednesday night? He can come after I get off of work."

Jo started cutting the butter in chunks. With both potatoes stuffed, she set the knife down and wiped her fingers on the apron she'd tied over her scrubs. She'd picked up so many shifts over the past month, I didn't know how she could still stand on her feet. Aside from the exhaustion hovering under her eyes, you would've never known how worn out she was. But she'd been worn out her whole life—for me. For us.

"I think I can swing that," she said and placed the potatoes back in the warm oven. "I'll cook—for all our sake. And I'll be on my best behavior. I promise."

I pulled some silverware out of the drawer in the island and made my way to the little dining room where I set the table.

As much as I wanted to help Evan and to get to know him, I still had an uneasy feeling in my stomach about agreeing to it. I couldn't help but feel that I was making a huge mistake.

My mind went back to the week before, when it all changed—to the pit in my stomach I'd felt the first day I'd seen her in homeroom.

At first, I knew I recognized her, but I didn't know where I'd seen her before. When her gaze passed me by with no sign of recollection, I assumed I must be mistaken, because she clearly didn't know me. She sat herself two rows in front of me, and I watched the back of her head, trying to think of why she seemed so familiar.

And then came the roll call.

"And you must be Jordan Carson, our newest student," Mr. Murphy said, his southern drawl dragging out the *ar* in Carson.

She nodded.

And my heart skipped a beat.

I knew who she was. I knew her well, even if she didn't know me. But I never, *ever* thought I would see her at my own safe, secluded Ivy Hollow High School.

"And you're in tenth grade, correct?" Mr. Murphy asked, but his voice sounded so far away.

"Yes, sir," she mumbled.

I felt like I could throw up. I all but jogged to the bathroom as soon as the bell rang to lock myself in a stall and gather my thoughts. My chest felt tight. I was shaking all over. Questions I hadn't entertained in years were now screaming for answers in my mind, yet I was terrified of learning the answers.

I'd found my belonging. I belonged here in Ivy Hollow with my people. I knew who I was. I knew what I wanted. Yet her presence alone threatened to shatter all that I'd built.

I crossed my arms over my chest in that bathroom stall, asking myself over and over again how in the world she got *here*. I would die if she ever found out who I was.

I'd hardly been able to get through my day.

"Jordan is really pretty," I said to Jo, brushing the memory aside while I set the table.

She shot a questioning glance at me, as though she wondered where this conversation had come from and where it was going. "So are you."

I placed the last plate down and crossed my arms over my chest, fighting the same uneasy, nauseating feeling I'd felt in that bathroom stall. "She looks a lot like her dad. She has his blonde hair and blue eyes."

For so long, I'd stared at her photo, admiring her and wondering about her. And looking—looking for the difference. Searching for what made her better than me.

And my imagination was so good at creating things.

There was a time in my life where I had idolized her. She was better than me in every way. And I was little more than the dirt of the earth.

I shook my head and busied myself straightening imaginary wrinkles in the tablecloth. I wouldn't go back to that pit again.

"Well, Reagan is gorgeous," Jo said. I could feel her eyeing me closely from her spot in the kitchen. "You look just like she did when she was your age."

I straightened my shoulders and forced myself to look Jo in the eye with an indifferent look on my face. I wouldn't give her any reason to worry about me. "Do you think Jordan will see the resemblance between Reagan and I?"

She shook her head confidently. "Not if she isn't looking for it. Besides, she doesn't spend a lot of time around you, right? Only homeroom and lunch."

I wished I could feel as convinced as she sounded.

I guess you could say I grew out of comparing myself to her; not that I got too old to care but that I'd grown enough to forgive. But now that she was here in Ivy Hollow, part of my imagination wanted to run with it again.

Jordan had gotten everything that should have been mine. It wasn't her fault, but I still couldn't deny that her presence was digging up the bones of a past I'd laid to rest long ago.

JORDAN

"Kindred spirits are not so
scarce as I used to think. It's
splendid to find out there are
so many of them in the world."

L.M. Montgomery, *Anne of Green Gables*

AT LUNCH, I SAT alone at a table in the cafeteria with my laptop
in front of me. Ever since my attic discovery, I'd been Googling
everything I could think of that would give me more clues to my
mom's secret, but I wasn't getting anywhere. I just didn't have
enough information to work with. I tried calling the hospital
and asking if they could share any information about my mom's
visit back in 1999, but they said the information was confidential,
which made sense even if it was irritating. I'd looked for Mom's
yearbook to see if I could find the Andy guy she doodled about

in the diary, but I couldn't find it. All evidence, aside from the bracelet, seemed to be completely gone.

I wished I could just ask her, but even before the divorce and the emotional wreck it had her in, I don't think I could have done that. We'd never been close, and I always felt like I was walking on eggshells when I spoke to her. I never knew what was okay to say and what could flip her switch.

Exasperated from searching and having nothing to show for it, I shut my laptop and looked around at the different cliques of Ivy Hollow High, but my mind was someplace else entirely. I was surprised to find a set of eyes staring back at me while doing a visual sweep of the room. They darted away quickly when our gazes met. I knew her. From homeroom for sure. She had a weird name and only one hand. But looking at her then, I felt certain I'd seen her somewhere else, too. Why did she seem so familiar to me?

I didn't get to look long because a guy, also from our home-room, made his way to sit across from her, blocking my view. Evan Lawson. I'd *definitely* noticed him before, as had every other girl at this school.

"Hi there," a voice behind me said, and I jolted upright. Breaking my stare at Evan and the girl, I whipped around to find a boy from my own grade behind me. He was in a wheelchair, and he was different—I'd gathered that much. He seemed slower than normal. Mentally, that is.

He chuckled at me as I settled, his eyes squinting curiously behind his glasses.

My hands found the bench beneath me and tightened around it in a deathgrip.

"Hi," I finally said.

"You're new." He didn't ask. It was a statement.

I reluctantly nodded before searching the room for a way to get out of the situation. "Yeah, I am."

His hand lifted in an awkward motion from his lap and pointed at the table. "Can I sit with you?"

Unable to think of a reason to deny him or to disappear, I nodded. He wasted no time pulling his wheelchair up to the table.

For a few minutes, he didn't say anything else. He methodically opened his lunchbox and began eating the sandwich inside.

He avoided eye contact with me, and I avoided it with him. The cafeteria was pretty full, and all of the tables had at least two people sitting at them. The guy needed a place to sit, and appeared to have little to no interest in carrying on a conversation. Which was fine by me.

In my effort to avoid eye contact, I resumed watching Evan and the girl again, who seemed to be talking about the painting on her hand.

"You're watching Rain," the kid sitting with me said. When he spoke, his voice was steady and almost monotone.

Rain. That was her name.

I pushed my laptop to the side of the table and pulled my lunch bag closer. I'd been so lost in my obsession with finding answers, I hadn't even gotten my lunch out of its bag yet. "Just looking around," I said.

"Do you know her?"

I met his gaze suspiciously for a second, wondering why he cared. "No. We're not even in the same grade. Do *you* know her?" At my old school, grades hardly ever mixed. It was sort of an unspoken rule. But Ivy Hollow was a small town, and I guessed kids around here probably knew every single other student. I'd heard that about small towns.

Thomas pushed a strand of his dirty-blond hair out of his eyes. "Yeah. We hang out sometimes. She comes to my house in the summer a lot. And she works with Mr. Clark. Mr. Clark sells the things I fix in his shop. I fix all kinds of stuff. Typewriters, old clocks, watches. Stuff like that." He spoke fast.

"That's cool," I said.

There was another long pause as he finished his sandwich and moved on to his apple slices. He seemed to put extra thought into every movement.

"You never told me your name," he said, his lips smacking as he chewed. "That's okay, because I know what it is. It's Jordan. But do you know mine?"

My cheeks went warm with guilt for not remembering. "I don't think so."

"It's Thomas. Thomas Helms. Do you wanna see what I'm working on right now?" He pushed his glasses up higher on his nose before reaching into his pocket to pull out an old pocket watch that looked to be ancient. The silver was almost completely covered in grime, and to me, it looked far beyond the point of repair.

"This is from 1855, and it doesn't work at all. Not even a little bit. When I got it, the hands were bent, but I replaced those. Now I'm working on what I like to call its 'guts.' That's the inside mechanics that make it run. And then I'll polish it up to look good as new."

"Neat," I said, looking it over in my hands. "Where do you find this kind of stuff?"

"Mr. Clark usually finds it broken and pays me to fix it."

"And he's the one who works with Rain?"

"Yep."

I had to admit I was impressed. My first impression of him was that he was slow, but I think it's me who's slow; I'd been slow to realize how beyond me he was.

"What's your favorite thing you've ever fixed?" I asked.

"I have to say it's a typewriter I did recently. It was all out of sorts, but now it runs like it just came from the manufacturer. It's so good, Rain has it on display in the store's front window." Thomas tossed half an apple slice into his mouth as he beamed with pride. His chest puffed out an extra few inches.

"I bet that's pretty cool. I've never used a typewriter before."

"They're super fun to fix."

"I'll take your word for it."

His attention fell back down to his lunch and his whole disposition changed in a matter of seconds. "I don't like to see people sit alone," he said abruptly, the shyness he'd displayed at first returning. It had disappeared as he talked about the different things he fixed, his passion for tinkering overriding his fear, making him seem more confident. But he'd become reserved again.

"Not unless they want to sit alone," he went on. "Sometimes when I'm working, I like to sit alone. And Rain likes to sit alone and read sometimes, I think."

It took me a few seconds to catch up with him. He was talking about me, sitting here by myself.

"So if you want to sit alone, I can leave."

"No," I said, shaking my head. I wouldn't let him feel out of place, even if I did prefer to be alone. "No, I'm glad you came over here."

He gave a smile in between throwing grapes into his mouth.

Thomas was my first real interaction at Ivy Hollow High. The first person to reach out and make me feel welcome in his own way. And I couldn't help but think that maybe he came over to talk to me because we weren't so different. He was a peacemaker. We were alike in that way. He wanted everyone to feel like they belonged, the same way I fought to keep my family from being divided.

And he was doing a far better job at it than I was.

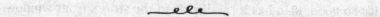

I never missed Florida more than when I was running. The hills in Ivy Hollow killed me, but I wasn't about to give up my after-school ritual. We lived just a little ways outside of town, but the house was off of a backroad of sorts that was long and almost always lifeless. It made for a peaceful jog, except for the parts where I thought I'd die of a heart attack because the hills were so steep. But it gave me a chance to clear my head and loosen up after school. I loved feeling my heart beating and the burning of my lungs. My body felt truly alive. I lived for it.

I was halfway home from my after-school run when my phone rang from my pocket. I slowed my pace and tried to catch my breath.

I stared blankly at the screen as I panted. It was Dad. He'd only called me a handful of times since we moved. I didn't want to answer, though I couldn't pinpoint why. I wanted him back in my life, and maybe he was finally making an effort. But not like this. I wanted things to go back to the way that they were, not this new, half-invested thing we still pretended was our family.

But I couldn't ignore him. So I slid a sweaty finger across the screen to answer.

"Hello?"

"Hey, kiddo," Dad's familiar voice said. Hearing it made my heart ache in my chest.

"Hey, Dad."

"You sound out of breath? You okay?"

"Yeah, I'm just running."

He chuckled and threw in the dad joke I'd heard a million times. "From what?"

I didn't feel up to faking a laugh, so I answered honestly. "My problems, I guess. And maybe a little homework."

The pause was brief but noticeable, and then when he did speak, he conveniently ignored the first part of my answer. "Homework, eh? How are you liking your new school?"

I pressed the toe of my blue sneakers against the asphalt. I just had to get through this phone call and then he'd leave me alone for a few more weeks.

"It's okay. It's really small."

"I'll bet."

"Everything about this place is small. Except for the view, I guess. The mountains are pretty incredible."

"Yeah, I'm sure the change of scenery has been nice. I've always liked the mountains."

We used to visit the mountains every few years when we would come and stay with Aunt Cass. We would all go spend a day hiking and shopping at antique stores and getting ice cream. Back when we all enjoyed each other.

"I'd like it better if I knew it was only a visit," I mumbled.

Dad heaved a sigh. "I'm sorry, hun. You know I tried. How's Mom?"

Now it was my turn to pause. I wasn't sure how much I should tell him. "I don't know. She's off," I said.

"Off?"

"Yeah. She's stressed, I think." Stressed was an understatement.

I could hear his voice becoming more tense. "Has she had any more of her fits?"

Telling him the truth would only divide us more. There was nothing he could do about it now, and I knew he'd probably end up calling Mom to tell her she was unfit to have us. And what good would that do?

"Nah, nothing like that," I lied. "She's just overwhelmed with her new business and all."

Another hesitation on Dad's side. "Do you promise you'll tell me if something's really wrong?"

"Sure, Dad." I said, rubbing my palm over my face. I felt overwhelmed all of a sudden. The weight of having to fill the gap Dad left behind was hard enough, then to top it off, I had to lie to him about what I was dealing with.

He left, but he still wanted control, and that's not how it worked. Instead, I was left to control it, and I didn't want to.

"Are you guys happy there? I know it'll take time, but do you think you'll like it?"

"I dunno. But it'll be fine," I lied again. I felt pretty certain I knew. I hated Ivy Hollow. There was nothing for me. But that was my job. Keeping the peace.

"I swear, your mom only moved you out there to keep you from me," he grumbled in exasperation, like he forgot I was listening. "But don't worry about it too much. Just try and get settled. We'll make the most of the holidays and breaks when you guys come home, okay?"

"Okay."

"I miss you, kiddo."

THE COLORS OF RAIN

"We miss you, too, Dad."

And that ended our conversation for what I figured would be the next week or two.

When I got back from my run, Maya was sitting in the front yard. I knew it was bad if Maya was bored enough to sit outside doing nothing. Neither one of us cared to be inside where Mom's nerves had us feeling like we were walking on glass that could shatter at any moment. That had pretty much been our life since we moved to Ivy Hollow: Mom was a wreck and life was boring.

I collapsed in the grass beside Maya, still panting.

Darn those hills.

"Have you met anyone at your school?" she asked, hardly giving me time to get situated. She'd probably been sitting there, thinking up a list of questions to interrogate me with the moment I got back. We were opposites. I was quiet and content by myself; she was always talking and always having to stay busy.

"One person. You?" I asked between heavy breaths.

"I met one girl today. She's new, too. She seems nice." Maya was in seventh grade, but I was sure I acted a lot older when I was in seventh grade. I guess I just grew up faster.

"That's good."

"Do you remember how to make those daisy chains that Grandma showed us?"

"Yeah, I think so."

"Can you show me?"

Our landscaping was nice. Trails of flower beds lined the driveway and surrounded the porch, full of shrubs and daisies and some other pretty things I didn't know the names of. Mom hated it. It was too much upkeep, she said, but she couldn't afford to neglect it. A relator's house had to look perfect. Simple and clean was better than artistic and messy. Imperfection was bad for business. So we all had to take turns weeding the beds and mowing the yard until she found a landscaper to take over.

I reached over and picked a handful of daisies from the flower bed before setting them in my lap to start my daisy chain.

"Does your school have a lot of kids?" Maya asked, picking blades of grass as she watched.

"No."

"Mine either. Ava—that's my new friend—she has a brother that goes to your school, but he's older than you. He's a senior."

"That's cool," I said before pulling out my sweaty ponytail to redo it. My hair was so thin and slick, it never stayed put for long. Especially not after a run.

"His name is Evan."

My ears perked up. "He's in my homeroom, I think." He was the one I saw sitting with Rain.

"Even though he's older?"

"There are a lot of different grades in homeroom."

Maya paused, probably because she needed a breather between talking. She watched my hands as I punctured a hole in the stem of one daisy with my thumb nail before sliding another stem through it. She grabbed a fist full of daisies and started her own.

"Do you like it here?"

I picked another flower and ran its stem through the hole I'd pierced. I pulled too hard and the hole ripped.

Dang it.

"No," I mumbled and discarded the daisy before starting on another.

Maya twirled her pointer finger through her hair absently. "I don't either, but I think I will. I just wish Dad had come with us."

"If Dad hadn't left in the first place, we wouldn't even be here." My tone was sharp. But Dad's conversation was fresh on my mind, and I didn't have the stamina to pretend with her the way I had with Dad. He should be here. He should've fought for us. He should've fought for Mom, too.

Maya dropped her brown eyes to her lap, where the start of her chain was.

The front door opened, and Mom walked out with a tray of glasses filled with lemonade and a plate full of sandwiches. Her knee-length lavender dress swished around her knees as she walked barefoot through the grass toward us. She was dressed nicely that day. She'd gone into her town office and was wearing business clothes like she used to. Lately, her wardrobe consisted mostly of pajamas.

"I made us some dinner," she said, plopping down in front of Maya and I. "What have you two been chatting about? Is that a daisy chain? I haven't made one of those in forever." She was using her overly nice voice. It's the tone she would take on after she lost it. It was her way of saying sorry without actually saying. She just pretended the outburst never happened and acted extra sweet after, expecting us to do the same.

I used to believe it, to accept the unspoken apology and as-sume the worst was in the past. Back when I'd been naive.

"We're talking about school," Maya said, her perkiness quickly returning as another set of ears was present to listen to her. It must be nice to have the luxury of forgetting your problems so quickly. She and Mom had that in common, I guess.

Mom set the tray in the middle of our somewhat-circle. "Oh yeah? And what do you think about your new schools?"

"We don't like them," Maya said nonchalantly. "But I've made one friend." She wrapped her half-finished daisy chain around her wrist like a bracelet.

"Well, you're off to a good start, then. What's her name?" Mom asked.

Maya took a glass into her hands and sipped it. "Ava. She's new and she hates it here, too, but her mom and brother like it a lot."

"Well, you can find common ground in hating it here together," I said, taking a glass of lemonade from Mom who shot me a displeased look.

"Who have you met, Jordan?" Maya asked.

I took my time answering, taking a swig of my lemonade. My face scrunched as I tasted it, the overpowering sourness giving me chills. Mom forgot the sugar. I looked at her to see if she'd caught my reaction, and she didn't. There was no use in bringing it up.

"Just a guy in my class," I told Maya. "He's in a wheelchair. He decided to sit with me today."

"That was nice of him," Mom said.

It grew quiet as we all started on our ham and cheese sandwiches. Mine had mustard which I hated and always had. Mom knew that. Or she used to. I wasn't sure she knew anything anymore.

I broke the silence. "Dad called me while I was on my run."

"He called me after school," Maya said.

Mom's shoulders tensed. "That's good. How's he doing?"

"Fine," Maya said.

"How old were you guys when you got married?" I prompted. I knew already, but I wondered if I could guide the conversation and get clues about the baby bracelet in the attic.

"I was twenty and your dad was twenty-three," she said coldly.

I knew she wanted to forget him. She'd be fine if his name was never mentioned again. I could tell by the way she avoided talking about him and how short she got when he was mentioned. But how? How do you spend so much of the most important parts of your life with someone and then leave them and their memory in the dust?

I swallowed a bite of my sandwich and wiped my lips with a napkin. "Did you have a lot of boyfriends before Dad?"

Mom narrowed her eyes. "I wouldn't say *a lot*."

"How old do I have to be to have a boyfriend?" Maya asked.

"Older than a seventh grader for sure."

"Can Jordan have one?"

Mom turned to glance at me with raised eyebrows. "Does Jordan want one?"

"No," I said, glaring at Maya. "And if I did, he'd probably be in Florida because I don't even know people here."

Mom was growing impatient with me. Like my attitude held a candle to how she'd acted since the move. But she changed the subject.

"What are we going to do for your birthday on Friday?" she asked, and something told me I wasn't going to get very far in learning about the baby today. Not knowing was killing me.

"I don't care," I said.

"Come on. We'll do whatever you want. Sixteen is a big deal." She gathered her curled hair and twisted it before laying it over her shoulder. Her hair was dark brown like Maya's and Aunt

Cassidy's. I favored Dad with my pasty skin, blue eyes, and blonde, flat hair. Mom was beautiful, and I always wished I looked more like her the way Maya did. Maya was a lot closer to her, too, and I envied that most. But then, Maya got along with everyone.

The part that really hurt was that Mom at least tried with Maya, but she didn't with me. Sometimes, I think I gave the impression of being self-sufficient so much that she never knew how much I needed her. Every kid needs their mom. But I was only self-sufficient because I never had her. I had to become that way. Why had she never tried?

I kinda felt like it was because I'd been an accident. I was never a part of her plan the way that Maya was. And it's like she never forgave me for it. I must have left some sort of a bad memory in her mind.

"I just want to get my driver's license," I said. That would be enough for me.

"Well, that's a given. What else?"

"Can we go shopping and out for ice cream?" Maya asked.

"If that's what Jordan wants."

I didn't say anything. What I wanted I couldn't have on my birthday. Dad wouldn't be here, my friends from back home wouldn't be here, and I was stuck in a place where there wasn't much to do even if I wanted to do something. But I would get my driver's license, and with that came a feeling of freedom.

Mom's phone rang, and she stood to her feet. "It's a client calling me back," she said, and began shuffling to the front door.

Maya and I watched as she disappeared inside the house.

"She seems a little more okay today." Maya kept her voice low.

"She'll be alright. She's adjusting just like we are."

Maya nodded and tried to smile a little before taking the last bite of her sandwich. I frowned, knowing that even though Maya could carry on with her life easier than I could, she'd learned to use her personality to hide what she was really feeling. She was worried, too; she just hid it well.

We were all hiding, even though we were all experiencing the same thing.

"We *will* like it here, I think." I lied for the third time that day. "All of us. You've already met a friend, it's beautiful, and we're closer to Aunt Cassidy. I bet she'll come visit a lot and that'll be fun."

Maya grinned. "Maybe she can come for your birthday," she suggested.

"Maybe."

Mom never came back outside, but Maya and I spent the rest of the afternoon in the grass doing homework, making daisy chains, and weeding the flower beds.

This was my life now. It seemed so insignificant. And yet something inside of me knew that I was close to the biggest and most significant discovery of my life.

Even if my birthday didn't hold all the things I truly wanted, maybe it would at least hold answers. Because maybe Aunt Cass knew the story I was looking for.

EVAN

> "The world calls them poets and
> artists and story-tellers; but
> they are just people who have
> never forgotten the way to
> fairyland."
>
> L.M. Montgomery, The Story Girl

THE WEATHER ON WEDNESDAY was amazing. It was perfect fall weather with a warm sun and a crisp, autumn breeze. I did my homework outside after school and spent some time in my garden before it was time for me to head for dinner at Rain's house.

Around five that evening, I sat outside the antique store in Dad's old truck with the windows down while I waited for Rain to lock up for the day. When we moved from Chicago, we kept Mom's car, and I got rid of mine so we could keep Dad's truck. There was no way I could've parted with it. It held too many memories. Mom let me have it when I sold mine, and I felt closer to Dad when I drove it with the windows down and a soda in the cup holder, because that's what we always did. He'd take me out for a drive, nowhere to go, and we'd get sodas to drink while we rode around. He taught me to drive in that truck when I was fourteen, and I was the only one of my friends who knew how to drive a stick shift because of it. I felt like the big man on campus back then. Back when times were simple and I took it all for granted.

Rain walked out of the store and locked the front door. She had asked if I could pick her up on my way to her house for dinner, because Jo used their truck for work.

Rain said that Jo was ecstatic about meeting me and apologized in advance for anything awkward she might say. But I knew all about that. If I were to have Rain over to our house, Mom would definitely have to be apologized for.

"Like a date to meet the parents?" Mom had asked when I told her my plans for the evening.

"No," I retorted a bit too quickly, putting the finishing touches on my sandwich and throwing it into a brown paper bag. "It's more like meeting after school to work on a project. That's all it is."

Mom eyed me suspiciously as she finished packing Ava's lunch. "Okay, okay. But maybe work on your project at *our* house over dinner next time so I get to meet your insignificant project partner."

I gave a sarcastic smirk before walking to the bottom of the stairs to yell for Ava. "Let's go, Ava! You've got three minutes to head out!" I turned back to Mom. "We'll see."

Moms will be moms, regardless of what you call them, and I was hoping to learn exactly why Rain called her mom Jo that night.

After double checking that the store door was locked, Rain hopped into the passenger seat. "Hey," she said with her usual, soft smile. "Thanks for loading my bike into the back of your truck."

I put the truck in gear and pulled away from the store and the neighboring downtown shops. "No problem. You gonna tell me how to get to your house from here?" The fact that Rain rode her bike with one hand all the way to school, to work, and then home again already impressed me, but when I drove to her house, I was blown away. It wasn't a short trip for a bike, and there were a lot of major hills. "You do this during the winter on your bike, too? When it's cold and dark?" I asked, making a left turn onto yet another backroad as she directed me.

Rain shrugged like it wasn't a big deal. "I don't do it every day. Only if Jo has to use the truck for work and Mr. Clark isn't able to take me home. Jo almost always takes me to school in the morning with my bike in the back, just in case. It's a small town."

It still didn't seem like an easy task to me, but her answer led to my other question.

"Why do you call Jo by her name? I feel like with her being your adoptive mom, you would call her 'Mom.'"

Rain had her face turned toward the open window, letting the wind play with her hair. "Jo never wanted me to. I've always known about my birth mom and that I was adopted. Jo was a foster kid growing up, and she felt like it was important for me to always remember where I came from."

"Jo was a foster kid?"

"Mhm. This next driveway on the right is us," she said.

The pale yellow farmhouse that came into view looked just like the sort of house I would imagine Rain to live in. It was old but well kept with a wrap-around porch holding two rocking chairs and brightly painted flower pots all over the place. I had no doubt that Rain had painted them.

When we got out of the truck and made our way toward the porch, I stopped to point out a vibrant rose bush in a blush-pink pot. "Looks like you've got a green thumb, too. I'll have to get you to help me in my garden sometime."

Rain gave a doubtful chuckle. "Oh no, that would be Jo's green thumb. Utilize my help at your own risk. If my thumb is green, it's only because I painted it."

I laughed as I followed her up the steps and through the front door. Inside, the floors beneath us whined under our weight, and the door creaked as it shut. I was immediately struck by all of the color. Rain's paintings in gold frames filled the white walls of their living room like a gallery, each piece so different from the one beside it. The couch was an emerald green, and there was a pink wingback chair next to the fireplace.

"Jo insists we hang up as many as we can," Rain said when she saw me admiring her art. "I can't say I like them being on display everywhere, but she's adamant, and I do like the color it brings to each room. Plus, we rarely have anyone over, so it's not too embarrassing."

"If I could paint like you, I'd show my work off to anyone who would look at it."

"I doubt it. The more I look at a painting, the more mistakes I find and the more I don't want them on display."

THE COLORS OF RAIN

I moved closer to one that specifically caught my eye. It was a view of the ocean, wild and alive, with a night sky nearly as majestic as the real thing. The constellations were all there and in place. It was done in her usual, slightly abstract style that suggested more than reality, but it almost combined what you would see and what you would feel if you were there.

"You're amazing," I said in an awe-struck whisper, looking it over. I guessed almost every home in Ivy Hollow had at least one of her paintings on display since she sold them at the antique store.

"Thank you," she said quietly.

I faced her. "Here I am giving you all the attention that makes you not want them on display, right?"

Her cheeks blushed pink as she pushed her black framed glasses higher on her nose. "Yeah, kinda."

I gave the painting one last look before following Rain into the kitchen, where we found Jo frantically pouring the water off some pasta. Rain immediately jumped in to help her by stirring the bubbling sauce on the stove.

Jo was a lot younger looking than I imagined her to be. She wore purple scrubs that now had a pasta sauce stain near her waist.

"Hi, Evan," she said with a slight flush to her cheeks. "I'm sorry you walked in on my crazy. Rain's a lot better in the kitchen than I am." She glanced over at Rain, who snorted at her apparent sarcasm. "Anyway, it's so nice to finally meet you."

"It's nice to meet you, too," I said. "What can I do to help?"

They put me to work setting the table while they put the finishing touches on dinner. After a few minutes, we were all sitting down to a hot meal of pasta, garlic bread, and salad.

Jo was easy to make conversation with. She asked about my family and our move here and invited us to church. She asked about my garden and told me about her flower beds, which she really enjoyed tending, and that gave us a common interest.

Rain was fairly quiet over dinner, piping in here and there, until Jo asked her about school and work.

"It was okay," she said, poking at the last few pieces of lettuce in her salad bowl. "Mr. Clark left awfully early. I don't think he was feeling well, but you know how he is. He won't tell you the whole truth."

"He seemed weak when I checked in on him Tuesday to bring him supper," Jo said, her brow dipping. "All he would say is that he always gets down this time of year with the change of the seasons, but I know his and Bonnie's wedding anniversary is coming up."

Rain frowned. "Maybe once it's behind him he'll be back to his old self. He didn't even want me to read to him before he left."

I wiped my hands on my napkin after taking my final bite and leaned back in my chair. "How long have you known Mr. Clark?"

"My whole life," Rain said.

"He's been more of a dad to me than anyone I've ever known, and the closest Rain has to a grandfather," Jo added, gathering our plates and taking them to the sink. "I think I'll make a pot of coffee. Rain, do you want me to boil water for tea?"

Rain stood to finish the task of clearing the table. "Yes, please."

"And what'll you have, Evan?"

"I'll have coffee," I said.

Rain gave me a look of disappointment. "Not you, too."

"You don't like it?" I asked.

She shook her head with a crinkled nose, and I noticed for the first time that she had a few freckles—dusted on her cheeks like faint stars.

"You would be a tea drinker," I said with a smirk. "You along with all your fictional characters from Barrie and Dickens and Austen."

"Frankly, I'm surprised you know who Jane Austen is," Rain remarked.

"I do know some things about literature; I just don't like it. And besides, my mom is obsessed with all things Austen."

"Well, tea happens to be the one thing that my reading *doesn't* influence," she said, walking behind the island to grab two mugs and a very regency-looking teacup from the upper cabinet. "I like tea because I like it, and I dislike coffee because it has an awful taste. I don't understand how anyone drinks it."

I looked on from my spot at the table as she and Jo measured out tea leaves and ground coffee beans. "I could say the same about tea. It's too watery. It's no good unless it's iced and sweetened in true southern fashion."

"Coffee tastes burnt. And only enjoying tea when it's covered up with cups of sugar is criminal. I'm disappointed in you."

"Well, get used to it." I crossed my arms against my chest. "You'll always find something in me to be disappointed about. Whether it's for reading CliffsNotes or drinking coffee or butchering your story."

She looked at me doubtfully as she poured the hot water into her cup. "I'll reform you yet. Give me time."

"You may get me reading and writing by the end of this, but I assure you I won't be drinking tea."

Rain dropped her diffuser full of tea leaves into her cup. Looking at it closely, I could see that there were paint smudges all over it. She had paint smudges on everything she owned—little bits of her creativity impressing itself on everything in her life.

Her mug nestled in hand, Rain looked over at me with reluctance. "We best get started on that paper. We can work in the living room, but I'll be honest, I'm not sure what we're going to work on."

I stood and rubbed the back of my neck. We were both reluctant. Neither one of us ready to take the plunge. I was terrified of her reading my awful writing, and she was terrified of sharing her story.

"I'd like to see more of your art for starters," I told her in an effort to procrastinate longer. She seemed as eager to put it off as me, and a few minutes later, I found myself following her up a set of stairs and to a hallway, the steps creaking beneath us. Even the walls going upstairs held art, but at the landing, I spotted a few family photos of her and Jo.

"I'd really like to watch you paint your hand with your mouth. That'd be cool."

We reached the top, and Rain turned her head back to give me a look that told me I was asking for more than I was going to get.

Inside Rain's bedroom was basically an art studio. Art supplies were scattered on her floor, and her work displayed itself from top to bottom. Color enveloped me, giving me the feeling of being surrounded by the stained glass windows of a great cathedral like the one in Chicago.

Mom grew up Catholic and was until college. Even though we were Protestant, when I was little, Mom would sometimes take me to see the cathedral during the day when the sun shone brightly through that colored glass. Even as a kid, I was in awe and felt a kind of reverence sweep over me. It was the same with Rain's bedroom.

"Wow," I said with a slight gasp which made Rain blush again, and she rubbed her right forearm with her left hand.

I moved in closer to one of the paintings. It was the silhouette of a girl holding an umbrella, walking down a street lined with trees. Her right hand was missing. The whole photo was black and white, except for the raindrops. Those featured an array of hues, falling to create puddles and dripping down the umbrella. The only other thing that contained color was the girl's painted left hand that gripped the umbrella.

"You're incredible," I whispered, sounding like a broken record. But she was.

Rain joined me in front of the painting with the girl and pointed to the raindrops. "Remember how I told you that colors bring emotion with them? It's a big factor that plays into each of my paintings and even how I see the world. It sounds kind of crazy, but just think about it: what sort of emotion or concepts do you think the color black portrays?"

It took me a minute of thinking to come up with anything. "Fear. Loneliness, maybe."

Rain nodded. "What do you think about green?"

Green was harder, but I looked around her room, and my gaze fell on a painting of a field of sunflowers. "Growth," I said. "Life."

Rain smiled. "That's what your garden does, right? It takes the black that came after your dad passed, and even if it's just for a while, it turns it to green. That's why you moved here, where there was more green."

I crossed my arms, feeling exposed, like she was seeing straight into me. "Yeah, something like that."

I wanted to change the subject, so I made my way over to three more paintings that grabbed my attention. They were side by side in round, decorative frames—portraits of three different girls. One I could easily tell was Rain, but I wasn't sure about the other two. Neither looked like Jo, and one of them was a child. Elementary school age, maybe. The other one was a little older, but still young, with bright blonde hair and eyes with varying shades of blue. I looked closer and found the ocean in her eyes, subtle waves of different blue hues. The detail was incredible.

"Who are they?" I asked. "This one is you, I know. But who are the other two?"

Rain's face drained of color as she turned toward the bookshelf on the wall opposite her bed. "Not yet. We've not gotten to that part of the story yet."

"We haven't gotten anywhere with your story yet," I reminded her.

"There's plenty of time. Besides, you still have some reading to catch up on." She pulled *Peter Pan* off the shelf and flipped through the pages. "How far have you gotten?"

I grimaced. "I haven't started it yet. Did you finish reading it again?"

As she fingered through the pages, I could see dozens of lines highlighted and marked. "Yep. It was just as good the third time as it was the first. Actually, I would say even better."

In all honesty, I'd only completed a couple of books in my lifetime. I couldn't imagine reading one twice, and definitely not three times.

"A good book can be enjoyed once just fine, but a great book leaves you never wanting to walk away, and so, every once in a while, you indulge in the pull to go back and relive it."

"I guess I've never read a great book, then," I said.

"You're right. You opted to read the CliffsNotes instead," Rain said with a smirk, pulling A *Tale of Two Cities* off the shelf to glance at it. "That's why we're here."

I couldn't help being slightly glad that I'd read those Cliffs-Notes, because it got me into a new story—the story of Rain Brooks. A girl with just one hand that always held palm-sized masterpieces, and everything in life she touched seemed to receive her color. The story of the girl who'd read everyone else's stories, multiple times even, but few had ever taken the time to read hers. Dickens created a cast of unique and compelling characters in A *Tale of Two Cities*, no doubt. But to me, there was no character more colorful and compelling than Rain herself. The girl who saw the world differently than most and gave me a small glimpse of it.

We never worked on the paper that night. Not really, anyway. We spent the evening going through her art and sitting on the living room floor, talking about everything under the sun. Everything except for my story and hers.

It was still research, you could say, because I got to know Rain better. I noticed things while she was here in her own home with her own people that I hadn't noticed about her at school. Like the way she blushed when I asked her about herself and how she laughed with her eyes almost completely shut behind her glasses. Or how she always followed every sarcastic comment with a smile or a wink to let others know she was only teasing. I don't think Rain could bear to offend a fly.

And the way she always knew what questions to ask me about myself to dig deeper than you really cared to go, because she was investigating my character as much as I investigated hers. I wondered if she did because she was looking to trust me, but I think she did it because she truly cared to know.

She was a reader. A reader of stories and of people, knowing that each person had their own tale to tell. She and my dad had that in common. The more I knew her, the more I was reminded of Dad. Reminded in the way where a memory comes to your mind, and while you enjoy it inside, you can't keep the smile from displaying itself outside. But even those memories can leave you in agony.

When I got home that night, I told Mom about Rain and Jo. She was dying to know what I'd learned about Rain's past. When I told her that we didn't work on the paper at all and that we just hung out, she smiled.

"That's even better. I'm glad you're settling in here and making friends," she said sleepily from her spot on the couch. She looked tired, and not just the kind of tired that comes when you haven't slept. The kind that happens when life licks you.

A twang of guilt pierced me.

I'd come here for all of us to start fresh and find a new life, but Ava was right—I was the only one getting it. I had my garden, and now I had friends, but I was leaving Mom and Ava in the dust.

That isn't what Dad asked of me. I was failing the one mission he'd given me. The purpose he gave me when he died. And that feeling was crippling compared to the ache left behind after the good memories.

Rain wasn't ready to trust me with her story, and I still didn't trust myself with mine.

RAIN

"IT'S PRETTY SIMPLE TODAY," Evan remarked, motioning to my hand as he caught up to me in the hallway.

I stretched out my arm to look over it again. I had gold paint on my fingertips and it got lighter the closer it was to my wrist. The paint was brand new. It wasn't just metallic gold, it sparkled like glitter.

"Yeah," I said. "Pixie dust." It was the very first thing to come to my mind when I saw the paint online, and I had to have it.

"Pixie dust," Evan repeated. "I should've guessed."

I stopped at my locker and started turning the knob on the lock. Around us, the hallways buzzed with motion as everyone darted to get their things and make their way to class.

"Are you going to finish *Peter Pan* over the weekend?" I asked. "I refuse to tell you any juicy details until you've at least put the effort in to finish *Peter Pan*. It isn't very long after all." I was stalling. Sure, I wanted to see Evan put in the effort before trusting him with the truth, but I was also buying time to back out. It was wrong, and I knew it.

I wanted to trust him and help him with this paper, but every time my eyes met Jordan's as we passed each other in the hall or as I took my seat in homeroom, fear made me want to become one with the floor beneath me. The thought of her knowing who I was and having to face her robbed me of all courage pushing me toward helping Evan.

And I couldn't help but feel like she was looking at me as suspiciously as I was at her. I got the feeling she knew something. Maybe not everything, but she was onto *something*. So I'd done my best to keep out of her path. I felt like an intruder in my own school, hiding in the shadows and avoiding the places she might be.

"Yeah, I guess I'll try," Evan said. "I have a busy weekend ahead of me though."

"Oh yeah? What will you be up to?"

He leaned against the locker beside mine, gripping the strap of his backpack on his shoulder. "I'm building a greenhouse. I want to be able to grow some stuff throughout the winter, so I'm gonna set one up in our field."

"That sounds like a big undertaking. Want some help?"

"Nah, I'm sure I can manage. I could always try getting Ava out there if I need to."

I smirked at him doubtfully. "Yeah, somehow I don't see that ending well."

I exchanged my history textbook for my science and dug through the spare pens and pencils I kept in my locker hoping to find an extra eraser. I'd worn my previous one down to a nub. Mostly a result of math class.

"Let me help you," I said as I fingered through my container of spare tools. "I'd love to. I don't have to work at the antique store until the afternoon. I'm not sure how helpful I'll be, but three hands are better than two, right?"

Evan glanced at my stubbed wrist and laughed nervously. People were always weird about my hand at first. It was way more awkward for them than for me, so I usually tried to joke about it. "Yeah, I guess so."

"Besides," I said, "I want to see you in your natural habitat. I want to see your garden."

"Well, it's nothing compared to what I'll do next year. But it's more than what I used to have. And I'll pay you for your labor in sunflowers and any veggies you want."

My eyebrows rose at his offer. "Sunflowers are my favorite flower. You have yourself a deal." I reached my left arm out, and Evan gave me his left hand to shake. It was so brief I can't say for certain, and maybe I imagined it, but I think he hesitated before letting go, making my face go warm.

Behind me, I heard someone call my name, and I was grateful for a reason to turn away from Evan to find the voice's owner, even though I already knew the culprit. There was no mistaking his stiff speech.

I turned to see Thomas making his way down the hall, smiling from ear to ear. "I have a field trip today," he said, stopping in front of me and Evan. His eyes were alight with excitement, but they kept landing on Evan curiously.

I leaned back on my locker to face him. "Are you going to that Civil War site?"

"Yep. And I'm bringing the pocket watch on the bus to work on it, so tell Mr. Clark I'll have it finished for him this weekend."

"Will do."

Thomas glanced behind me at Evan and then back to me expectantly, and I knew he was only here to get a formal introduction.

"Have you met Evan yet?" I asked. "He's new, and he loves the typewriter you just brought into the shop."

"Thomas," he introduced himself, reaching his hand out formally. "Thomas Helms."

Evan shook it firmly. "Evan Lawson."

"A pleasure." Thomas copied etiquette from his favorite movies which mostly dated back to the thirties and forties. He considered himself a true gentleman. But he turned it off and on, spending half of his time mimicking dialogue from Cary Grant and the other half being an average kid. It was endearing.

I glanced up at the clock on the wall. Class would start in three minutes. "When does your bus leave?" I asked Thomas.

His gaze followed mine, and he quickly began reversing his wheelchair. The fear of being tardy drew his face into a determined scowl as he heaved at the wheels. Thomas hated being late. "Right now or so. I'll catch you two later. I'll see you this weekend sometime, Rain." And with that he was off, abrupt as always.

94

Thomas was unpredictable and yet unchanging, and I loved that about him. You never knew what to expect from him, but you always knew who he was and where his heart was. The world around him could flip upside down, and you wouldn't know how he'd respond, but you knew he would be the same ol' Thomas.

I slid the last few books into my bag and closed my locker. "And now you've met our Thomas."

Evan smiled. "Seems like a cool kid."

"He is."

"Maybe I'll stop by the shop on Saturday after we're done with the greenhouses so I can take another look at that typewriter, if it's still there."

"It's right where you left it."

Even though we'd had multiple people stop in for a look, no one had actually made the plunge to buy it. I believed it was supposed to belong to Evan, and there in the window it would stay until he had it.

He crossed his arms. "I still don't know what I'd do with it aside from writing this paper with it. I just think it'd be cool to put it in my room to remind me of my dad."

"You never know, you might fall in love with words and take up a hobby of composing stories by the time you're done. Maybe you'll follow in his footsteps."

Evan smirked. "Fall in love with words? I don't think so."

I started making my way toward history class, Evan close beside me. "Think about it. We have markings—a set of lines and scribbles—that we call letters. We pair a few together to create what we call words, and they officially have meaning. Put together enough of those and you create a sentence that means even more. Compile those and you can tell a story; you can create

95

worlds and lives and people. I think it's pretty easy to fall in love with words." I glanced at him briefly to read his expression, and I saw a thousand questions in his eyes. "I'm determined you'll agree by the end of this."

He let out a short laugh and shook his head. "You have higher expectations for this paper than Mrs. Jones does, I think."

"Maybe so. But I told you you'd be biting off more than you can chew. You can't say I didn't warn you."

In history class, my mind was anywhere but on the history of British monarchs. I'd been that way since Jordan arrived, always thinking about her and wondering if we'd cross paths when the bell rang. Wondering if I'd run into her in the bathroom. It wasn't like me. I loved school. Well, except math and science, that is.

Then, I realized Jordan was probably on the field trip with Thomas. I wouldn't have to spend my day trying to hide from her. A burden lifted from my shoulders.

She and Thomas were in the same grade, and I'd noticed them sitting together at lunch a few times. I wanted to ask Thomas about her and what she was like, but I didn't want to tell him why I cared to know. I didn't want him tugged in two directions if he'd truly found a friend in her. If she was at all skeptical of me, I didn't want Thomas feeling like he had to pledge his loyalty to me instead of her. I felt it was best to just keep him out of the middle as much as possible. I just hoped he truly had found a friend in her. Kids could be brutal, and he knew that better than anyone. But Thomas was smart, and I figured he wouldn't continue hanging out with her if she wasn't worth his time.

But maybe not.

After school, Evan followed me outside to the front of the school. Kids surrounded us as they made their way to buses or waited for their names to be called from the carpool line. Those of us who drove weren't allowed to leave until after the carpool line had gone through, so Evan and I sat together with our backs against the brick walls of the school, watching and waiting.

"You've been in this little town your whole life," Evan said abruptly.

"I have."

"Do you know everyone in town?"

"Almost everyone. I'd say most."

Evan opened his mouth to reply, but his face slowly fell. His eyes squinted, fixed on something in the distance. "Do you know her?"

My gaze immediately tried to follow his.

Jordan was at the end of his stare. She stood awkwardly as if wondering what she was supposed to do, her eyes fixed with concern on someone. She was watching Thomas.

Thomas was in the middle of the crowd. His eyes were red and puffy, his expression heated.

I stood to my feet with a jolt and made my way over to him. I'd seen this before and chills ran up my arms in rage as the memory began to play itself in my head.

"What happened?" I asked once I was leaning over him.

The other instance had been when he and I were both in middle school. I'd found him crying in the hallway, and Drake Anderson had stood over him with a devilish grin. The things he'd said to Thomas, the way he made him out to be little more than an animal, had made me angrier than I'd ever felt in my life. I ended up in detention for slapping Drake, and I've never once regretted it.

"Forget it, Rain," Thomas said. There was a bite in his tone.

"Come on," I pressed him. "What's going on?"

He refused to meet my eyes, keeping them fixed on the carpool line. "You don't have to protect me all the time."

"We're friends, aren't we?" I asked. "That's what friends do. You'd protect me if I needed it, right?"

He didn't answer.

Evan walked up behind me and nudged my arm. "We aren't the only ones concerned," he said and nodded his head forward.

I followed his gaze back to Jordan. She stared at the three of us nervously until our eyes met, and she looked quickly away.

My head darted back to Thomas. "What did she do? It was Jordan, wasn't it?"

"Rain, I said to forget about it." He was getting agitated, but so was I.

Jordan's name was called, and I watched as she made her way to a black SUV in the carpool line.

And time slowed down. My hand gripped tightly to Thomas' wheelchair armrest. I couldn't keep myself from holding my breath and waiting for her to open the passenger door. The situation at hand disappeared from my mind as I strained to see the driver. I swallowed, but the saliva felt stuck in my tightening throat. I watched with eyes wide as Jordan's fingers grabbed the doorknob.

After all these years, here she was. In the carpool line at my school. I would finally see her. In flesh and blood. The woman whose choice changed the entire course of my life.

"Are you alright?" Evan asked, and I turned to face him with a flushed face.

I tucked my hair behind my ear nervously. My hand was shaking. "Yeah. I'm fine."

When I looked back at the car, Jordan was already in, and she shut the door before I could get a glimpse.

It's fine, I told myself, exhaling. *You don't want her here anyway.*

I looked back down at Thomas, who was still searching the line for his mom's car. He was retreating into himself. I'd seen it before. He would shut the world out and process all of it internally until he became nothing but a shell of the Thomas we all knew and loved. Getting him out of the pit was never an easy task.

I kneeled in front of him so that he had no choice but to meet my eyes. "Thomas, I'm your friend. You can tell me."

"My only friend, I guess," he said. "I thought she was. She made me think she was." His name was finally called, and he didn't hesitate to steer himself around me and make his escape.

I stood to my feet, feeling queasy. Getting over this wasn't going to be easy for Thomas.

And I had been so close. So close to seeing her.

"What was that all about?" Evan asked as we watched him roll his chair onto the ramp of his car.

"I'm not sure yet," I said, determination laced in my voice. "But I'm gonna find out."

JORDAN

> "Oh, sometimes I think it is of no use to make friends. They only go out of your life after awhile and leave a hurt that is worse than the emptiness before they came."
>
> L.M. Montgomery, _Anne of Avonlea_

MY SIXTEENTH BIRTHDAY SUCKED.

I asked Mom if Aunt Cassidy could come stay for the weekend. She said she'd think about it, but since there was still so much to unpack, she really didn't feel up to hosting just yet. And that was the end of it.

Dad called me before school to tell me happy birthday, and he promised a card and money was on its way. "I'm not sure how long it takes for mail to arrive in Ivy Hollow or if it arrives at all," he joked, "but it's coming nonetheless."

Aunt Cass called me, too. "Sixteen!" she cried over the phone. "My gosh, time flies! But at the same time, you've always acted so grown up. I'd think this was your twenty-first birthday if I didn't know any better."

"Thanks, Aunt Cass," I said.

"So... What are you doing to celebrate?"

"I don't know. Hopefully I'll have a driver's license by the end of the day. And technically I get out of school because we have a field trip. It sounds boring, but it's better than going to class." I wanted to sound mature and indifferent. Like it didn't really matter that Mom had made zero effort to make the day special. Being obsessed with birthdays was for kids anyway.

"That's lucky," she said. I could hear her smacking on chewing gum over the phone. "Make sure your mom does something special for you though. This is a big one. Next time I see you, we'll party big. I promise."

I believed her, because she was the one person in my family who still kept her promises to me. The one person I still felt I could count on.

When I got to school, we started loading up into the bus right after homeroom. My field trip was with my history class to some war site from the Civil War. It was a pretty day, so being able to spend my birthday outside instead of in a stuffy classroom really was a win.

Thomas couldn't have been more excited about the trip. "I've been here twice with my parents, and it's so awesome!" he told me on the bus. We sat together, and I watched as he tinkered with his pocket watch to pass the time.

I played with the small gear he handed to hold for him as he worked. "I've never been."

"You'll love it. There's the coolest old stuff that I would love to pull apart."

There were two guys sitting in the row in front of us, and one turned around to face me. I knew his name was Drake and that he was super tall for our age. I didn't know him well, but I'd gathered that his ego was even bigger than he was.

Thomas glanced up briefly from his tinkering.

"You're the new girl," Drake said to me. "It's Jordan, right?"

"Yeah," I said.

He looked me up and down. "Let me guess, you're the athletic type."

My face went warm under his analyzing stare. "I like to run," I mumbled.

"Really? I hate running, but I do it anyway. I'm on the football team."

"Nice," was all I said. I tried to keep my answers short. I had no desire to encourage any sort of friendship between us. The one friendship I *did* have I hadn't even encouraged. It just sort of happened.

"Maybe we could run together sometime. I bet I'd like it a little more if I had some company."

"She probably doesn't want to hang out with you, Drake," Thomas retorted, still focusing on his watch.

Drake rolled his eyes.

"Thanks for the offer," I said. "I'll think it over."

Drake winked. "Sure," he said, and turned around in his seat.

Thomas held his hand out expectantly, and I dropped the gear back into his palm. "Drake's bad news," he muttered, just quiet enough to keep the conversation between us.

"Oh yeah?"

He gave two rigid nods. "He's a jerk."

"Well, maybe I'll take you running with me next time I go, then."

Thomas looked up at me like I was an idiot. "I can't run. Wheel-chair, remember?"

I smirked at him. "Of course I remember. But I could push you, couldn't I? I'd get a better workout that way."

His eyes lit up, and a smile crossed his face. "Sure. That'd be cool."

I smiled, too. There was something about Thomas and being around him that made me genuinely happy—and that was a rarity for me these days. In all honesty, I never would have thought I'd enjoy hanging out with someone like him, but something about him had drawn me in from the first day he sat with me at lunch. I loved watching him work and seeing the determination he put into his tinkering. I liked to see his face brighten when he finally figured it out. And I loved his heart. He hated to see someone left out. He was always looking to be the friend someone needed. I guessed it was probably because he'd been the one without a friend so many times. I'd always been the sort to stick to what I knew. I never branched out. I was never the one to introduce myself first. I built a wall around myself. But Thomas made me want to be a bit braver and kinder.

The ride to the war site was nearly an hour long, and Thomas had his pocket watch ticking away by then. He would only have to clean and polish it before it was ready to go to the antique store where he sold his refurbished items.

The war site was pretty cool, I guess. Or at least Thomas made it feel that way. His commentary made me laugh as we walked the long trail, cannons and open battlefields around us.

"Virginia and North Carolina had the most Confederate deaths during the Civil War. But New York had even more deaths," he told me as I pushed him along. "Over four hundred thousand soldiers were wounded. And ya know what?"

"What?"

"Some of their wounds glowed in the dark."

I rolled my eyes and pushed my bangs behind my ear. "Yeah, okay. Whatever."

"No, I'm serious!"

"I'm not falling for it."

"I swear it's true!" he argued passionately, and he turned in his chair to look up at me with eyes lit up with excitement. "There's science to back it up. After the Battle of Shiloh, soldiers said their wounds were glowing in the dark, and no one could figure out why, but the ones that glowed healed faster."

"Some sort of magic, I suppose?"

Thomas's facial expression transitioned to a glare. "Really, Jordan? Magic? Are we babies still?" He rolled his eyes with an air of drama before continuing. "It was science. They later figured out it was because the wounded men became hypothermic, and their body temperatures were perfect for a bioluminescent bacteria called *Photorhabdus luminescens* which has pathogens. And that's why the wounds glowed. So then the generals made all of the wounded men walk ahead so they could see where they were going in the dark."

He lost me at the word "bioluminescent," but I said, "Well, I guess that makes sense."

"You have no idea what that means, do you?"

"Nope. And that makes you proud, doesn't it?"

Thomas did a miserable job fighting a smirk. "I like knowing more than people."

"Well, I'm glad to hear that making me feel stupid brings you joy."

"Ah, come on." He waved a dismissive hand and turned forward in his chair again. "I'm trying to make you smarter. Toughen up a little. And push a little faster; we're falling behind."

"Yes, sir."

Silence hovered between us almost a full minute before he finally fessed up. "I did lie about the part where the generals made the wounded guys walk ahead. I don't think that they glowed enough for that, but maybe all of them together did. That would be pretty cool. But making them walk ahead would be kinda cruel since they were hurt. I'd say they were lagging behind, kinda like we are. Didn't you say you were a runner?"

I stifled a laugh and purposefully slowed down, the gap between us and the rest of the class growing. Thomas turned his head back again to look at me with his left eyebrow raised.

I shrugged. "That's what you get for lying to me."

It didn't take long for Thomas to recover from his irritation, because he was back to spitting facts and statistics within a few seconds.

As we followed behind the group, Drake eventually slowed down to fall into step with me. "I think it's great you're so nice to him. A lot of people wouldn't be. Least of all the new girl," he whispered into my ear, as if Thomas wasn't right in front of us.

I shrugged, and didn't bother to lower my voice. Thomas couldn't walk, but his hearing was just fine. "He's the one who was nice to me. He was the first person to talk to me."

I saw Thomas's head turn slightly, and I knew he listened in on our conversation. Drake noticed, too.

"So what do you think of Ivy Hollow so far?" he asked, taking on a normal tone of voice.

I'd been able to escape thoughts of the move, the divorce, and my home life for a few blissful hours. Drake's unwelcome reminder immediately smothered out my unusually pleasant mood. "It's alright," I slurred.

"You're from Florida, right? I'm sure it seems pretty boring in comparison. But maybe you just need to get to know some people. I'd love to show you around sometime. There are a few interesting things to do, believe it or not. With the right crowd, you can make the most of it."

Thomas shook his head, and I felt sure he was rolling his eyes.

"Thanks for the offer," I said.

"Sure thing."

"We're coming up on the best part," Thomas said, pointing ahead of us. "You see that statue?"

"Yeah, I see it."

"You know who that is?"

I exhaled with a smile. "Nope. But I bet you'll be more than happy to tell me."

"He's the best general of the whole war. I'm literally named after him."

I thought through the different names of the men we'd been talking about in class. "Thomas Jackson?" I asked.

He clapped his hands slowly. "Wow. You must have actually been listening yesterday."

"I do try."

I looked over the statue as we passed it by, but Thomas was all but drooling, as if it were the most sacred monument ever created. I couldn't keep from feeling a little secondhand joy as a result of his delight.

Drake put his hands in the back pockets of his jeans. "I think we're coming to the end now. Finally." For the first time, I noticed he wasn't unpleasant to look at. He had a sharp jawline and dark, wavy hair. His eyes were a matching shade. Too bad about his inflated ego.

After a little while longer of walking, the group came to a halt, and we caught up as men in costumes began to line up in the field for a reenactment.

Thomas's eyes grew wide, and his lips curved into a smile as we watched them take their positions.

Minutes after the battle began, I felt Drake grab my elbow. "Come this way," he whispered, nodding his head toward a small, old building.

I eyed him suspiciously.

"Unless you're just dying to see how this act ends. I'm sure Thomas will be happy to tell you who wins back on the bus."

Red flags waved fiercely in my head, but for some reason, I ignored them. I don't know why. I was content to stay right where I was. I had no desire to get to know Drake, and I didn't want to risk getting in trouble. But I snuck away with him behind the old log cabin and sat next to him in the grass anyway. Maybe it was because I hated saying no. Maybe it was to avoid the embarrassment of resisting. Whatever the reason, I did it.

Drake leaned his back against the historic logs at a slight angle so he could face me. "So tell me about yourself."

I drew my knees to my chest and wrapped my arms around them. I watched over my shoulder and over his, waiting for a teacher to catch us. "There isn't much to say," I told him.

He ran his fingers through his hair and fluffed it a little. "Relax. No one saw us. And I'll take the blame if they did. We're just hanging out. We didn't commit a crime."

I sure felt like we had. My over-cautious, anxiety-driven mind was reprimanding me fiercely. "Thomas will be upset when he finds out I ran off."

"You sure are uptight, aren't you? Loosen up. Thomas is fine. He's on cloud nine right now and doesn't even know you've left. Didn't you see him watching those soldiers?"

The corner of my mouth lifted. "He was pretty into it."

"Yeah, he's fine."

I looked ahead of us at the rolling hills and thought of the soldiers that had marched and traveled them so many years ago. They had real battles to fear. Real problems to have anxiety over. The thought didn't make me braver; it only made me feel weaker than before.

Drake tried to strike up a conversation, bringing me out of my thoughts. "You haven't really answered my question. I know you like to run and you're from Florida—and that you're really nice—but that's all I know."

"Who says I'm nice?"

He picked a few blades of grass and rubbed them between his fingers. "Well, you choose to hang out with Thomas for starters."

A frown turned my lips for a brief second, but I didn't say anything. I should have. I didn't hang out with Thomas because I was nice and a better person than most; I hung out with him because *he* was nice and I liked being with him. Sometimes, peace-making was my gift. Other times, it was just a cop-out.

"I've heard you live in town and your mom has a real estate business," Drake said.

"Yeah. I live with my mom and little sister. We're on Third Street."

"Cool."

An awkward silence came next, filled only by the fake gunshots from the battle reenactment behind us. The result of following Drake behind that building wasn't amounting to much. Not that I exactly expected it to.

"So who was the guy you sat with on the bus?" I asked when I couldn't take the cringey quiet any longer. I wasn't sure which was worse, the cringey silence or the desperate attempts of Drake to flirt—if you could even call it that.

"That's Andrew. He's on the football team, too. His dad used to be the coach, but now my dad is," he said, swishing his hair out of his eyes again. "You should come to one of our games sometime. If only you'd been around last year—dang, that was our best season yet. I scored the winning touchdown in the last game of the season. It was also Dad's first year coaching, and he really improved the team a lot. The last coach was trash, and we never won."

I was internally rolling my eyes. He was every bit the egomaniac I had suspected he was.

"Aren't you in ninth grade?" I quizzed him suspiciously. "How were you scoring touchdowns for the high school football team last year?"

Drake's insecurity started showing as he brushed his fingers through his hair over and over, but he tried to play it cool by shrugging it off. "I was held back. Andrew and I both were. Got into a little trouble, if you know what I mean." He stopped to wink at me.

I *didn't* know what he meant, but I definitely didn't care to find out, so I never asked.

"Cool with us though. Just makes us the oldest in our class. The kids respect us more, you know?"

I brought my attention back to the rolling hills. I couldn't look him in the eye anymore. Nothing about Drake commanded my respect, and yet he got me to follow him behind some old building for no other apparent reason than to try and sweet talk me. I didn't respect him, but I gave him what he wanted anyway. That made me respect myself even less.

Drake inched himself closer, a mere two inches away from my spot in the grass, making the hair on the back of my neck rise and red flags wave wildly in my head. "You know, Andrew and I are going out tonight with his younger sister. You should come with us."

I didn't even take the time to think about it. "I'm good, but thanks," I said. I was majorly regretting following him back there.

"Gosh, you sure are uptight," he mentioned again for the umpteenth time.

I brought my knees a little closer to myself and hugged them tighter. I didn't want to agree with him, but it was true. I'd never cared much about having a busy social life. The one I'd had back in Florida just sort of found me, like Thomas had. I was never the one to seek it out.

"You'll always hate it here if you don't get to know the place," he said. "We're just going to the movies and out for dinner."

"It's actually my birthday." I said it a little too quickly. "My mom has plans for us." Truthfully, I'd be surprised if Mom even remembered to mention my birthday again.

Drake looked like he caught my excuse, and his eyes went down to the grass as he tried to hide a smirk. I felt like he was mocking me. "So why Thomas but not me?"

My eyebrow lifted, and I couldn't resist a short laugh. Was that what this was about? He was just trying to compete with the guy in the wheelchair. To prove he could win my attention.

"Why *not* Thomas instead of you?" The question came out with more bite than I'd intended.

Drake caught the bite, too, and he blinked at me before trying to hide his shock with a forced smile. "Come on. You're no idiot. I don't know much about you, but I can guess that much. There's not *one* thing about him that makes me want to hang out with him."

Drake had officially bitten off more than he could chew. I refused to give in to his ego. He might have been the football team's best player, he might have been the oldest in our grade, but Thomas would win this game.

I stood to my feet and prepared to exit the situation before it grew worse. I just had to figure out how I was going to sneak from behind the building without being seen.

"If that's the case, I'm probably not your type either," I said, peering around the building. The reenactment was over already, so I didn't have a cover up anymore. "I think he and I have a lot in common."

"You're joking," Drake said.

I turned to face him again. "Nope."

He let out an exasperated laugh, but it seemed like he was trying to cool down. "Look, I'm trying to make friends with you, and you're making it kind of difficult."

"I didn't ask you to try and make friends with me. I don't really care to have friends. I feel like I've made that pretty clear." I didn't even want to be here. Not at this school, not in this town, and definitely not behind this log cabin.

"Except for Thomas," he said.

"Exactly."

"Maybe you are an idiot."

"Or maybe you're just a jerk. Thomas is ten times a better person than you could ever think about being."

Drake stood, and I suddenly wanted to back down, but I couldn't now. I felt my knees tense as he towered over me, his eyes locking on mine. A mixture of anger and fear brewed in my chest, making me nauseous. Not to mention, he was so close I could smell his cheap cologne, which made me want to gag. I wanted to run, but I couldn't even look away. I wasn't sure what to prepare myself for.

"Thomas is retarded and does nothing but get in the way. He gets special treatment from everyone and can do no wrong—and for what? All because he's *special*. Yeah"—Drake paused to cackle and his eyes grew darker—"he's special alright. A special kind of stupid."

My cheeks burned to hear him talk that way about Thomas, but I bit my tongue until I tasted the metallic twang of blood. I was afraid of him and what he'd think of me if I spoke out.

I've said enough. I'm a peacemaker, I thought over and over as Drake stared into my eyes, daring me to react. But it had far more to do with people-pleasing than peace-making.

Finally, after what seemed like a full minute of Drake's face hovering over mine, his hands slipped into his back pockets, and his gaze broke. "If you want to hang with a moron, go for it," he muttered fiercely under his breath, giving me one last look up and down. "Such a waste." And then he walked off, not even bothering to peer around the building to see if anyone was watching.

I exhaled once he was gone, my nerves on edge, and leaned my weight on the building next to me. I felt like all the blood had rushed to my head—throbbing and dizzy. It was my own fault; I shouldn't have followed him back here in the first place.

I peeked my head from behind the log cabin again to see what the others were doing. I wasn't as brave as Drake to just make an entrance. The others were heading down the trail back toward the buses, except for Thomas.

Thomas sat there, looking right at me. Waiting for me.

I jogged toward him and swooped behind to grab the handles of his chair.

"Have fun with Drake?" he asked. His back was to me in his chair, so I couldn't see his face, but jealousy laced his voice.

"A smashing time." I tried to lighten the mood with sarcasm in my tone, but my voice shook. I hoped Thomas wouldn't hear it. "Drake is just as pleasant as you made him out to be. Yet another fact you were right about."

"Did you think I was lying to you?"

"No."

"But you had to go figure it out on your own?"

I pushed him up the hill with the sun beating on the back of my neck. I freed one hand from the wheelchair handle to wipe the building sweat from my forehead. "I don't know. He just asked me to come, and I did. Don't overthink it."

"As long as you didn't catch any of his cooties like everyone else who hangs around him." Thomas's hands came together and folded in his lap. "They all start to degenerate and become more stupid and mean the longer they're with him."

I smiled, his returning humor calming me. "Don't worry. I don't think I caught any of his cooties."

On the bus ride home, we laughed and talked, and I ignored the few glares I got from Drake. Thomas gave me a thoroughly detailed account of the reenactment, while he scrubbed his pocket watch with a little cleaning cloth.

The first thing I did when we got back to school was head toward the bathroom. I'd had to go for almost an hour. Class was still going, and the hallways were quiet except for the two chatting girls, also from the field trip, who followed behind me.

In Florida, my old school had been sort of like a second home. I was there almost as much as I was at my house, after all, but that familiarity and sense of belonging was missing here. I couldn't imagine this place would ever feel like that.

But homes could shatter, and people could move on in your absence like you were never there. I'd already experienced both. Part of what made a place feel like home was the people there. My friends had been like family to me. My best friends, Molly and Savannah, had been like sisters. And where were they now? Sure, we kept up for a while. We'd promised never to drift apart, no matter the distance. Besides, I'd be coming back to Florida a lot during my allotted times to stay with Dad. But they got into their own routines again, and slowly but surely, the effort to stay together felt one-sided. We drifted. All day, I'd wondered if either one of them would even remember to text me on my birthday. In the bathroom stall, I listened to the two girls chat like Molly, Savannah, and I used to, and it made me ache for home even harder.

When I went to find Thomas and the others in the gym where we were supposed to wait until class was over, Thomas was off by himself in a corner facing the wall. His posture was slumped, his head was low. Something wasn't right—that much I could tell.

"Thomas," I said warily, walking to his side. "Are you okay?" When I peered down at his face, he looked angry. Tears were running down his cheeks.

"Don't bother," he barked at me.

I stared blankly at him in shock. We had been laughing with each other ten minutes ago.

"Thomas," I repeated. "What's going on?"

"Back off," he said a little louder.

From the corner of my eye, I could see people turn their heads to watch the commotion. I didn't want to make a scene, but I didn't know what to do, so I just sat with my back against the wall, facing him.

"Leave me alone," he growled, quiet again. His thumbs were twiddling, one around the other, quickly in his lap.

I stared him straight in the eye with all the determination I could muster up. "I'm not going anywhere. Are you mad at me?"

Thomas looked back at me like I was the dumbest person in the world. "Look, it's obvious, okay? You don't have to pretend anymore."

What in the world was he talking about?

The school bell rang, and Thomas quickly turned his chair around to dart to the front of the gym. I followed after him but got stuck in the sea of exiting students. I shuffled impatiently, trying to get outside. The only thing I could think of that might have ticked him off was me running off with Drake, but that was hours ago, and he had seemed fine since then.

I finally made it outside and began scanning the schoolyard for Thomas, but I'd been beaten to the punch. Rain and Evan were there talking to him. Something inside me retreated. Rain had been his friend longer than me, and she probably knew the right thing to say. I didn't know what to do for him, and it was clear he didn't want me there.

I spotted Mom's car coming up in the carpool line and made my way to the front of the crowd. I watched Rain and Thomas while I waited. She didn't seem to be getting any farther with him.

Then, she looked up at me.

It struck me again. I had seen her before—before Ivy Hollow.

My name was called, and I jolted back into the moment, heading for Mom's car. I turned back one last time to look at Thomas. He met my gaze with a glare that crushed my soul.

What did I do?

"How was school?" Mom asked as I closed the SUV door and buckled up in the passenger seat.

"Fine," I said, but I wasn't even paying attention. I looked out the window to find Rain still watching. She knew me, too. I felt certain she did. But how? I'd never met her before or I would have remembered. Rain Brooks isn't the sort of person you forget. She has one hand, and it's always painted. And her name is Rain for crying out loud. It's like we knew each other from a dream or another life. It wasn't even like she seemed slightly familiar; it was more like she was someone so important I should have never forgotten her in the first place.

"How was the field trip?" Mom asked as we moved forward in the carpool line. Rain and Thomas disappeared from my view.

"It was fine."

"Gosh. You make it sound thrilling. Easy on the details."

I had too much on my mind to carry the conversation. Thomas was mad at me, and I wasn't sure why. And Rain was apparently a ghost I'd met somewhere before. Maybe I was imagining that she knew me. After all, if someone stared at me the way I'd gawked at her, I'd probably stare back, too, wondering who in the world was stalking me.

We picked up Maya, and for once I was thankful for her non-stop talking about every single second of her day. It filled the silence and kept me from having to.

We swung by the diner to grab takeout before we got home, and I took my meal to my room, claiming I had loads of homework. I shut the door behind me and laid my burger, fries, and drink on my desk before plopping on my bed with my phone.

Thomas and I had exchanged numbers the day before at lunch, so I immediately went to text him.

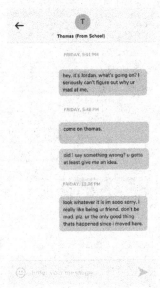

He never responded.

And I was right: Mom never mentioned my birthday again that day.

Molly remembered, but Savannah didn't. I almost wish Molly had forgotten, too, because it showed she remembered but didn't actually care. She ended the conversation before it even began.

It was the one day a year I was supposed to celebrate my life, but nothing about that day made me want to be alive. Everything was wrong.

So, yeah. To say my birthday sucked was an understatement.

green

growth; life; creativity

EVAN

"A wonderful fact to reflect
upon, that every human creature
is constituted to be that
profound secret and mystery to
every other."

Charles Dickens, _A Tale of Two Cities_

"A WONDERFUL FACT TO reflect upon, that every human creature is constituted to be that profound secret and mystery to every other."

Charles Dickens, A _Tale of Two Cities_

Saturday morning, I was wide awake at five o'clock, and nothing good was running through my head.

Each night, I hated the time between getting into bed and falling asleep. My mind went over memories and dwelt on the emptiness I spent all day trying to distract myself from. So when I woke up at five, I decided to just get up and start my day.

After a cup of coffee and some toast with an egg, I spent a few minutes reading A *Tale of Two Cities* until I couldn't stand it anymore.

"*Up the broad flight of shallow steps, Monsieur the Marquis, flambeau preceded, went from his carriage, sufficiently disturbing the darkness to elicit loud remonstrance from an owl in the roof of the great pile of stable building away among the trees.*"

Ugh. I didn't understand how Rain and my dad could appreciate this stuff. I had to look up three words in my phone's dictionary just to know what was going on.

I set the book down and made my way outside to the barn. There was no reason I couldn't get started on the greenhouse while I waited for Rain to arrive.

From one of the stalls, I pulled out my dad's old tools and hoped I could do this. I'd never done anything like it before, and I wished Dad was there to show me. He'd been good at this kind of stuff. He'd been good at a little bit of everything. I'd printed out the greenhouse building plans I found online and had studied them over and over again. The only way to know if I could do it was to try and see if I failed. So I got started.

I started with a basic frame, long and rectangular, out of the lumber I'd gotten from the hardware store. I knew I'd need some help securing the cattle panel over the top to create the dome shape, so I decided to start on my raised beds, where I'd plant the vegetables once it was finished.

The sun began to rise and beat down on my bare arms and neck. Sweat was beading down my face and soaking through my shirt. My hands were blistering from the rough wood and from gripping the tools. My whole body felt alive and stimulated. More alive than I had felt since Dad passed. I was creating. I was building. I was watching something come together that would bring life and produce growth.

Mom walked out wrapped in her bathrobe around eight, coffee in hand, to watch me as I worked. "Your father would be beyond proud of you, Ev," she said, and the words burned worse than the blisters on my hands. "You've worked so hard to get us here and make this place home."

"It doesn't really feel like home, does it?"

She hesitated, and that was all the answer I needed. I was failing. "It'll take time," she said. "But we're getting there."

I pressed my toe into the dirt. "I don't know. I'm beginning to think Ava's right. I may have been a fool for dragging you two out here."

Her eyes narrowed. "Ava was dragged, but I wasn't," she said.

Maybe it was true. I didn't drag her, but I convinced her. I'd been the one to assure her the move was exactly what we needed. And she was so fragile and lifeless in her grief then, the wind could have picked her up and navigated her where it wanted. She'd joined me without a fight because she didn't have one left in her. She'd been fighting since Dad's diagnosis. And she was desperate. Desperate to believe in anything that might help us heal.

"Have you regretted it?" I asked.

She paused again and took a sip of her coffee. She didn't have any makeup on, and her loose hair blew gently around her shoulders. Before Dad died, I can't remember ever seeing my mom without makeup. Not that it mattered, but it just wasn't her. She was the type to get up before the sun to get herself ready and make the bed before she ever left her room. When Dad died, there was a piece of her that died with him, and it slowed her down. It made her care less about the little things I never even noticed until they were gone, like makeup before she came out of her room, making the bed, candles lit in the living room after dinner, and the radio playing old country music during lunch on Saturdays.

"I haven't regretted it," she told me, tightening her grip on her mug. "I've missed things, but I haven't regretted it. I think that place would've destroyed me if we'd stayed." Her eyes fell to the grass in front of her, but she was looking far away. She was traveling through memories—years of time. I know. I'd done it, too. "He was everywhere there. I kept expecting him to walk through the door after work, or bump into me in the hall, or leave his socks lying beside the laundry hamper instead of in it. I was always waiting for him—or at least signs of him." Mom smiled, and her eyes grew moist before she lifted them to meet mine. "But he's here, too. He's in you. And Ava. I just don't expect to see him at every turn, and that's better somehow." She paused, and the sun hit her face in such an angelic way that I wished Rain could have painted it for me. "At one point in my life, that little Chicago townhouse was the happiest place on earth, and I've left it. It turned into a nightmare, but I still miss it for the days where it was my happy place."

I think we were all waiting for him there. When every day for your whole life your dad walks through the same front door at the same time, you don't know what to do when he suddenly stops. You can't stop waiting because it's the way it's always been.

I felt certain again that I was right to get us out of Chicago. We would have waited forever.

"We'll make this place happy, too," I promised. "Even if I have to offer Ava the moon to get her on board."

Mom smiled, and I could see her mask going up again. The raw and vulnerable face I'd only seen a handful of times in the past few months started to fade. "I know we will. Besides, nothing feels homier than eating veggies grown from your own backyard, and we have an abundance of that. When will Rain be here to help?"

I hesitated. I felt I should say something else. Something that would let her know she didn't have to wear the mask. But I also knew she might want to, because there's that weird fight in grief between wanting to remember and wanting to forget.

I dusted my dirty hands on the front of my jeans. "Within the next hour or so."

"I'll make sure to have snacks and drinks ready for when you need a break." She raised her eyes expectantly. "And *do* plan to give her a break, please. Not everyone enjoys working 'til they're dog tired like you."

I glared at her for assuming I'd be so thoughtless. "Yes, ma'am."

"Besides," she busied herself readjusting the tie of her robe, "I still haven't met her, and I'd like to get a chance."

"I'll be sure you get plenty of time with her," I said with sarcastic dread in my voice.

Mom offered a satisfied nod, and I watched her go, her robe blowing around her frail form.

I would make Ivy Hollow home to her if it killed me.

An hour later, Rain showed up in a pickup truck that looked at least twice our age, and I heard it long before I saw it make its way up the gravel driveway.

I was waiting in the front yard for her when she slid out of the front seat. She wore a pair of overalls covered in different colors of paint splashes, and her hair was in two braids with a yellow bandana tied around her head. Her hand was painted blue with bright yellow sunflowers.

"Sorry I'm a little late. I stopped by the antique shop," she said, and walked to the passenger side door. "I brought you something." From inside, she pulled out what looked to be an old black suitcase and handed it to me.

It was heavy, and I opened the tailgate of the truck to set it down and look it over, eying her quizzically even though I knew exactly what it was.

Rain watched eagerly as I opened it. Inside was the vintage typewriter.

"I told you I'd come by today and look at it," I said. "You shouldn't have gone through the trouble."

She waved her hand dismissively. "Now you don't have to. And you don't have to make a decision on it either. I've decided for you. That typewriter is meant to be yours. It's a gift from Mr. Clark and I."

I'd seen the price tag for the typewriter when I first stopped by to look at it. It was worth every penny after how well Thomas had refurbished it.

"I can't accept it," I said, shaking my head.

She frowned. "Why not? You'll hurt my feelings."

I ran my fingers around the edge of the case. I didn't even want to touch it with my dirty hands. It glittered in the sun like new. Dad would have loved it.

I let my hand drop to my side and shook my head again. "It's too much."

Rain rolled her eyes and shut the case. "Just say thanks and let's move on," she said, a smirk on her lips. "I swear, you're acting more and more like a southerner every day—too polite for your own good."

I slid my hands in my front pockets and met her gaze. "Thank you, Rain. I won't dread the writing process nearly as much now."

She shrugged. "It was nothing. But if you want to thank me, you can type up a note to Thomas as your first practice page and slide it in his locker on Monday. He'll love knowing that you liked his work enough to get the typewriter."

Rain Brooks. She was always looking out for someone other than herself. Always wondering whose day she could make a little better. In some ways, her name was the opposite of who she was. She evoked nothing of rain clouds. She was bright, sunny, and warm. The darkness faded when she walked into a room. Her name would be the first question I asked her about when working on her story.

"As you wish," I told her, and she seemed satisfied. "Have you heard from Thomas? Is he okay?"

She shook her head. "He won't answer my phone calls. I'm gonna call his mom if I don't hear from him today."

"Who was that girl? The one who was looking at us. He always seems to sit with her at lunch." I'd noticed her staring as Rain tried to talk to Thomas during carpool. She didn't even look at me. Her eyes were glued on Thomas with a combination of concern and guilt.

"Jordan. She's new," Rain said. Then, she turned her head slowly with her hand on her hip, taking in her surroundings. "I like your place. Now where's this greenhouse we're supposed to be working on?"

My brow furrowed at the sudden change in subject, but I led her behind the house and through the barn to my worksite. The tall grass in the fields around us shook in the wind, and gray clouds were already beginning to block the sun. I hoped the rain would hold off until the evening.

"You started without me," Rain said, and she walked a circle around the base of the greenhouse, looking over my work. Loose wisps of hair blew around her face in the wind. She looked natural here. She belonged to this place as much as the soil under our boots. I envied that. Even though I'd only been in Ivy Hollow a few short months, I wanted to belong to it the way she did. She was as much a piece of this place as it was a piece of her.

I leaned my shoulder against one of the boards attached to the base. "I guess I was just restless, but don't worry—there's still plenty to do. Besides, we always have a story to work on if we get bored." I had the frame finished and some of my beds were done, they just needed the dirt and plants.

"This is gonna be a pretty good-sized greenhouse," Rain remarked, straining her neck upward. "Larger than I expected."

I wanted to be able to provide lots of produce throughout the winter, but even more than that, I wanted lots to keep me busy. I knew I wouldn't last long cooped up in the house over the colder months with nothing to do or get me out. My garden had become my drug. It removed the maddening pain in my mind and chest that immediately came when I had the time to let my thoughts wander, and it brought my focus to the work of my hands instead. It made me think of the sweat and the ache of my bones, instead of the memories that threatened to replay over and over if I was left idle. It taught me something, too.

The first batch of seeds I'd tried to plant when we moved here failed to sprout. I'd done everything right—babied them, kept them moist. But they never came up. I was furious. All this time I'd been dying to plant something on my own piece of land, and I couldn't do it all of a sudden. The wound of Dad's death was more raw then, too, so it felt like just another event to add to the list of things that hadn't gone my way. But I providentially read the book of Mark in my Bible a few mornings later. Getting myself to read my Bible had been hard since Dad died.

As a kid, when I first learned to read, Dad started waking me up early before he left for work, when he made his coffee and read his Bible. He would pour me a glass of orange juice and sit me down across from him at the kitchen table to read mine.

"Don't neglect this discipline, Ev," he'd said, tapping a finger on the black leather cover. "You can do without a lot of other things in your life—even a little extra sleep—but you can't do without this."

Eventually, it became a discipline of my own, and he didn't have to wake me up anymore. He'd come down to the kitchen table, where I'd have both our coffee cups poured and ready.

Since he'd passed, God became harder to approach. I wasn't angry, but I didn't understand. When I opened my Bible to Mark four and read the brief verses of the farmer who sowed seeds, slept, and woke up to find them sprouted, I snickered. Mine hadn't done that at all. When I read the passage a few times over,

I realized the responsibility of the farmer and the sovereignty of God.

By waking me up every morning and having me read my Bible, my Dad had sown a seed in my life. God brought the harvest when He saved me at twelve years old.

But sometimes, we don't see the harvest. Sometimes, the seeds don't sprout in front of our eyes. Like when we prayed for Dad to be healed and he wasn't.

And then we have to decide. Do we only trust God's wisdom when He gives us what we want? Or do we trust that His harvest is far bigger than the kind we're looking for?

The next batch of seeds I planted, I prayed over. "Bring them up Your way," I whispered, my fingers covered in the damp soil as I gingerly set the seeds into the dirt. "I know Your harvest isn't always the kind I have in mind. Your plans involve a kingdom far greater than the one I live in, and Your way is far more abundant."

When I walked toward the house at the end of that day, I smiled. Those first seeds that never came up *had* brought a harvest, because they taught me something about my Heavenly Father. That's what a heavenly harvest looked like, and it had been far greater than strawberry plants.

All that to say, I wasn't going to give up my garden over the winter. It had brought something to my life I couldn't go without.

"What can I do?" Rain asked, lifting her boot to rest on one of the boards set at the foundation. "I have to say, I've never done much more than simple home projects with Jo."

"Good," I said. "Because that's about all I've done, too. I'm a city boy, remember?"

"Oh yeah, that's right. So I need to show *you* how it's done?" she said with a smirk. I glared and threw a pair of work gloves at her, which she caught between her arm and her chest. She snickered and threw one of them back. "I only need one, remember?"

Now that it came down to it, I felt a little nervous about asking her to help. I didn't want to ask her to do something that she was incapable of because she only had one hand. But I also knew it hardly limited her. She could paint with her mouth after all. "Why don't you work on cutting the tarps," I said, pointing to my right. I had stacks of clear plastic that would cover my frame and allow sunlight to shine through. "I have the measurements printed, and there are scissors and a measuring tape over there."

Rain got down on her knees in the grass and began the task. Watching her work was pretty remarkable. She used her one hand to do the more dominant work while her other arm, feet, and sometimes even her teeth helped her do the rest. I discreetly watched her as she used her handless right arm to hold the measuring tape in place against the tarp, while her left hand used the scissors to cut. She looked so natural, and it took her little time and effort to get it done.

I walked back and forth from the barn, carrying out some of the plants I wanted to put in the new greenhouse beds. The sky overhead began to look more and more fierce, so I went ahead and filled a bucket with as many sunflowers as I could for Rain to take home as payment for helping me. By the time I had a bucket full of flowers and the plants gathered at the greenhouse site, Rain had all of the tarp cut.

Together, we secured the cattle panel over the frame to create a large, wire dome, and then wrapped the tarp pieces snugly against the panel, Rain holding the tarp tightly in place while I used the nail gun to secure it.

"Have you made any progress on *Peter Pan* yet?" she asked me as I lifted the gun. Once on target, I pulled the trigger, feeling the jolt through my palm and wrist.

"I've started it, but I haven't gotten very far. I've been catching up on *A Tale of Two Cities*, too."

"What did you think of Sydney's confession of love to Lucie? I think it was so well written."

I turned to face her with a smirk, lowering the gun to my side. "I haven't read that yet, but thanks for giving it away."

Rain let her head fall backward with sarcastic irritation. "Good grief, Evan! Your lack of commitment to get through these books is driving me crazy. I can't keep all of the plot twists a secret forever."

I couldn't wrap my mind around loving to read the way that she did. Did she love books so much because she was lonely? Rain didn't have many friends, and I wondered if books and their characters fought off loneliness the way that my garden kept my grief at bay.

"Well," I said, almost as a sigh, and lifted the nail gun back up to its point, "there's a story I'm crazy interested in reading, but I can't write it until you tell it to me. I want to read the story about the girl who keeps her nose in a book and paints her hand with her mouth." I glanced over at her to read her expression. She looked like she wasn't sure if I was being genuine or teasing her. "I think that would be one of my favorite stories of all time," I added, with all the seriousness I could muster. I wanted her to know I meant it. Truly.

Her face relaxed, and she let out a long breath as though she'd been holding it a while. "I'm sorry. You probably think I live a double life by the way I've acted about this story. If you'd asked me to do this last year, it would've been fine. But this year..." She must have seen my confusion and gave a reassuring smile. "It's really complicated. For now, we'll just start with the basics."

I put down my tools, having attached the last bit of tarp, and nodded my head toward the opening. Rain followed me inside, and I pulled off my gloves before sitting down in the grass, prepared to listen. I was ready to hear whatever she could tell me, because the more nervous she became, the more intrigued I grew. She really was like a book with plot twists, excitement, and interesting characters. One of the few I had interest in diving into. Nothing about her was just *plain.* Her life was pretty normal, but normal through rose-colored glasses. Normal with abstract colors thrown in. Normal in an intentionally romanticized way. Whenever we spent time together, and every time I learned something new about her, she left me on the edge of my seat, dying to turn the page. I felt certain her backstory, whatever it was, was the climax of the whole thing.

Hesitantly, Rain joined me on the ground, the clear plastic and wood enclosing us. Our greenhouse was nearly complete, needing only a door. But it was enough to be a shelter from the raindrops that started to patter on the plastic overhead. We listened and watched as the droplets hit and then slowly fell down the cloudy material. It reminded me of the question I'd thought of earlier, and I faced Rain to ask her.

"Did Jo name you, or was Rain your name before you were adopted?"

"I guess my name is as good a place to start as any," she said, bringing her knees to her chest and wrapping her arms around them. "My name is something I think about a lot, actually. My birth mother named me Rain Olivia, but I don't know why. The first time I ever asked Jo about it, I think I was six. I was staring out the window, wishing the storm outside would go away so I could ride the new bike I'd gotten for my birthday. It made me wonder why anyone would name their daughter Rain." She looked overhead at the raindrops falling harder against the tarp. "I still wonder. Was I just a storm cloud that threatened to destroy her plans? I think I probably was."

Being named Rain before being given up for adoption would probably make me wonder, too. Adoption can be loving, but it isn't absent of doubt. Sometimes, you're given up for justifiable and even good reasons. But sometimes, it's just because you weren't wanted. I couldn't imagine walking through life wondering which one it was.

I ran my fingers through the moist dirt, thinking of what I would call her if she wasn't Rain. I couldn't come up with anything. She didn't deserve a normal name, that much I knew. She had too much personality to fit into something average. But I couldn't imagine calling her something like Summer or Sunny either. They didn't fit. And that's when I decided I had been wrong about her name. It fit her perfectly. She was unpredictable and wild like a thunderstorm, but she went about bringing life with her wherever she went.

Rain. That's who she was.

"I guess at six years old, being named after the rain does seem pretty discouraging, but on the other hand," I said, turning behind me to pull one of the long sunflower stems out of the bucket I'd brought in, "it's the rain that brings growth. No rain, no flowers. Our world would be missing a lot of beauty and color without it." She studied me, and I thought I spied tears gathering in her eyes.

But they never fell, so maybe not. I handed her the sunflower. "I believe I owe you your heart's content of these."

"I'll just take a bundle and leave the rest for your mom. You had most of the work done by the time I got here anyway."

When she reached to grab the flower from my fingers, I studied the intense detail of the sunflowers she had painted on her hand.

"You know," Rain began, "I don't think I believe you anymore."

I looked up to find her watching me.

"You've assured me that you don't have a creative bone in your body, but I think you do. You think deeply, and I believe you just need practice getting your thoughts out, and then you'll be surprised at their beauty."

There it was again. That strange, beautiful, yet understandable stuff that she threw into conversations. It reminded me of how songs are sometimes. The ones that have lyrics that aren't really talking about anything specific, but they're deep and seem to be speaking directly to you and whatever it is that you're going through. She was a walking book of poetry.

I stood to my feet and began pulling the best of sunflowers for her to take home. "Well, if anyone can teach me, it's you."

Rain stood, too, and took each stem from my hand to bunch them together. "Perhaps. But you have to cooperate and actually do what I tell you. Like read *Peter Pan* and *A Tale of Two Cities*." She placed her flower-filled fist on her hip.

"And you would have to tell me what it is I'm actually writing about," I retorted.

"And so I will," she promised, "but I need to see you put in some effort first before I give you my entire life and let you run with it. Besides, I don't want just anyone writing my biography; it has to be someone I know can handle it. And," she paused to smell the bouquet, "I expect your own story in return."

I chuckled. "Well, that's fine by me, but it isn't nearly as interesting as yours, I promise."

"Then why do you avoid it?"

I felt my face flush, feeling like her gaze was going through the archives of my mind, looking for the memories I'd hidden in the cobweb infested corners.

She smiled tenderly. "It hurts still. So does mine. Maybe this will be good for both of us."

I had a strange feeling that Rain Brooks was going to be for me what the rain was for my garden—the type of rain that brought life, growth, and color.

"I guess I better head to the antique store," Rain said.

"Will you be working by yourself today?"

Her expression fell slightly. "I wasn't supposed to be, but Mr. Clark hasn't been well the past few days. I told him I would take over and let him go home and rest after I finished helping you."

"Let me help you," I said. "You've helped me a lot, and now that it's raining, I've got the rest of my day and nothing to do with it."

"I'm used to running it alone. It's really not bad."

"You can put me to work, or you can just let me keep you company."

Rain's eyes gave a sparkle that suggested she knew something that I didn't. "A bookworm in an antique store is never in want of company, for she always has plenty of familiar friends about her."

"I suppose Captain Hook and Mr. Darcy make better company than I do, then."

She hummed, bringing a finger to her chin. The dirt from my garden clung to her hands, dirtying her painting, and had made its way under her fingernails. "I wouldn't for sure say 'better.' Especially not when they arrive at the same time. Their personalities don't mesh very well."

"I can't imagine what will happen if you add me to the mix."

Rain grinned as though the thought amused her greatly.

"If nothing else, you can work, and I can read *Peter Pan*. You can slap my hand if I start to doze off."

"Deal," she said, and walked out of the greenhouse and into the rain.

I felt ready to start this paper. Ready to know who Rain was and the events that made her who she was.

I determined I would finish *Peter Pan* that night.

RAIN

"There is nothing I would not do for those who are really my friends. I have no notion of loving people by halves; it is not my nature."

Jane Austen, Northanger Abbey

"ANY SUGGESTIONS FOR WHAT to put on the desk in the window display now that the typewriter is gone?" I asked.

Evan stopped his dusting and looked around the store. "What about that old record player?"

Mr. Clark's head lifted from the book he read. "Yes, we've had that one a while now, and I've got another for Thomas to fix. I'd like to get rid of it." I had found Mr. Clark on the bookshelf ladder when Evan and I had walked in. He hated for me to boss him around, but I couldn't help it. He'd been so weak the past month or two and complained of dizzy spells. That ladder was the last place I wanted him. Evan helped me convince him to sit and read while we worked. It wasn't without a fight, of course.

"Yeah, maybe I can do that and some vinyls." I crossed the store to grab the record player off the credenza. We had an abundance of vinyls I was always having to reorganize, and I wouldn't mind getting rid of some of those either.

"Does it work?" Evan asked.

"Yep. It's another recipient of Thomas's handiwork."

Thomas. He'd been on my mind all day. He'd ignored all of my texts and calls, and I was worried. I hated it for him. He'd seemed to really like Jordan, and in spite of my reluctance about her, I truly hoped she would be a friend to him. I was graduating, and I wouldn't be able to keep an eye on him after the school year was over. He could handle himself, but everyone needs a friend of some sort.

Evan nodded toward the record player. "Can we try it out?"

I walked over to the wood trunk where I had the vinyls sorted in alphabetical order and began fingering through. "Have any vintage favorites?"

"I like The Beatles."

"You look like you like The Beatles."

He laughed, but his cheeks went a light shade of pink. "What does that mean? Don't tell me it's my hair. I'm not *that* overdue for a haircut."

"No." I laughed along. "You have better hair than The Beatles." I found a Beatles album and put the vinyl on the record player. If seasons were albums, The Beatles were summer to me, along with The Beach Boys. Frank Sinatra was fall and spring. The Andrews Sisters were spring, too. Dean Martin was winter, of course. I placed the needle on the edge and "Paperback Writer" started playing like a closing chapter to the summer days, because they were quickly disappearing.

"You would pick this song," Evan teased.

Mr. Clark snickered his agreement over the top of his novel. *War and Peace* held his attention again.

"Mr. Clark doesn't like The Beatles," I said, walking across the room to sit at his feet.

He laid the volume on his lap upon seeing me, and I watched as his left hand rubbed absently at the plum-colored velvet of his chair's arm. "Bonnie liked them, but they were never my taste," he said, his hazel eyes meeting mine. "I've always preferred the '40s era of music."

So did I, but I thought The Beatles had their place, too.

I laid my hand over Mr. Clark's on the arm of the chair. "Today's your anniversary, isn't it?"

The smile on his lips remained, but it softened as he nodded slowly. "Would've been married fifty-four years today." And if they could have lived forever, I know their love would have outlasted time itself. Not because they were perfect and always got along, but simply because they had chosen to be in love. Every day, they chose it. Bonnie had told me so.

"The world could learn a thing or two from you and Mrs. Clark," I said, stroking my thumb along his wrinkled knuckles.

With his other hand, he pushed his glasses higher on his nose, giving me a knowing look. "I don't have to teach the world, but I get to teach you."

My head tilted toward my shoulder. I knew something was coming. One of his lessons. I'd spent a good chunk of my life sitting at his feet to glean from his lessons.

143

His hand slipped from mine and reached out expectantly for my other arm—my right arm. I gave it to him, and he held the stub at the end gently in his fingers, like it still held the pain and he didn't want to inflict more. "Love is a choice far more than a feeling. You'll get to choose soon," he said as he lightly tapped the stub. "She made her choice, but your turn is coming, my dear. How will you use your choice?"

From the corner of my eye, I saw Evan turn away from his dusting to look at us, listening.

I swallowed hard. "I'd rather just avoid the whole thing," I admitted. "I've moved on."

"But it's time to move forward and fight the battle you've been enlisted for." Mr. Clark let go of my arm and leaned back in his seat to recline a little. "God has prepared you. He's spent your whole life teaching you and training you. He's brought mentors and trainers at opportune seasons. And now He asks you to move forward. To take the training He's given you and use it. It appears He's requiring you to face this battle head on."

My throat tightened. I couldn't. I wasn't ready. I didn't think I'd ever be ready.

Evan dropped his feather duster, the tapping of the wood handle hitting the floor reminding me that he was in the room with us.

Mr. Clark knew I hadn't told Evan anything yet, and he shot a vague smile in Evan's direction as he slowly stood to his feet. "He still prepares you, even in the last hour." Once he was steady, he looked down on me and pressed my nose with his thumb like he used to when I was little.

My cheeks lifted at his affectionate gesture.

"He's brought along a comrade to go with you. Don't underestimate that gift. 'Friendship is one of the sweetest joys of life. Many might have failed beneath the bitterness of their trial had they not found a friend,'" he quoted. "Faithful old Charles Spurgeon said that. He was probably right, of course. He usually was."

I didn't doubt God was preparing me. I didn't doubt His training and His timing. I doubted myself. But I also couldn't ignore the Bible verse that told me His power was made perfect in my weakness. It didn't leave me much of an excuse to run and cower like I so desperately wanted to.

Mr. Clark pulled his keys from the pocket of his jeans. "Since you two seem to have things under control without me to pester you with life lessons, I think I'll head home. If it somehow becomes busy enough to need backup for the first time in this shop's history, feel free to give me a call." With a wink and a smirk, Mr. Clark left, and my attention turned to Evan's pent up questions that I could feel filling the room.

Evan propped his weight against the shelf behind him and eyed me like he was trying to read my thoughts on the conversation. "He sounds like a wise man."

I considered telling him then. He'd proved himself to me, and Mr. Clark was right; he could be the comrade I needed to face the coming battle. I swallowed hard and ran my braid through my fingers. As I opened my mouth to tell him, the pit in my stomach felt nauseating. How do you even begin a story like mine?

Evan could tell. He leaned back a little more, easing into the shelf. His eyes were expectant and encouraging.

But the bell above the door rang, and I turned away from him with relief, regaining my composure to greet the next customer.

To my surprise, Thomas and his mom entered.

Thomas still looked hard as stone. Unbreakable. Everything about him translated that he refused to talk about what had happened yesterday.

But I was determined. No one knew Thomas like I did.

"Good afternoon," I greeted them with a smile.

Stacy smiled back, but even she seemed uneasy, like she didn't know what to do about him either. "Afternoon, Rain," she said, her southern drawl thick as ever. If there was only one southern belle in Ivy Hollow, it was Stacy Helms. She reminded me of myself in the sense that she was born here, raised here, and never cared to leave here. She was a genuine product of our little town.

"I finished the watch, so I came to bring it by," Thomas said, his voice monotone. He reached into his pocket and pulled out the old watch that Mr. Clark had given him only three weeks ago. In that time, he'd found parts for it online, learned how it worked, pulled it apart, put it back together, and had it glittering like it was brand new.

I reached out to take it from him and looked it over, and Evan made his way beside me to see it, too. "You've done an incredible job, Thomas," he commented.

Thomas was silent.

I wrapped the gold chain around my finger absently, trying to come up with something to say that might shatter the wall he'd built. "Mr. Clark won't want to part with this one. What year did you say it was?"

"Nineteenth century."

"You don't think it belonged to ol' Stonewall Jackson do you?"

Thomas rolled his eyes. "That's impossible."

"Shoot," I said. "I probably could've made a fortune if it had." I walked over behind the counter and counted out the two hundred dollars that he and Mr. Clark had agreed upon.

"The typewriter isn't in the window anymore," Mrs. Stacy observed, crossing her arms over her bright floral blouse. "Did it sell?"

"It did." I nodded my head in Evan's direction. "Evan's the proud owner now."

"I'm really excited about it," he told Thomas. "It's the coolest thing I own."

Thomas didn't even glance in his direction, and Mrs. Stacy gave a defeated shrug from behind him.

With the wadded cash in hand, I walked over to Thomas and sat on the floor in front of him, legs crossed into a pretzel shape. "Alright, spill the beans."

He glared at me, his blue eyes like arrows. "I already told you; I'm not gonna talk about it."

I crossed my arms stubbornly. "Yeah, well, I'm telling you I won't leave you alone until you do."

"You're bossy."

"You're selfish."

"How?" Thomas had always been like a little brother to me. Despite being in different grades and not getting to hang out all the time, we could always come back together like family. We could argue like family, too.

I leaned a little closer and set my eyes on his, unwavering. "You have a lot of people here who care about you, and until we know what's going on, we're gonna be worried sick. Do you really think I can just forget about it? Until you're happy, I can't be. So stop being so selfish."

147

I saw it. The slight softening of his features. The hint of conviction in his eyes.

"What did Jordan do?" I asked, not wanting to hesitate and lose the hold I had on him. He looked caught, and I tilted my head with a prompting stare.

After a heavy exhale, he caved. "I thought we were friends, but I was wrong, okay? That's it. She made me think we were friends, then she hung out with Drake and ditched me."

Any friend of Drake's immediately lost my respect after what Thomas had dealt with in the past thanks to him. It had taken me weeks after the last incident to get Thomas to even smile again—and I'd tried everything. I even binged every cringey Star Wars prequel with him. *That* was an act of love.

"Did she tell you she didn't want to be friends anymore?" Mrs. Stacy asked.

Thomas had reached the point of exasperation. "She didn't have to. And I don't care anymore. She's stupid. Now, can I have my money so I can go home?"

I shifted my weight onto my arms behind me. "I think you care a lot. You wouldn't be acting like this if you didn't care."

"I *don't* care."

"Well, I care," I said. "And I'm getting to the bottom of it if I have to ask Jordan myself."

Thomas groaned. "Stay out of it. I'll look like a tattle-tale if you ask her. Tattle-tales are stupid babies."

"Okay, then. Go home, think it over, and then decide if you want to tell me everything that happened or if you want me to ask her." I handed him the money, and he snatched it angrily. "And I really don't want to hit her like I had to hit Drake, with her being new and a girl," I said with a wink and a smile.

He didn't find it funny. He just rolled his eyes as he stashed the money in his pocket and mumbled the word, "Blackmail."

I rested my hand on his knee, and he stiffened at my touch. "You know I'm your friend, right?"

"You aren't acting like it."

"Yes, I am, and you know it. I care about you, Thomas. I won't stand by and watch you get hurt."

He swallowed hard, and I wondered if he was fighting tears, but he didn't stick around. He turned his wheelchair and made his way to the door.

Mrs. Stacy smiled at me, though it didn't hide the defeat in her expression. "Thanks for trying, hun."

I nodded and gave her a reassuring smile. "He'll get there. He always does."

They left, and I leaned against the counter, running the pocket watch chain through my fingers.

"You're good with him," Evan commended, taking a place beside me.

My shoulders lifted and fell with a sigh. "He's no different than you and I. He hates being babied, which is what a lot of people tend to do because of his situation. He wants tough love. He wants to be taken seriously and treated like everyone else."

"I wonder what happened. That girl seemed to really like hanging out with him. Why would she just ditch him like that?"

"It feels pretty obvious to me," I said. "She's new. She wants to fit in with the right crowds. Drake probably made her feel like she belonged, and it got to her head." I'd thought about it a lot since yesterday, and that seemed the most likely situation. Besides, I knew Drake and how he worked.

"You must know what that feeling is like," I said, and turned to give him a half-questioning, half-joking look. "You opted to join the weird crowd when you made friends with me. Surely by now you're wishing you'd tried to fit in with cool kids instead."

Evan's eyes sparkled with amusement. "And miss afternoon tea with you, Captain Hook, and Mr. Darcy? You kidding?"

I laughed until my eyes watered.

JORDAN

> "It isn't what we say or think that defines us, but what we do."
>
> Jane Austen, <u>Sense and Sensibility</u>

THOMAS WASN'T AT SCHOOL on Monday.

All weekend, I'd worried myself sick over him. I felt guilty, and I didn't even know what I'd done wrong. I texted him over and over and got nowhere with it.

Guilt. Anger. Confusion. Disappointment. Loss. Those were all the feelings I'd experienced over the past four months, and they were getting to be too much. No one in my life stuck around for very long. My friends abandoned me, my dad left, and my mom may as well have been on another planet. I'd never been much of

151

a people person, and I was beginning to see the benefit of that. I was ready to close the world out. It had nothing for me anyway.

At lunch, I sat alone. I missed Thomas's dry sense of humor, his sarcasm, and his punchlines. I tried to busy myself on my phone, Googling more terms and names that might lead me to solving my mom's mystery, but I'd hit a wall, and I couldn't see any way around it aside from asking her or Dad or Aunt Cass. I decided that if I didn't have it figured out by the time Aunt Cassidy came for a visit, I would ask her. I felt sure she would tell me. She'd never been one to hide things from me, and she was always the one I went to with the hard questions.

I didn't even eat my lunch that day. My bowl of soup sat in front of me, untouched. I just sat there scrolling to keep from making eye contact with anyone and to keep my mind from thinking about Thomas.

I was doing just fine ruining my own day without help, but Drake decided to come over and give me a hand anyway. "Where's your little friend?" he asked, taking the seat in front of me. He brought over what was left of his lunch, which told me he planned to stay a while. I had to fight to keep from rolling my eyes.

"I'm not sure where he is."

"Some friend you are. Don't you even know why he's out of school? What if the little guy is sick or somethin'?"

I ignored him and went back to my phone, though I couldn't help but wonder why he cared. I doubted he did. He was probably only back to attempt winning me away from Thomas again. Why it mattered so much to him was beyond me.

"He's bipolar or somethin'. The kid's emotions change about as often as he breathes. He's laughing one minute and crying the next."

I glared at him over the top of my phone. "Shut up."

Drake brushed some invisible dirt off his faded red jersey. He grinned at me with a teasing look in his eyes that dared me. Dared me to stand up to him. "Come on. You know exactly what I'm talking about. He's different. He'll be fine, and then he'll just lose it. I saw him do it to you in the gym on Friday."

I kept ignoring him, but my teeth were grinding. Inside, I was fuming.

"You don't feel bad, do you?" he said, fake pity now donning his expression. "Look, don't take it personally. It's just the way he is. Now you know why no one has the patience for him. It's not your fault. You tried."

"It's *you* I don't have the patience for," I sneered.

"Ouch. I'm just trying to make you feel better." His eyes narrowed into slits, then he repeated with a sly grin, "It wasn't your fault."

Suddenly, it hit me. Drake knew more about this mess than I did.

Gosh, I'm so stupid.

I put my phone down on the table, giving him my full attention. "*What* isn't my fault, Drake?"

His smile grew as if I'd finally hit the mark. I'd finally gotten what it was he came over here to tell me. He wouldn't just tell me—I knew that. He would hang it over my head like a carrot on a string and watch me try to get it until he'd been humored enough. I wasn't willing to wait for it.

"You've got three seconds to tell me why Thomas is mad at me."

Drake took a bite of his sandwich and chewed slowly. "Now I know something else about you. You're bossy."

"I'm serious, Drake. Spit it out."

He continued to gloat, spitting his bite of sandwich onto his plate, real mature-like.

I didn't have the patience to sit and watch a teenager act like a two-year-old. My fuse was ready to blow, and I was about to make up for all the things I should have said behind that log cabin.

The pent up anger inside me had been building for so long. It started with the divorce and then the move. It continued to build when my friends quit texting and when Dad called less than before. Then, I found out Mom had been lying to me my whole life, and the worst part was that I didn't at all feel welcome to come to her with questions. Then, I made a friend, and Drake ruined it—my one good thing in Ivy Hollow.

Later, I would feel kinda bad, because only one of the collective triggers was Drake's fault, but I let it *all* out on him. I guess he was just in the wrong place at the wrong time. But I still believe he deserved it.

I stood from my seat, and Drake's amusement faltered just slightly. It was barely noticeable, but I saw it. The slightest hint of fear smothered the confidence in his eyes as I grabbed my soup bowl and leaned over the table before pouring its contents over his head.

Gasps echoed through the cafeteria as people watched and pointed out the excitement.

Drake's eyes were closed tight as the thick broth dripped from the ends of his hair down to his lap.

My first instinct was to run before I had to deal with his wrath. Stares focused in on me from around the room which made my cheeks go pink.

Then, my eyes met Rain's, and I wasn't sure, but I thought she looked proud of me. A small smile was forming in the corner of her mouth. Her gaze somehow prompted me to continue my show of bravado. So I fought the urge to run.

I stood firmly, prepared to take whatever came next. I wouldn't be a coward. I'd take what I'd dished out. For Thomas, I would.

Drake wiped his eyes with the back of a clenched fist and gave me a stare that grew goosebumps on my arms. "What the heck is wrong with you?" It came out like a growl.

"If you're gonna be a jerk, expect it to come right back to you. At least from me." He stared at me but kept silent, like he was trying to decide how much he could get away with. "I think we're plenty acquainted now, Drake. Wouldn't you say so? I know the kind of guy you are, and now you know who I am."

The teachers arrived then to break it up, which was good because I had a million words I wanted to spew at him that would have probably gotten me expelled instead of just detention. Drake got off the hook, even though I told them I'd been standing up for another student.

"But violence isn't the answer," the principal said—a big man with a receding hairline. His impatient look gave the impression I was the last person he had the time of day for.

But *please*. Pouring cold soup on a guy's head was hardly violence. An inconvenience, maybe. But Drake's lies had hurt my friendship with Thomas more than my soup had messed up his hair.

But I could handle detention. I sat in a classroom alone and did homework, which is what I would've done when I got home anyway.

Mom was the worst part. She lost it on me worse than I did on Drake. She told me she didn't understand. I was a good kid.

I'd never been violent. This wasn't like me. What had gotten into me? Why hadn't I just ignored him?

I didn't answer her. I knew she wouldn't have agreed and didn't even want to hear my answers. I did it because I felt like it was the right thing to do in the moment. But maybe I wouldn't have if I wasn't such an angry person these days. And whose fault was that?

But I'd had enough confrontation for one day, so I just took it on the chin and let her fizzle out.

I wasn't allowed to use my phone during detention, so the minute I got home, I ran to my room and started texting Thomas.

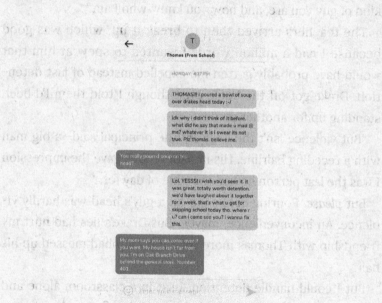

Thomas (From School)

k b there soon. just gotta smooth things over with mom. she didn't find the soup as funny as i did.

What kind of soup was it?

haha only u would ask that. broccoli and cheese

Ew. Gross. Okay, you may have been a little too harsh, Jordan. Even for Drake :)

Enter your message

I got lucky. Mom was on a business call when I went downstairs to tell her I was going to see Thomas, so I wrote out on a sticky note that I was going on my run and laid it on her desk. I walked out before she could finish glancing over it.

The run did me good. It cooled me down. All the anger and frustration and guilt that had built up over the weekend seemed to release a little as I ran, especially knowing Thomas was willing to talk to me again.

I arrived at his front door, heaving for air, and took a minute to catch my breath. His house looked like a southern dream. It was one of the historical homes in town, probably built in the late eighteen-hundreds or early nineteen-hundreds. It was painted a pale yellow with white trim and looked to be three stories tall. One of the upper bedrooms had a large balcony overlooking the perfect lawn and charming street.

I knocked on the door after I finally felt like I could breathe well enough. A woman I assumed to be Thomas's mom answered with a smile. Thomas had her glittering blue eyes.

"Hey, Jordan," she said with a deep, southern drawl. "I'm, Stacy. It's so nice to finally meet you. Thomas has talked so much about you." I wondered what all he'd said. I can't imagine he'd had many good things to say over the past few days.

"It's nice to meet you, too." I was terrible at talking to most adults. I'm not sure why, but it always made me so anxious.

Her hair was a honey blonde, even more than mine, and it was pulled into a perfect ponytail with a teased bump at the back of her head. Not one hair was out of place. "Honey, you're panting like a dog! Come on in, and I'll get ya some water. If I'd have known you were plannin' to run all this way I could've picked you up."

"That's alright. I always take a run after school," I said, following her into the living room. It was themed Kelly green and fuchsia pink.

"More power to ya," she said. "Have a seat. I'll get you some water and find Thomas. I think he's working in the garage on some sort of broken trinket." The couch was printed with green palm branches and accented with pink throw pillows. It felt too pretty to sit on, but I obeyed.

The walls held photos in gold frames of Thomas with his parents. Some of them were dated back to when he was a baby. Even when he was little, he wore tiny glasses with blue, plastic frames. I couldn't help but snicker. He was adorable.

Mrs. Stacy walked back in with a glass of ice water and handed it to me before taking a seat across from me with a cup of coffee. "Thomas will be in soon. He's finishing up something. I won't pretend I know what—it's all too complex for me. But whatever it is, it's apparently time sensitive." She shook her head and stared up at the ceiling. "My gosh, it's a wonder he hasn't blown us all up yet."

I stifled a laugh. "I don't mind waiting," I said, then chugged my water. The icy liquid made my head swell.

Mrs. Stacy watched me finish my water, her polished pink fingernails rubbing her ceramic mug. "Thank you for coming," she said when I set the glass on a cork coaster on the end table beside me. "Thomas has been so out of sorts the past few days. I told him there had to be some misunderstanding."

"I never would have hurt him intentionally," I assured her.

She smiled and adjusted the coffee mug in her hand. "I think he's a little paranoid sometimes. He assumes all people think the worst about him just because a few people have in the past."

People like Drake. I wondered if this was the first time he'd ever picked on Thomas or if it was a reoccurring thing.

"It's understandable. After a few times of being let down, it's hard to trust again," I said. Something about the way Mrs. Stacy looked at me, the way she searched me with her eyes, told me that she guessed I knew it for myself.

"Well, I'm glad he's found a stable friend in you, and I'm glad you have him, too. I know it must be hard movin' all the way out here and not knowin' anyone. Maybe you'll be good for each other."

She was right. I felt out of place here, and in some ways, so did Thomas, and that brought us together somehow.

"He's the only person who's been a friend to me since I got here," I said.

Her eyes swelled with pride. "That's how he is. He has the hardest time *making* friends, but he's always the first to *be* a friend. It's my favorite thing about him."

Hearing her talk about her son that way made my heart ache. I couldn't imagine Mom talking about me like that.

"It's hard to watch. I've known him his whole life and know every special thing about him; I want others to see it, too. The ones who don't give him a chance because they can't get over the fact that he's different than they are miss it completely."

"I guess most people see being different as a bad thing, but we're all different in some ways. It'd be boring if we weren't."

"I wish people saw it the way you and I do. But they don't. Not really." She looked down into her mug like she was thinking of something specific. Something that hurt. "Our world is so broken. So blind to beauty. Even before Thomas was born, the world was against him."

My brow furrowed. "What do you mean?"

Mrs. Stacy gave an apologetic look. The same kind Dad used to give me when Mom was all out of sorts and I tried to help. A look that said, "You shouldn't have to worry about this." But she ran her finger around the rim of her cup and went on, "Even the doctors couldn't see his value. They tried to convince his dad and I to have an abortion as soon as they found out he would be different. They made him sound like a leech on society. They made judgments before they even knew who he'd be. Gosh, I'd bet now he's smarter than some of those doctors. I can't wait to see what he brings to the world. Lord knows how much he brought to our family."

Abortion. I knew what it was, of course, but I'd never heard many people talk about it. It was one of those taboo topics no one liked to discuss because everyone felt so differently. What I *had* heard seemed to always be good things. I'd always heard that since it was a woman's body, she should be able to decide if she wanted to be pregnant or not. But what if Mrs. Stacy had decided on abortion? I felt like she should be able to decide things about her body, but we wouldn't have Thomas if she had.

That felt like a right more powerful than I wanted access to—choosing whether my body or the baby's was more important.

Mrs. Stacy's smile returned, and she sat up a little straighter when we heard the garage door open. "Regardless," she whispered, "I'm glad he's found a friend in you."

Thomas appeared around the corner and eyed me a little skeptically. "Hey, Jordan." His voice was flatter than usual. I'd learned he did that when he was nervous, like he was trying to hide the emotion he felt.

"Hey, Thomas."

His mom stood. "I'll give you guys some space. I'll be out in the garden if you need anything."

Thomas watched his mom leave before turning his head to face me. He got straight to the point. "So what exactly happened when you ran off with Drake behind the log cabin?"

"Nothing really," I said, leaning back in my seat. "He asked me about myself and invited me to hang out with his friends, but I turned him down. I didn't really like him even then. But I made him mad."

"How?" Thomas pulled some kind of battery out of his pocket with all kinds of cords and wires attached and began messing around with it.

I felt warm. I didn't really want to tell him that Drake had made fun of him and I'd been standing up for him, but he needed to know the truth. "He was picking on me for hanging out with you and not him, like the ego-maniac that he is," I said. "And I didn't play along."

Thomas didn't look up. The movements of his fingers grew faster. "In the gym, he said that you told him you didn't really want to hang out with me. He said you only hang around me because you didn't want to hurt my feelings."

I shook my head, my ponytail sticking to my sweaty neck. "Well, he lied. He was mad at me and decided to hurt your feelings to get me back. I'm sorry, Thomas."

He looked up briefly, like he was evaluating my words. He was testing them.

"Who is more likely to lie to you—me or Drake?"

Thomas shrugged. "Drake is."

"And who just went to detention because they poured broccoli soup on someone's head for you?"

He let out a chuckle, then straightened his face like he hadn't meant for it to escape. "You did."

"Right," I said with a half smile. "So don't I deserve your trust?"

His lips gathered to the side of his mouth as he nodded. "Yeah. You do."

Relief made the tightness in my chest melt away. "Thank you. Because I don't want to go back to that stupid school if you aren't gonna hang out with me anymore."

I could tell Thomas was fighting a smile now. It made me want to beam. Who'd have thought that this unlikely friend would have meant so much to me after just a few weeks?

"Okay, so tell me about what happened at lunch today," he said. And I did. I told him the story with a few minor exaggerations and made him laugh until it was contagious. And we spent the rest of the afternoon like that. I went to his garage, and he showed me all the crazy projects he was working on, and I pretended to understand until he called me out. Then, we went outside and sat in the garden with his mom. Even his dad joined us when he got home from work, and he was super nice and funny like Thomas. Honestly, the resemblance was crazy.

When I left, I felt an emptiness. They had what I'd lost. As I jogged home, I went slowly, not at all eager to reach my destination. My mind went over Mrs. Stacy's story again. Thomas was worth every hardship she and her husband had ever gone through for him. It had to have been crazy hard, but they did it. They stuck together through it, and I was willing to bet they were stronger because of it. Why hadn't my parents been able to do that?

By the time my feet pounded against my driveway, the joy I'd felt with the Helms family had been replaced with the all-too-familiar longing for what I once had.

That night, I unpacked the last box in my bedroom. The one I'd been avoiding. The one with all my pictures and mementos. Things that reminded me of Molly, Savannah, and Dad. I cried as I took one last look through the scrapbook that Molly and Savannah made for me as a parting gift. It was kind of like Mom's sequin diary—full of the remains of the most important parts of my life. But they turned out to be disposable.

Mom's sequin diary was left alone and untouched by her in our attic. I shoved my scrapbook under my bed, where I hoped I would forget about it in the same way. Once-important memories are only *sort of* disposable. The mementos and photos would still haunt me. I knew they would. I wondered if Mom's haunted her. The other boyfriend, the baby, and her entire life before there was us.

I needed to busy my mind. Sitting around and thinking about it was going to drive me crazy. If it hadn't been dark already, I'd have gone on another run, but I decided to go to the attic and look around for more of Mom's stuff. Maybe I'd missed something that would point me to solving the mystery.

Basically, I went from one toxic obsession to another. One haunting box of memories to the next.

I found the little shoe box right where I'd left it before. Nothing had moved, shifted, or changed. Some of the pages in the diary had dates on them and went as far back as her middle school days. The more recent ones were her senior year. But still, none of them stood out as being anything important.

Until I found that photo again—the one of Mom with the guy on the couch. But this time, it wasn't Mom I saw. It was Rain Brooks.

I dropped the diary into my lap and shook my head. "No way," I whispered out loud. I had to be crazy. But the resemblance was unbelievable. *This* is where I'd seen Rain before. It had to be a bizarre coincidence... Except, the fact that the Richmond hospital was so close to Ivy Hollow seemed a little too weird to ignore.

I pulled out my cell phone.

EVAN

"Suffering has been stronger than all other teaching, and has taught me to understand what your heart used to be. I have been bent and broken, but—I hope—into a better shape…"

Charles Dickens, <u>Great Expectations</u>

I NEARLY FELL OVER when mom told me that Ava had made a friend and was inviting her over after school on Tuesday. "Her name is Maya, and she's a new student, too. I think they sort of had that in common and clicked," she said.

I shook my head and raised my eyebrows. "I guess I'll believe anything now."

The antique store was closed Mondays and Tuesdays, so I decided to invite Rain over after school on Tuesday, too. We agreed that this would be the day where we both put all our cards on the table.

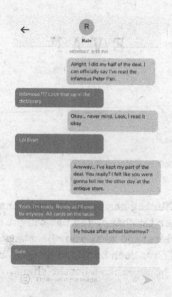

I'd finished *Peter Pan*, practiced typing on my typewriter—producing the promised note for Thomas which I slid into his locker on Monday—and had even caught up on *A Tale of Two Cities*. My weekend was spent almost entirely on reading and writing. Each morning, I woke up before the sun, made my coffee, and read a few chapters before Mom and Ava got up. I'd spend the first few hours of the day outside working in my garden and greenhouse before reading again in the barn. I didn't enjoy it, but I respected it. Rain was right—it took a lot of talent in penning words as artistically as Dickens and Barrie did. I just hoped all the reading would somehow rub off on me when I went to pen my own words.

And as much as I didn't want it to, reading made me think of my dad. He was a storyteller by nature. As I read in the barn, I pictured Dad doing the same thing. He'd wanted to get out of the city to someplace quiet where he could pen the novels trapped inside his mind. I pictured him sitting in the loft with my typewriter, clicking away to master the stories he'd told me as a kid, perfecting them on a page.

On Tuesday, Rain's hand was painted in black and gray again. This time, it was dark clouds outlined in jet black with black raindrops spilling from them. She seemed even more quiet than usual. I, on the other hand, was ready to actually get started on the project. The suspense would finally be over.

After school, we hopped in my truck and headed toward the house, but Rain's mind seemed to be elsewhere. "Are you okay?" I asked after a full minute of silence. I hoped she wasn't clamming up again.

She glanced at me with a smile that was anything but convincing. "Yeah, I'm fine. I guess I'm just a little reluctant to get started on this paper." She adjusted her posture as if in an effort to try and seem more pleasant. "So, tell me... What did you think of my *infamous Peter Pan*?"

I ignored her teasing, pretending to check my blind spots to hide my blushing, and shrugged. "I won't say it's my favorite book I've ever read, but it's good. Barrie was a talented writer. It made me think that your mind and his are similar with your colorful imaginations."

"I don't think my mind holds a candle to his." Rain looked back out her window as we drove by old buildings turning into rolling hills. "Didn't it make you want Neverland though? A place where things stay the same and nothing changes?"

I thought about my dad and the life we'd had together when our family felt complete. Life was easy then, and I'd taken all of it for granted. I wondered what she was thinking of and what changes she was fighting. "Yeah, I guess it does in some ways."

"Jo says the best is always yet to come. I like the thought but not the reality. I hate change." Her voice cracked slightly as she spoke, and I tried to catch a glimpse of her face, but she was turned away from me.

"I guess you probably haven't experienced much change around here."

"No, not much. But senior year always changes things, whether we like it or not." Her hand went to her forehead, massaging it with her fingers, as if just thinking about it brought her anxiety. "What are you going to do after graduation?"

I'm certain I noticeably winced at the question. It's one I'd been tossing around for months, and it felt more complicated now that Dad was gone. "I'm not sure, but I don't think I'll be going to college. At least not for a while. I plan to stay here with Mom until Ava's graduated. Dad made sure we were pretty well cared for, but that money won't last forever. We used most of it to buy our place here. I don't want my mom having to carry that, so I'll get a job of some sort and take care of her and Ava."

Rain was looking at me with what seemed like admiration. "Most eighteen-year-old guys wouldn't do that."

I kept my gaze forward, feeling my face grow warm. "I bet they would. When you lose someone in your family, the family that's left becomes a lot more important to you." We turned into the driveway, and I turned the conversation to her. "What about you?" I asked, unbuckling. "Do you have big plans after graduation?"

"I'm not sure yet. Mr. Clark has always told me one day the store will be mine if I want it, but I'm not sure that will be enough.

I guess my dilemma is similar to yours; I don't want to leave Jo. I'm all she has, and she's all I've got, too."

"The antique store and Jo's job is enough for you now, isn't it?"

"Well, yeah," Rain said, hopping out of the car and meeting me in front of the house. She brushed out the creases in her knee-length skirt from sitting. The bright floral of her fabric contradicted the dark scene on her hand. "But it doesn't feel like enough after school—you know, like a career."

"Why can't it be a career?" I paused by the front door to face her, and she seemed unsure how to answer. "Just because it's not the norm doesn't mean it's not good enough. You have a way of creating a life you love right where you're at, Rain. Most people are looking for the next big thing, and you're finding the best in life right where you are. Don't lose that just because you're graduating high school."

Rain smiled sheepishly, her eyes darting to her sneakers.

I turned away to open the front door, and inside, I could hear Ava chatting away with her friend. I could hardly believe it was my own sister. She hadn't sounded so happy in months. Part of me was glad, but I had the feeling that as soon as her friend left, she'd be just as moody as she was this morning, and I didn't have the patience to put up with it. If she could act normal with her friends, I definitely wasn't going to cater to it anymore.

"Ava has a friend over," I told Rain as we walked through the hall to the kitchen. "We can grab some drinks and snacks and do our work in the barn, if that's alright with you."

Rain nodded as we turned the corner, but her face froze in horror when we entered the kitchen and her gaze landed on Ava and her friend. Her mouth opened slightly in shock, but she quickly caught herself and closed it.

"I didn't know you had a girlfriend," Ava said, taking a sip of her lemonade, the bite in her voice immediately returning.

I heard her, but my attention was mostly on Rain. Her complexion had lost all its color. "Well, maybe if you came out of your room every once in a while, you'd know more things," I bit back a little absently. "But she isn't my girlfriend. She's helping me with a project at school." I turned to the fridge to pour two glasses of lemonade.

Rain quickly followed me, looking eager to turn her back toward the girls.

I passed her a plate of cookies, trying to get her to meet my questioning gaze, but her eyes remained fixed downward as she took it into her trembling hand.

"Tell Mom we're in the barn when you see her," I said to Ava, leading the way to the back door.

Ava ignored me, not even bothering to glance in our direction as we walked out.

Once the door was closed behind us, I fell into step next to Rain as she shuffled to the barn. Our boots squished in the mud from the downpour we'd experienced early that morning.

"Who was that girl?" Rain asked in a low tone, her voice shaking.

I moved closer to her so I could hear her better. "I don't really know. One of Ava's friends. I think my mom said her name was Maddie. Are you okay?"

"It's Maya," Rain corrected me. Her hand still carried the plate of cookies, but she used her other arm to swat at the gnats. They were swarming like crazy after all the rain.

My eyes narrowed into a squint. "You know each other?"

"No, but I've seen her before. In pictures."

"Pictures?"

We entered the barn, and I jumped in front of her to climb the ladder to the loft. Once up, I reached down to take the plate of cookies and watched nervously as she climbed with her one hand effortlessly. I wasn't sure I'd ever get used to her doing dangerous things.

My typewriter, journal, and books were already up there, and we settled in with our drinks and snacks before I began interrogating her. "Alright, explain. Where have you seen her in a picture?"

We both leaned against the back wall, Rain to my left and the large shuttered window to my right. The wood shutters were practically falling to pieces, and they let in more light than they kept out. The sun hit Rain's colorless face as she ran her dark painted fingers through the front wisps of hair that had long since escaped her braid. When she looked up at me—moist eyes glittering in the light shooting from behind me—I could see she was afraid. Truly scared.

"If I tell you, you have to promise you won't tell a soul. Especially your sister."

"More secrets, eh?" I shuffled in the hay beneath me uneasily, trying to figure out what was going on. I didn't want to be the one to pressure her, but at this point, I was truly concerned. Something wasn't right, and it would eat away at me until I could help. "Yeah, I promise. Is everything okay?"

Rain leaned heavily into the wood behind her and brought her knees to her chest like she was trying to go through it and disappear. "I was going to have to tell you all of this today anyway, but I wasn't expecting to encounter Maya at your house."

My eyebrows shot up. "Wait, the girl in my kitchen has something to do with your adoption story?"

Rain heaved a sigh and pointed to my journal and typewriter between us. "You ready to take notes?"

I grabbed the notebook and opened it, waiting.

R A I N

"There is a prodigious strength in sorrow and despair."

Charles Dickens, *A Tale of Two Cities*

SEEING MAYA IN FLESH and blood sent a wave of nausea over me. Evan saw my face but thankfully didn't draw any more attention than necessary. Maya seemed to be looking at him, not me. In my fear and surprise, I hadn't noticed much about her except that we had the same eyes. Reagan's eyes.

I couldn't get out of that kitchen fast enough, and when we finally made it to the barn loft, telling the truth was the last thing I wanted to do. I looked down at the stub where my right hand was missing and rubbed it with my left palm. I had been at peace.

I was happy and content. It was like Evan said—I'd always found a way to create a life I loved right where I was, but now everything was out of place. Every wound once healed had been reopened.

Evan took his notebook and pen in hand, waiting, eyes still peering at me in utter confusion. I buried my head in my arms, trying to decide once and for all if I still wanted to do this.

"Rain, you can trust me with whatever's going on," he repeated. "Are you sure everything's okay?"

Nothing had been okay since the day I'd realized where I'd seen that girl in my homeroom. My life began falling apart that day. "Evan, if one person finds out—"

"No one is going to find out. I swear." He was sitting next to me, his typewriter filling the gap between us, and he leaned on his left hand to move in slightly closer. "Whatever's going on, don't face it alone, Rain. You're not okay."

I searched his eyes one last time. If I started now, there was no going back. I was afraid, but I believed Evan was worth the risk. He'd become my friend—that much I knew—and he deserved my trust.

And God was worth my trust. My story was hard, but He'd always done what was best. Each time the pieces seemed too shattered and too broken to repair, He'd rearranged them to create something more beautiful than before. Every single time. Now, He'd brought Evan into my life—perhaps when I needed him most. I had to trust Him. He'd proved Himself faithful time and time again, so why was it so hard this time?

"I was born in Richmond," I began. Evan's sturdy gaze prompted me to be brave, yet there was a quiver in my voice. "My biological mom checked into the hospital there to be induced into labor. She was just out of high school." I raised my right arm to show him the stub. "She'd attempted to have an abortion, but it failed." I fought the sobs that I felt gathering in my throat. I hated the feeling of wanting to cry, especially in front of someone. But this was the first time in years that I'd told the story out loud, and somehow it was much harder than processing it internally. It brought the story to life again. It reminded me of its reality. It wasn't just the story I'd been told all my life. It really happened, and it was a part of me. A single tear escaped despite my efforts, and I quickly brought my hand to my cheek to brush it away. "I had a twin that didn't make it, and they'd missed me, except for my right hand."

Evan's eyebrows came together as he looked on me with shock and disbelief. "Wait, what?" His knuckles went white as he gripped his pen tighter. I stared at them, wanting to look anywhere but into his eyes. I needed to get through this as quickly as I could.

"When I was born, they didn't expect me to make it through the night. I was really premature, but they were afraid that waiting any longer would cause infection for my birth mother, so they induced her. The NICU fought for my life. That's where Jo worked at the time."

"That's where Jo met you," Evan said, processing the story out loud. He wasn't taking notes, just staring at me with sympathy in his eyes—a look of brokenness.

I nodded. "Jo fought for me harder than anyone." She'd told me that my mom didn't even come to see me the first day, and it broke her heart that I was so alone in the world.

I swallowed and went on. "I made it through the night, of course, and each night after that. Jo says that my mom's sister was the only one with her at the hospital. She thinks her sister had more to do with the abortion than my mom did. It wasn't until her sister left for a few hours one day that my mom finally asked to see me for the first time, three days after I was born. She refused to touch me or hold me when Jo offered; she just looked down at me with a blank expression. Jo finally asked what she was going to name me so they could put it on the birth certificate. She hardly hesitated and didn't even blink. Rain Olivia is what she wanted on the birth certificate."

"She never said why?" Evan interrupted.

I shook my head. "Apparently, the week I was born, there were tons of terrible storms and flooding. Every time one of the nurses went into my mom's room, she was just sitting there, staring out the window. Jo wonders if postpartum depression and trauma from the failed abortion were affecting her mind. She'd just given birth to the person she'd tried to kill, and my twin didn't make it. That's a lot for someone to process."

Evan rubbed the back of his neck. All of the color had left his face, and his eyes seemed glazed over. "Yeah, I'd say so."

"My mom and her sister ended up leaving me. Just up and deserting me when they realized I was going to live. They told the hospital to let DSS step in. Jo had grown so attached that she ended up adopting me. It was a long process, but Jo had been a foster kid all her life. She'd worked hard to get through school and to get an apartment, but she said she couldn't watch me get lost in the system like she had been."

Evan's head leaned back to rest on the wall behind us. His eyes were fixed on the roof of the barn, but his mind seemed far away. His fingers rolled the pen against his thigh absently. "How long have you known?"

I leaned back, too, trying to relax a little. "Always. Jo never hid it from me. Being a foster kid, she knew how important the truth was. She knew I needed to know. She's always felt that knowing where we come from helps grow us into the sort of people we should be. It makes us stronger. So I've always called her Jo and known about my real mom."

"She's braver than most people in her situation would have been," he said.

Jo had always been my hero. The world had fought against Joanne Brooks most of her life, and when she finally got up on her feet, she took up the battle of fighting for me. And I swore I would never forget that or take it for granted.

"I never wished things any other way," I said. "We ended up moving to Ivy Hollow when I was two. Jo saved the money to buy our little house, which was an absolute wreck when she got it. She met Mr. and Mrs. Clark at church, and they sort of adopted both of us. They never had children of their own, and Jo was about the age their own children would've been if they'd had any. Mr. Clark repaired the house by himself while Jo worked at the hospital, and Mrs. Clark would watch me at the antique store each day. We became each other's family."

For the first time since we arrived in the barn loft, a small smile formed in the corner of Evan's mouth. But the hollow look in his eyes stayed the same, making the smile seem out of place. "It's interesting to see stories like that come together. You all completed each other."

There was a pause that grew between us, as all that I'd told him soaked in, but he rolled the pen in his fingers faster. I could see the wheels turning in his head. "And what does all of this have to do with Maya?"

A soft sigh brushed my lips. I dreaded this part most, but there was no retreating now. "As I got older, I did a little social media stalking to learn who my mother was and what had happened to her. My mom was seventeen when she got pregnant with me. She went off to college, met a guy, and ended up pregnant again, not very long after I was born. They kept that baby and eventually got married. A few years later, they had another. My mom became a realtor and her new husband is a doctor. I have no idea if any of her new family knows that I exist.

"When I was fourteen, I obsessed over their social media photos. The beach pictures, the birthday parties, the family portraits... I wondered what made me so awful that my mom had tried to take my life and then abandon me. What made her two new daughters more worthy than me?" I twisted the hem of my skirt around my pointer finger. "Eventually, I just forgave her and moved on. It didn't matter. It was probably my dad or just bad timing, but that wasn't my fault. Regardless, things turned out the way they were supposed to. I was wanted by Jo and the Clarks. They loved me, not because I'm their flesh and blood or because they had to, but just because they chose to.

"But as for Maya..." I continued, and Evan seemed to know what was coming. "You aren't the only new student at Ivy Hollow High. I recognized Jordan on her first day. She's my half-sister. My mom's second baby. The one she kept." My face went warm. It almost felt shameful again, saying it out loud to Evan. I knew I shouldn't, but that didn't keep me from feeling embarrassed, like I was the ugly duckling. "Maya is the youngest daughter."

Evan looked like he had a thousand questions but was trying to decide which ones were most important. The barn air was already stale, but it seemed to grow thinner with the weight of the silence between us. And yet I sat there feeling a sense of freedom come over me. What was done was done. And Evan was right; I didn't have to face it alone anymore. Of course, I'd had Jo and Mr. Clark to go to since Jordan arrived, but there was something nice about having a friend. Not just a parent and grandparent—someone who went to school with me every single day. Someone who would walk the halls with me and face the problem by my side. Each day, I went home and told Jo about every almost-encounter, every suspicious look, every mini panic attack. Evan would be there to brave it alongside me.

I shifted to change positions and crossed my ankles in front of me. "A bit more of a story than you planned to tackle, huh?" I asked, trying to smile a little.

Evan gave a dry laugh. "I don't know what I was expecting, but it wasn't that." He ran his fingers through his dark, wavy hair before turning to face me. "I didn't know something like that could happen—surviving an abortion. I've always been against abortion, but I never really thought too much about it."

"It happens more than you think. Those of us who survive are just walking proof that abortion kills *people*. It takes lives. We aren't clumps of cells or 'potential' people. We're *people*." Evan was studying me closely as I spoke, and I avoided his gaze, scuffing some hay with the heel of my sneaker.

"What was the hardest part for you? Knowing you weren't wanted by your mom? Seeing your sisters live the life you didn't get?"

I shook my head and swallowed the tears that rose in my throat. "Knowing my twin didn't get a chance at all. *Nothing* has hurt more than that guilt. Sure, I've been jealous of Jordan, but my twin didn't even get the opportunity to be jealous of me." I could forgive my mom. I could accept that my life had turned out better in the long run. I could get over the jealousy of being wanted by my mother the way that Jordan and Maya were. But I'd never been able to accept the death of my twin. I'd never been able to shake the guilt that came with that. There were nights I would even dream about him or her, and I'd wake up and sob my eyes out until my chest couldn't take the tightness anymore and my throat was raw.

Evan rubbed at a smudge of dirt on his jeans with his thumb. "I guess you're bound to run into your mom at some point."

"Probably. I don't even know how I would react if I met her face to face. I don't know what I'd say. All my life I've had things I wanted to ask her and things I thought I might tell her, but I never expected to actually get the opportunity. Now that it's here, I don't think I want it." I'd played the scenario out in my mind a thousand times in the past few weeks. Would she recognize me? I looked a lot like her, but she had nothing to base me off of. She might see my missing hand and remember the baby she'd abandoned eighteen years ago with the same handicap. Maya or Jordan could go home and talk about the girl they'd met named Rain. Would she look for me and seek closure? Or would she pack her bags and abandon me again as soon as she realized I was right here in her own town? Or maybe she knew I was here and had been looking for me all along.

It was the unknown that brought the anxiety.

Evan rubbed his chin thoughtfully. "I feel like I'd want the answers after wondering my whole life. I don't know how you can stand it—being so close to her for the first time in your life and still not having answers."

I chewed on my lip. Some things were better left unknown. After all, she'd tried to take my life. It wasn't like she placed me for adoption and hoped I'd end up in a loving, stable home. I was disposable. "I don't know," I said. "I finally accepted the first time she left me, and I'm afraid she'll do it again. Then, I'll have to start from square one."

"Yeah, I guess so."

I picked up his leather journal and passed it to him. "I think I've given you enough to keep you busy for a while." As I held it out to him, I noticed it had initials engraved into the right hand corner.

J.H.L.

"What do the letters stand for?"

Evan traced a finger over them. "Jacob Henry Lawson. My dad. He was always going through journals. Ava and I got him this one for his birthday right before he passed, and he never got to use it. Figured I'd not let it go to waste."

That's what was really holding Evan back in this project. It wasn't a lack of time or skill, it was grief. This was his dad's thing.

"He wanted to move out here to write novels. If you'd given *him* your story, he'd have taken it and done it justice," Evan added, grabbing a cookie from the plate we'd long forgotten about in the midst of our conversation.

Outside, a gust of wind blew into the barn, rattling the tin roof and whistling through the grassy fields around us. Evan left Chicago to escape the memories of his life before, but he was finding his dad everywhere here. Ivy Hollow had a way of doing that—bringing back the people we left behind. And as much as it was happening to him, it was happening to me, too. Because new beginnings don't always mean forgetting the past; sometimes they mean facing it.

"I trust his son to do just as well," I said, offering a reassuring smile. "Besides, it's you who needs the story written, not me. I'm just letting you use me as a subject."

Evan looked me in the eye. "And I appreciate it. I didn't know what I was asking when I got you into this, but you agreed, and I promise it'll stay between us. I won't let you down."

I believed him.

Evan spent the next little while taking notes on everything I'd just shared with him, asking questions and clarifying details.

While he worked, I pulled out the watercolor palette and sketchbook I'd brought in my backpack to keep me busy. On the blank page before me, I began the outline of a face in various shades of green and brown. I always painted abstractly when it came to color. I liked to fill the eyes and face of my subject with colors that displayed the personality of my subject. Colors brought life and emotion to something flat and one-dimensional.

"What about your biological dad?" Evan asked. "Do you know who he is?"

"I've tried to find him, but I don't even know his name. I'm pretty sure he doesn't know I exist." I glanced up briefly from my painting. "Jo said she felt certain that my mom's sister was the only one to know about the abortion and my survival. I'm sure she was trying to hide the pregnancy from my dad."

Evan bit the cap of his pen in thought. "She was our age. Can you imagine?"

I brushed light, wavy strokes of forest green and a golden brown, framing the face of my portrait with hair. "No, I can't."

Evan's face went pink, and he rubbed his forearm with his other hand. "Do you think she could have been raped?" he asked hesitantly, his voice lower.

"It's possible," I said, looking back down at my sketchbook. "I'm not really sure. It was hard to find any information about her life in high school and college."

Next, I worked on the eyes, which was always my favorite part. Shakespeare said the eyes are the window to the soul, and I think it's true.

I looked up and watched as Evan wrote, his eyes fixed on his own page. The intentness of his gaze showed determination and focus.

I traced out an almond shape in dark green and filled the iris with a pool of deep hues of green, rich brown, and gold. The pupil I did in dark brown, too. The colors entangled to create a warm portrait that made me feel the hot summer sun. It made me see the tall brown grass, blowing in the wind on the hills. I could feel the moist soil between my fingers. I could see buds of life poking through the earth. I could smell the black coffee in a clay mug. Hear the clicking keys of a typewriter. Feel the ache of something missing—the absence of something vital.

"How should I write this?" Evan asked, pulling my attention back to him.

"What do you mean?"

"Do I write it from your perspective? Do I fictionalize your thoughts and reactions? Or do I do it as a narrator?"

I took my brush and smoothed out a rigged stroke on the lips of my portrait. "I think that's up to you. What way do you feel most comfortable writing it?"

He studied the notes before him.

I spun the paintbrush between my fingers, wondering if I should give my honest thoughts. I knew his grief was still raw, but I truly believed that facing his story in this way would help him move forward. But then, who was I to tell him so when I was struggling to do it myself?

I exhaled deeply, causing Evan to look up at me, and set my brush down. "If you really want my opinion, I would say to write it from your perspective. Add your own story. Start with moving to Ivy Hollow, why you came here, and what you've found. Write about why you neglected your studies in the first place and the grief that's been holding you back. Write about the people you've gotten to know through having to write this paper." I gave him an intent stare. "Evan, you're looking to my story to drown out your own."

He smiled and leaned his back against the wood behind him. "No, I'm looking to your story because mine isn't nearly as interesting."

"Says who?"

He shrugged. "Anyone. Rain, didn't you just hear yourself?"

I held his gaze as if willing him to see what I saw. "I don't read stories *just* for plot twists and action. It's a big part of it, but it isn't the biggest part. If I hate the main character, I'm not going to finish reading the book. I read the book because something in me wants to see the main character get what he wants. I want to see him succeed, no matter what happens in his story. The character has far more to do with how we love a book than the events. If you only focus on the events of my birth, your paper is going to be a thousand words at most. It'll take you no time to list out my family history. What are you going to do with the other nine thousand?"

Evan spun his pen in his fingers again as he thought. "So what is it *you* want?"

"I think you'll get farther if you ask yourself what it is *you* want."

"But this story isn't about me, and I have no idea how I would tie them together. What does what I want have to do with your adoption?"

I sighed. He wasn't seeing it.

He'd told me he and his mom had wanted to move out here to start again and to fulfill a dream of his dad's. Here he was, living that dream. He sat in this barn with the chance to write the story his dad didn't get to and pen the words that would mark his new beginning.

Evan pointed at the sketchbook in my lap. "What have you been working on?" Reluctantly, I passed it to him and watched for his reaction. His eyebrows lifted and he grinned. "This is amazing. You make me look better than I do in real life."

"Or maybe you and I just aren't seeing the same thing," I said.

He glanced up at me briefly, then back down at the painting.

"However you decide to write this paper, it's going to be great. I know it."

"I feel like I'm way overthinking it. It's just a school project."

"Yeah, you probably are. But if you're going to have to do it, you may as well give it your all, right?"

"You never answered my question earlier," he said, looking up again. "What is it you want?"

I hesitated and lifted an eyebrow. "First, tell me what it is you want."

"What I want I'll never be able to get back. At least not in this life," he said, swallowing hard.

"What I want is equally impossible," I said. "I'll never meet my twin or even know why things happened the way they did. So I have to come up with a new goal to chase after... and that's to take the broken pieces and arrange them to create the most beautiful life I can. To make the most of what I've been given and use it to bring God glory. I have to trust that He's the Master Artist, creating me the way He did purposefully and tastefully, even if my mom didn't love me. And I have to trust He's the Master Storyteller, and He wrote it this way for a reason." I crossed my arms over my chest and nodded toward the typewriter. "I recommend you do the same. And then write about it. I bet those words will come a lot more naturally than trying to get inside my head and pen my story."

Evan listened intently and then rubbed his face roughly with his palm. "But I still don't believe I have anything in my life worth writing about."

I took my sketchbook back and placed it on the wood floor between us. "I paint portraits abstractly when it comes to color. From the different shades of green and gold and brown, I see a personality. A story. Your life is as full of meaning as mine.

"In the color green, I see life and growth and creativity. In brown, I see hard work and determination. In the gold, I see your surroundings; I see the sun you toil under, the fields in Ivy Hollow you bought to start new. This is Evan Lawson—to me at least. You have talents, dreams, and desires. You have heartache, goals, and something to fight for. What more do you need for a good story?"

He considered my words, staring at the sketchbook in front of him.

"You can use my story if you want, but I'm just saying, thanks to this project, they intertwine now. You lost your dad and moved to the middle of absolutely nowhere to fulfill a family dream and find healing. You met me, right as my own life started coming apart at the seams. Now both of us have sort of been thrown together to figure out what's next and where we're supposed to go. Doesn't that sound like a more complex and rich topic than just reciting what I told you about myself?"

Evan's eyes lit up as I spoke, and I knew he'd caught on to what I was getting at. "So I write both of us."

"That's what I would do."

"From whose perspective?"

I tapped my knee with my brush. "Try writing it a few different ways and see what fits best."

"And how does it end?"

End. What a word. So short. So abrupt. So final. At the sound of it, the cold fingers of anxiety took hold of my heart and tightly clenched it in its fist.

How *would* it end?

"Just start writing first. I don't think you have to decide that yet," I said, hoping it was true of me. I didn't have to face it yet.

I watched Evan's forest green eyes as he scribbled in his dad's journal. Green—the color of creativity and growth. Behind them, ideas were starting to take root.

JORDAN

> "You need not be sorry for her. She was one of the kind that likes to grow up. In the end she grew up of her own free will a day quicker than the other girls."
>
> J.M. Barrie, Peter Pan

MOM FINALLY TOOK ME to get my license. I think she felt bad after yelling at me for detention. Two weeks after my birthday, she picked me up from school a little early and took me to the DMV. After a small panic attack, I passed my test and had the driver's license to prove it. Mom let me drive the SUV home.

"To think my first baby is sixteen and driving," she said nostalgically as we rode. I immediately thought about her *real* first baby who was—or would have been—eighteen now. "Where did the time go? It seems like just yesterday your dad and I brought you home from the hospital. We were practically babies ourselves. I was so young." There was wistfulness in her voice. Was she thinking of my dad and the days we were a real family? I wondered if she thought about her first baby and how young she'd been when it was born, not even two years older than I was now.

I turned my blinker on and loosened my grip on the steering wheel. I couldn't tell if I was nervous because I was a new driver or because I couldn't stop thinking about my mom's secret. I wanted to ask her so badly. I wanted to see how she reacted and hear what she'd say. I wanted to know if the baby had died and if the girl at school was just a bizarre coincidence.

I hadn't found anything on Joanne Brooks when I started Googling except that she worked at the hospital here in Ivy Hollow. Neither she or Rain had social media.

The thought that Rain was my mom's first kid seemed too crazy to be true, but the parallels couldn't be altogether ignored either.

Thomas had asked what was going on the day after I texted him, of course, but I didn't tell him. I just sort of brushed it off like I thought I recognized her, but I was wrong. Maybe I should have told him; we're friends after all. But I couldn't. He and Rain were friends before he and I were. If I told him, I knew he would tell Rain. My own mom didn't even know that I was snooping around in this secret. Rain was the last person I wanted to know. It would be a mess for everyone involved.

But then, I couldn't shake the feeling that she already knew—if it was her—and she knew exactly who I was.

I kept reminding myself I was basing all of this off of the resemblance to my mom in an old photo. It was definitely not the most trustworthy method of finding long-lost sisters. I hoped I was wrong.

"Your father was so in love with you. He still is, Jordan. You know that, don't you?" Mom said, bringing my thoughts back to the present. She pulled her loose, dark brown hair to a bun at the top of her head and tied it off with a hair tie she wore on her wrist. Rain wore her hair like that a lot. And it was the exact same color.

I didn't answer. I knew Dad loved me in some ways, but love is more than a feeling. It's action. And neither he nor my mom were acting like they loved Maya and I, regardless of how they felt about us and what they said.

"I know it doesn't seem like it now, but one day you'll understand that things are best this way."

"I know, Mom. You keep saying that."

"But you don't really believe it, do you?"

Again, I didn't answer.

"I know. And that's okay. You need time." She sounded like she was trying to convince herself, not me.

It was silent for a long, uncomfortable minute. This was the most Mom and I had spoken one-on-one since we came to Ivy Hollow.

"Maya is at her friend's house again today for a few hours. Why don't you and I take a detour and grab some coffee before we head home? Just us, for your birthday. Even if it is a little late."

"It's fine, Mom. I have a lot of homework to do."

She hesitated as she looked me over but reluctantly nodded her head. I knew she wouldn't fight me on it. She didn't want to endure an awkward coffee date any more than I did. "Well, maybe you could use your new freedom to take on some responsibility and help me out by picking Maya up in a few hours. Then, maybe the two of you could go do something fun."

I wasn't really sure what she could mean by "fun" in Ivy Hollow, but at five o'clock, I went to pick up Maya from the address Mom gave me. Ivy Hollow was already in the middle of nowhere, but this house was *really* in the middle of nowhere. As I drove, the hills seemed to roll on forever. Somehow, I couldn't help but love it. Maybe it was because I was the one driving and felt free. I rolled down my window to let in some of the crisp fall air, and I filled my lungs with it. I turned up my radio and let the music saturate my mind.

I wasn't going to think about my parents, or Maya, or my mom's big secret, or Molly and Savannah, or school. I just drove.

My phone's GPS let me know I was nearly at my destination, and I turned left onto a long, winding driveway. It led to a farmhouse with a barn out back, surrounded by fields of pasture.

Out front, I saw Evan from homeroom, painting the front door. The guy who always hung around Rain Brooks. I'd forgotten he was the older brother of Maya's new friend.

Self-consciously, I ran my fingers through my wind-blown hair and pushed my sunglasses on top of my head. I shrugged after a quick glance at my reflection in the rear view mirror; it would have to do.

Evan turned to look at me as I got out of the car and seemed to recognize me, too. "I guess you're probably here to pick up Maya," he said, rubbing his paint-covered hands on his jeans.

"Yeah, I am."

"We're in homeroom together. It's Jordan, right?"

I nodded.

"I'm Evan. I'd shake your hand but..." He lifted his open palms to show the remaining green paint with a smirk. He seemed friendly

194

enough, but his eyes made me feel like he was suspicious of me. But maybe I was paranoid. I was *definitely* paranoid.

From the garage, I heard a door open and close, and Rain walked out in paint-stained overalls with two glasses of iced tea in her arms. She startled when she saw me and nearly dropped both of them, half their contents spilling over her arm.

"Sorry," she said, and Evan walked over to grab them from her. "I wasn't expecting to see anyone else out here."

Evan glanced from her to me and smiled slightly. "You remember Jordan, don't you? She's in our homeroom."

"Yeah," Rain said, and she gave me an uncomfortable smile. "Yeah, I remember. It's nice to actually meet you."

I was starting to feel convinced that Rain was as suspicious of me as I was of her. But if Rain was my mom's first baby, why in the world would she move us right where she lived? Unless she didn't know Rain lived here. But how could a coincidence that big be possible?

Not to mention, she may have just been skeptical of me because of the whole situation with Thomas. I'm sure he told her everything that happened. Maybe she didn't trust me. Thomas had told me she was like an older sister to him and was super protective.

I swept a piece of hair behind my ear, feeling very out of place, and put my hands in my back pockets. "Maya has really enjoyed getting to know your sister," I said, directing my gaze to Evan. "I'm glad she found someone to hang out with, being new to the school and all."

"We're new to the area, too, so I'm glad Ava found your sister. She's been a handful since moving in, but I feel like making a new friend has helped a lot."

"Maya mentioned that you lost your dad a few months ago. I'm really sorry about that," I said to fill the void and immediately regretted it. But Evan didn't seem to mind.

"I think this place will be good for us. A new beginning, I guess."

A new beginning. He sounded like Mom. What was it about Ivy Hollow and new beginnings? It's the last place I would have chosen to start again. There was nothing to do. Nothing to keep your mind busy. All I ever did was sit around the house and reflect on what we used to have.

Almost like she was reading my thoughts, Rain asked, "Are you liking it here? You said Maya's getting settled, but what about you?" She picked up a paintbrush in her left hand and began painting the door where Evan left off. Her hand was painted, like it always was, but I could hardly make out what it was. The paint was smudged, probably from typical wear and tear throughout the day, and parts of it were covered with the olive paint they were using on the front door.

"I'm getting there, I guess," I finally replied, leaning on the hood of my car. "I can't really say I'm much of a small-town girl. I miss beach life."

"This is a big adjustment, then. You don't get a smaller town than Ivy Hollow," she said.

"Tell me about it."

For the first time, I noticed a black typewriter sitting on a table in the garage with two chairs nearby. I wondered if it was the typewriter Thomas had told me about.

"I already painted that while you were inside," Evan said, watching over Rain's shoulder.

She laughed, her shoulders rising and falling. "I can tell. You'd better let me take care of the painting."

Evan laughed, too. "Alright, have it your way." He bent down to grab his iced tea—what was left of it after Rain's spill—and directed his attention back to me. "I've seen you spend a lot of time with Thomas."

"Yeah. He's a really nice guy. Did he fix that typewriter?" I asked, nodding my head toward the garage.

"Yep. Evan's using it for a writing project," Rain said.

"Fingers crossed that using it will give me extra credit 'cause I'll need all the help I can get."

From an open window on the second floor, we could hear an outburst of hysterical laughter from Maya and Ava. I looked up to see a blur move past the gap in the blowing curtains.

I envied Maya's ability to adapt so easily. But then, I knew she could only do it because of me. I took on the responsibilities of holding everything together so that she didn't have to.

"I guess I'll go get your sister," Evan said.

"Thanks."

He closed the garage door behind himself, and I let my gaze fall back on Rain. I hoped maybe I could get some answers from her now that we were alone. I let the silence build between us for a few seconds. I didn't want to sound too desperate.

"So, Thomas told me you were adopted. That's pretty cool."

Rain didn't hesitate or do anything out of the ordinary, but her back was to me so I couldn't see her face. "Yeah, I am."

I nervously twisted the hem of my T-shirt around my pointer finger. "I bet it was hard though. At times, anyway."

"Sure. But I was always thankful for the way my life turned out. I have an awesome family." This was getting me nowhere, and I felt rude prying. What if she had nothing to do with my mom? But I had to try. I had to know.

197

"Have you always known you were adopted?"

"Yeah, I have."

"Do you know anything about your birth mom? I feel like I would be super curious about that." My palms were sweating. I knew I was coming across as invasive.

Rain turned to face me and sat on the front step. She seemed far cooler and collected than I felt. "I know a little about her." It didn't confirm or deny my suspicion, but I could tell by her disposition that she wasn't about to spill her life story for me any more than I was going to let on to Mom's secret. And why would she?

Evan came back with Maya trailing behind him before she could say anything else.

After a few awkward goodbyes, I slid into the driver's seat and exhaled the breath I'd been holding. My face felt hot.

I shouldn't have asked. It didn't get me anywhere except looking nosy. The whole way home I mentally kicked myself while Maya dragged on telling me about her day.

When we got home, we were welcomed by the eerie sound of moaning.

Mom was drinking, and it didn't take long for me to tell she'd had a lot.

"Get to your homework," I mumbled to Maya, closing the front door behind me.

"I already did it with Ava."

"Well then, go clean your room."

She began to protest, but Mom erupted in a sudden outburst of sobbing that made my blood curdle and Maya's eyes open wide. She obeyed me and made her way upstairs.

Mom was in the living room, hunched over her knees on the couch. She clutched her abdomen with one hand and held a nearly empty bottle of wine in the other. Her stringy hair hid her face from my view.

Where is Dad when I need him most?

I'd seen this twice before. Both times, I was the one sent upstairs while Dad tried to console her. I was eleven the last time it happened, and I sat hidden on the stairs, listening as he tried to soothe her, asking her what was tormenting her. She never said. I think it had happened more than twice though. There were days I'd come home from school and find the remnants of her drinking. She'd be locked in her room. Later, when Dad got home, he'd just say she wasn't feeling well.

When the divorce happened, Dad tried to convince the judge that she was crazy. That she'd have these episodes and she was unfit to care for us, but he didn't succeed. The judge just required Mom to start seeing a therapist. It was her therapist that suggested our "new beginning," which led us to Ivy Hollow. And a lot of good it did us, because here we were, too far for Dad to come pick Maya and I up and no one to control her but me.

Once again I would pick up the slack and fill in the holes, even though I was never rewarded for it. Most of the time it just put me in the line of fire.

Mom hadn't even noticed us come in. With each breath, she was working herself up more and more with deep cries that got louder and louder. I wanted to walk over to her, but I felt glued to where I stood. And when I got there, what would I say? I could hardly make conversation with her on a good day, so what could I say now that would make any difference? And why should I try? She hardly ever made an effort on her part to be the parent I needed. She was supposed to be my emotional support, and here she was, falling apart for me to swoop in and save her.

But guilt pulled at my heart and won. It always won.

Cautiously, I made my way toward the living room, afraid to make any sudden movements that might send her into a fit of who-knew-what. Mom remained hunched over, sobbing and mumbling things I couldn't make out. I eased my way onto the couch beside her and placed a shaking hand on the small of her back.

"Mom," I whispered. Her head lifted slightly at the sound of my voice. "Mom, it's alright. You just need to lay down a while."

She shook her head in a jerky motion and started to bring the bottle of wine to her lips again. I stopped her, wrapping my fingers around it and trying to pull it away, but her grip tightened.

"You'll be sick if you have any more. I'll take it." Her head shot up, and her bloodshot eyes dared me to continue. I hesitated but held my grip. "You need to rest now," I said, my voice wavering.

Her head went down, her eyes squeezed shut. When she spoke, it was through her teeth but seemed to come from the depths of her soul. "Do not tell me what to do. I know what I want. I'll do what I want. I know what's best for me. I have to do what's best for me." She seemed so far away, like she wasn't talking to me about the bottle at all. This was more than just being drunk.

"What is this about?" I whispered.

Mom froze, then turned her head to stare at me like she was trying to figure out who I was. She looked wild and dangerous.

I'd never seen that look in her eyes before, and I was terrified. My stomach tied in knots as I attempted again to pull the bottle from her fingers.

Again, her grip closed in. Her other hand raised in a flash of movement and slapped me across the face.

I stood to my feet in pure shock. It didn't hurt, not badly, but my mother had never hit me before. My first instinct was to cry, but it turned quickly to rage.

The rage I'd felt since the day she and my dad told us about the divorce.

I took a step forward and slapped her back—not as hard as she slapped me, but it was enough. Taking it out on her was far more satisfying than taking it out on Drake, and the satisfaction I felt made me hate myself.

She returned the look of sheer surprise, and I snatched the bottle from her hands. I threw it to the floor, glass shattering around us, the remaining wine staining the carpet and sprinkling the leg of our cream couch.

"You aren't the only one in this family," I said, and it came out as almost a growl. I'd never heard myself like this. Never felt a rage like this. The monster emerging from myself almost scared me more than Mom's monster. Who was I becoming? What happened to us? To the perfect, happy Carson family?

Tears burned my eyes. "Pull yourself together. Go take a shower and get in bed."

The shell of my mother continued to stare back at me with eyes full of shock, but I didn't wait to see how she'd respond. I spun on my heel and ran to my room, where I curled up in a corner on the floor and cried harder than I ever had in my life.

We all have skeletons in our closets, they say. My family included.

But ours hid in the attic, not the closet. They hid among the journals, photos, shoe boxes, wedding dress, and board games.

Ours were tumbling out.

I had to clean up the mess alone—hide the evidence.

If this is what new beginnings looked like, I didn't want one. If starting over meant facing the ghosts that haunt the past, I wanted to keep the past.

But there was no going back. I knew too much.

I'd seen the bones. I'd met the monsters.

My parents wore masks to make them look happy, to hide secrets, to tell us they loved us. Even I wore a mask to hide my own monster. But now the masks had fallen off, and sliding them back on wouldn't hide the truth anymore. What was seen could not be unseen.

The new beginning was here to be faced, like it or hate it.

EVAN

"'I say, Peter, can you really fly?'

Instead of troubling to answer him Peter flew round
the room, taking the mantelpiece along the way.

'I say, how do you do it?' asked John, rubbing his knee.
He was a very practical boy.

'You just think lovely wonderful thoughts' Peter
explained, 'and they lift you up in the air.'"

J.M. Barrie, Peter Pan

"MAYBE SHE WAS JUST making conversation," I suggested. Rain and I
were sitting in the garage after watching Jordan's car disappear
down the gravel driveway.

Rain's brow was furrowed, and I could tell she was on the verge
of freaking out the way she had when she first saw Maya in my
kitchen. "I don't think so. I think she knows."

Almost two weeks had passed since Rain and I sat in the barn
loft where she first told me her story. I'd spent the time since
writing like crazy. At first, I just played around, writing the story

in different ways and starting at different points. I tried writing it from different perspectives like Rain suggested. Eventually, I took her advice and wrote it from my own, starting the story when I moved to Ivy Hollow. But I added her perspective, too. I felt both were vital.

It was messy. Really messy. But I'd started, and that was the important thing—at least, that's what Rain said. Rain hadn't read it yet. It still felt too messy, and I couldn't get myself to share it with her. She was indignant about it, of course, but I knew I wasn't ready to hand it over.

I took the last sip of my sweet tea and smirked at Rain. "Well, there's only one way to find out how much she knows."

Rain's fingers gripped the edge of the blue folding table between us. "But what if I'm wrong and she has no idea? I can't imagine Reagan would appreciate me telling her daughter about her secret abortion and the baby that survived. I would burn the bridge before I even had a chance to meet her."

I rested my elbows on the table and laced my fingers together.

"But the look in her eyes... She was prying. Why would she be so curious unless she knew?" Rain covered her face with her palm.

"Well, if you aren't going to straight up ask her about it, I say don't stress over it. Let her wonder. It'll be fine."

She removed her hand to look at me, at first like I was crazy for suggesting she not worry, but eventually she sighed and gave a short nod. "You're right. I'm just... being flighty."

"I think I'd feel the same if I were in your shoes. But I'm not in your shoes, so I'll just try to keep you as grounded as I can."

Rain grinned in the way that brought a sparkle to her eye. Ever since I started writing Rain, I began noticing things about her that I hadn't before. I was always observing and listening for the little things unique to her personality.

And the more I did that, the more I felt like she was becoming the love interest in my story.

I ran my finger along the edge of the table. "What's Jo doing tonight?"

Her eyebrows came together at the sudden change in subject. She wasn't wearing her glasses; they sat on the table next to my typewriter. I think it was the first time I'd seen her without them. She almost didn't look like herself. "She's supposed to get off work around six. Why?"

"My mom wants her to come for dinner. She thought it'd be nice for us all to get together."

Her eyes lit up, and if I looked hard enough, I might have found the second star to the right in them. "That would be fun. I'll text her and have her come over after work. Jo could use a break. A friend and a night to enjoy herself would be good for her." Rain pulled out her phone and started texting. She used only her thumb to text and was still faster than I was.

"I figured Mom would enjoy someone else to talk to other than me and Ava for once," I said, "so I suggested she try and meet Jo." It had been part of my mission to make this place home for Mom. Ava was still being ridiculous, but Maya helped; she at least had a friend. Mom was practically on an island.

Rain dropped her phone to her lap and leaned back in her seat, looking outside the garage in thought. "I feel like they'll get along well." She tucked a stray wisp of her hair behind her ear. That piece was always bugging her, never going up into the bun on her head or staying twisted into her braid. It had a bit of olive paint on the end of it—the paint we'd just used on Mom's front door. "We've started to get along pretty well ourselves, haven't we?"

"I like to think so," I said. "Though you were determined we wouldn't. Admit it."

She blushed, and my stomach did somersaults. "I won't say I wasn't reluctant, but it wasn't your fault," she said. "I was scared."

She was still scared. Her entire disposition changed any time Jordan or Maya passed by. I'm sure I would've been the same way if my half-sisters showed up and threatened to shake the entire foundation of the life I'd built, but I hated to watch her go through it, always worrying.

I crossed my arms over my chest and met her eyes. "I can't say I blame you. But truly, I'm honored you decided to trust me."

Rain let out a short laugh. "I don't think you would have left me alone until I did."

"Probably not."

"Why?" she asked, squinting. "Why were you so persistent? You didn't even know me or if my story was worth the effort. It would've been easier to come up with some other idea."

I tapped a finger on the table absently as I thought. Why *was* I so persistent? After a while, it was her secretiveness that sparked my curiosity. The more she tried to hide, the more I wanted to know her secret.

But before that... What was it before that?

"I guess maybe it was your hand," I said finally.

"Which one? The one I paint or the one that's missing?"

I chuckled. "The painted one." I looked down at it. Earlier, it had been painted in wild, bright zig zags in all different colors. It was hardly noticeable now, covered mostly in green paint from the door, and I think her hand mirrored my own head that day. Wild abstract colors filled my mind when I thought about her, and I was doing my best to keep them from showing through.

Rain lifted her right arm and looked at the stub. "Usually, it's the other one first. People want to know what happened."

"Well, I wanted to know why it was stars on Monday and gray blobs on Tuesday. And how the heck you did it without the other hand."

Rain's smile grew softer, and her eyes grew more intrigued. "And when you learned all of that, why did you stick around?"

The colors of my mind were showing through. I could see it in the way she looked at me—like she was seeing something in me for the first time. I didn't care. Why should I? She would be able to read me no matter what. That's how she was.

I shifted slightly in my seat and met her gaze. "I guess I learned you wore your heart at the end of your sleeve. Literally. Every day, I wait to see what colors and shapes will appear and what they'll tell me about you."

She was searching, like she often did. Maybe for a sign that I was telling the truth or if I was just trying to flatter her; but I knew she wouldn't find any sign of a lie.

There wasn't a lie to find. "I'm glad I hated A *Tale of Two Cities*. And I'm glad I pushed through *Peter Pan*," I said. "Because I'm glad I know you, Rain Brooks."

Her cheeks went pink, and she looked down at her lap.

I'd have given anything to know what colors were going through her own mind then.

A silence followed, but I imagined her thoughts were as loud as mine.

"I like to think I'm one of the few people who knows your story," I said. "I like to think I know you like nobody else, now that I've gotten into your head and written about you. But I'll bet I'm not the first guy you made feel special." I crossed my arms over my chest, and Rain gave a suspicious glare. "So tell me. How many unfortunate Ivy Hollow boys' hearts have you broken?"

Her right eyebrow lifted. "I think you've gotten into my character enough to know I'm not that kind of girl."

"You're right," I said, nodding. "I think you're content to sit and read about fictional guys until some Prince Charming comes along to sweep you off your feet."

Rain shot an accusatory look. "You make it sound like a bad thing."

"You may be waiting an awfully long time. Maybe forever."

A thoughtful frown tugged at her lips. "Really? I don't think so. Maybe you have the wrong idea of the sort of guy I consider to be a Prince Charming."

I laced my fingers behind my head. "Alright, enlighten me, then. I consider this further research on your character."

A wistfulness crossed her face. She looked like she was imagining something wonderful. "He won't be like all the boys I've read about. He'll be like himself, and getting to know him will be like reading something entirely new for the first time. And I'm certain I'll know him when I see him."

I shook my head. "You're a puzzle."

"And yet you've made it your goal to figure me out," she said playfully.

I'm glad the tables didn't turn, and we moved on to other topics, because I knew that if she returned the question, and asked me the kind of girl I was looking for, I couldn't tell her a lie. She'd have read it as easily as she reads the pages of a book.

What I was looking for, I'd already found.

The realization had come slowly but surely. It wasn't anything grand. It happened there in my garage as we sat talking about nothing incredibly deep. But it was the simple moments of nothing special with her that I looked forward to most these days.

All I knew was that I never wanted to live without her color again.

RAIN

> "There are far, far better
> things ahead than any we
> leave behind."
>
> C.S. Lewis

"YOU'RE PROBABLY READING MORE into it than what's actually there," Jo said, brushing my hair.

"I don't know. She seemed weird. And she asked questions about my adoption as soon as Evan was gone," I said.

"Well, maybe she does know. But, Rain, you know it's gonna have to be faced at some point. You can't both live in Ivy Hollow and not have it come up somehow. Better sooner than later, I think."

"I guess so," I said, but I wasn't thinking it. Everything in me wanted to run and hide. I wanted everything to stay just as it was. I didn't want to face the unknown of how my mom would react to meeting me. I just didn't want to be rejected again.

Jo called it Peter Pan Syndrome. I always wanted everything to stay as it was. Never change. Never grow. Just freeze.

I say if it isn't broken, don't try fixing it.

But there was, of course, the curious part of me. The part that wondered if Mom would apologize. If we could mend. But was it worth the risk?

"She could end up being your best friend," Jo said, beginning a French braid in my wet hair.

We sat on Jo's bed at nearly midnight with popcorn and chocolate while she played with my hair. It was a sort of tradition we'd had since I was little. Any time Jo could tell I had something on my mind, she'd tell me to go take a shower while she got her room ready for "girl talk." By the time I was done, there were snacks and sweets on her bed waiting for me to munch on while she did my wet hair.

"Don't put walls up before you know what she's like and what she knows," Jo said, combing back some stray pieces.

"You're right."

"Of course I am."

I opened the sketchbook I had laying in my lap to a blank page. "Enough about my friends. What did you think about Mrs. Lawson?" Jo had been able to join us at Evan's house that night after work, and we all enjoyed dinner together. It was perfect. Evan even said that Ava seemed in higher spirits than normal for Maya not being there.

Jo loosened some of the braids to make it fuller. "I liked her a lot. She's got a sweet personality."

"I think so, too," I agreed. "Evan texted me a few minutes ago and said she really enjoyed meeting you. I don't think she's met many people since moving here."

"I invited her to church. She said they've tried a few but haven't settled anywhere yet."

"That was a good idea."

"Did you make any headway on Evan's paper?"

I began sketching an outline with my pencil. "A little. He asked a few more questions. I still haven't read any of it yet."

"He sure looked awfully smitten tonight. Don't you think?" Her voice changed in pitch, rising and falling.

I felt my face turn warm.

Jo wrapped around me to meet my eyes. "Don't you think?" she repeated.

I shrugged, keeping my gaze fixed on my paper. "I thought maybe I noticed something. But I don't know."

Jo blew a puff of air, and I imagine she was rolling her eyes behind me. "You can play blind if you want to, but I'm not blind. I know what I saw."

On the page, lines and curves slowly became the outline of a feminine hand.

"Has he told you he likes you?"

"Sort of. But not in that sort of way. I mean, I think maybe he was hinting at it."

"If you think he was hinting at it, he probably was."

The sketched hand had a wrist and an arm now, that trailed off the page.

I knew what Evan had meant. I'd seen it in his eyes—a look toward me I'd never noticed before. Even thinking about it now made my stomach swarm with butterflies.

But something held me back. Something *always* held me back.

My face scrunched as Jo's comb got caught in a knot in the tail of my braid. "Sorry," she said. "What do you think about him now that you've gotten to know him?"

I set my pencil down and looked up at the ceiling in thought. Jo finished my braid and leaned back in the bed to face me better. "I'm not sure that I want to decide yet," I said finally. "We still haven't known each other long."

"No, but you know each other *well*."

"He knows *me* well," I corrected her. "He's still reclusive, but I think it's more out of pain than fear."

"It may be that way for a while still. But I think you'll be as good for him as he's been for you."

"You think he's been good for me?" I asked.

She nodded, breaking a square of chocolate off the bar she snagged from the bed. "I like seeing you have a friend." She popped the chocolate into her mouth with a piece of popcorn. She liked salty and sweet together in one bite; I preferred them separate. "One your *own* age."

I grabbed a handful of popcorn from the bowl. "I see no problem having friends of a variety of ages. You learn more that way." I thought of all the days I sat at the feet of Mr. Clark, gleaning from his experiences and stories.

"I wouldn't be so sure. I think we can learn from peers, and those younger than us, too. Sometimes, it's learning from their mistakes, but I can sure say I learn from you every day."

"Mostly from my mistakes though, right?" I teased.

She smiled and tugged my braid before laying it over my shoulder. I could feel it leaving a wet spot on my shirt. "No. But only because you learned from my mistakes first so you didn't have to make them yourself."

On the hand I'd drawn, I began to sketch a pattern.

"Rain," Jo said seriously, "you've never been one to rush into anything new. But I think you should give Evan a chance. Take your time if you want, but give him a chance."

She was right. Reluctance was in my nature. I wished I was more like the heroes and heroines I read about in books—the ones who jumped at any opportunity for adventure. But I wasn't. I was just Rain. And bravery only comes naturally in fairytales. Peter Pan Syndrome is what's true in reality.

"And what if I do?" I asked, refusing to look up at her. "And what if it's wonderful and I decide to love him forever? Then, what about us—you and me?"

Jo giggled, but she was searching my face. "What about us?"

I could feel my eyes brimming. "I don't want this to change. I never have."

Jo placed her hand on my knee and rubbed it affectionately. "Rain, I've always prayed you'd find someone to love hard with that big heart of yours. If it's right here, don't fight it. Embrace it."

I met her eyes. "You've done fine without loving someone. We've had each other. That's always been enough."

"That's my story, and I've loved every second of it. But that doesn't mean it's yours."

My heart ached. I didn't know why. I wasn't leaving Jo anytime soon. But the thought of one day being apart from her broke me.

"Don't let fear hold you back from what God has for you, Rain. What if I'd been too afraid to say yes to you? Too afraid to adopt you when I was alone and almost penniless? We wouldn't even have what it is you're afraid of losing."

I spun my pencil between my fingers. Jo *was* brave. She always had been, and I'd always looked up to her for that. She was the sort of character that made a good heroine—always jumping in to save the victim, just like she had done for me, even while she was in need herself.

She moved closer and cupped my face in her hands. "You'll never get rid of me, Rain. I promise. But nothing would make me happier than seeing you spreading your wings and charting your own course. And that's regardless of whether or not Evan plays a part in it all." She kissed my forehead, and I smiled.

After the chocolate had disappeared, the popcorn was gone except the few unpopped kernels at the bottom of the bowl, and it was one o'clock in the morning. I sat on my own bedroom floor for a few minutes, painting the sketch I'd drawn as I replayed Jo's words in my head. I used an array of vibrant colors to fill in the pattern of paint splatters on the hand.

At the top of the page, I wrote out Evan's words:

I guess I learned you wore your heart at the end of your sleeve. Every day, I wait to see what colors and shapes will appear and what they'll tell me about you.

The thought made me smile without meaning to.

Was it the cleverness of what he'd said, or was it him that made me smile?

Was Evan my happy thought?

If he was, would embracing him mean letting go of what I already loved? I had a friend in him; that much I could confidently say now.

But did I love him?

J O R D A N

> "I would ask you to believe that he has a heart he very, very seldom reveals, and that there are deep wounds in it. My dear, I have seen it bleeding."
>
> Charles Dickens, _A Tale of Two Cities_

I FELT LIKE MOM was going off the deep end, and I didn't know what to do about it. Each day she seemed a little more overwhelmed. Each night she stayed in her office a little later. Most of the time, Maya and I were on our own with homework and dinner. There were nights we only crossed paths with her a single time before bed.

We went on pretending her drinking episode never happened. She put the mask back on. But I could see through it.

She called Aunt Cassidy almost every night after we'd gone to bed, and I'd lay on my stomach, listening through my bedroom floor, which was over her office. I listened as Mom cried, saying she didn't know how we'd make it. She was ruining mine and Maya's lives. She kept saying how she was a terrible mother.

Finally, Aunt Cassidy came to the rescue. She decided to come and stay a weekend with us to help Mom get some business things in order, but also to get us to enjoy ourselves.

Aunt Cassidy wasn't married and didn't care to date anyone. She had a nice job and always dressed really well. She wore outfits like skin-tight leather pants with hot pink heels, a hot pink top, and a black blazer, even when she wasn't working. She was funny, and she always made me feel like an adult. She let me do things when I was with her that Mom would never let me do, like drink a little wine and talk about celebrities and wear her clothes and shoes.

Aunt Cassidy was more like an older sister than an aunt to me. She'd explained puberty to me. She asked me about boys I knew. She listened to me. She asked questions. She did all the things my mom never bothered to do for me but should have done.

I needed her now more than ever, and I fully intended to ask her what happened to my mom's first baby. She would know, and I felt way more comfortable talking to her than to Mom.

When Saturday morning finally came, Aunt Cassidy was at the house before lunch. She walked in the door wearing a pink dress with nude flats and an olive green blazer. I loved her blazers.

"Hey, Aunt Cass," I said, stepping forward to greet her. Completely unexpected to me, my eyes began welling with tears. Seeing her lifted the weight off my chest that had been smothering me since the divorce. An adult was here to take over. She would take care of Mom, and everything would be okay again. I felt sure of it.

"Jordan!" She dropped her bags to wrap her arms around me. "Oh my gosh, you're taller than me! You look great!"

She hugged Maya next and then Mom.

Mom seemed to tense up when Aunt Cassidy arrived. I didn't understand why, but her entire disposition changed. She became more quiet, almost more submissive, as soon as Aunt Cass entered the room. I wasn't sure if that was a good or bad thing.

We spent the morning getting ready to go out for a nice brunch and for a "self care Saturday," as Aunt Cass called it.

She did mine and Maya's hair and makeup, and we wore our favorite outfits. Aunt Cass said there was a "no jeans" rule on girl days. We had to feel beautiful.

I never wore dresses. I was always in jeans or sweats with a T-shirt of some sort, but I did have a few on hand just in case. My favorite was one Grandma had bought me the previous spring to wear on Easter at her church. It was one of the few times a year we went to church. The dress was a sunshine yellow, which is my favorite color, with little white flowers. It almost hit my knee, and it was flowy at the sleeves. With it being fall and sort of cool outside, I decided to add an oversized white cardigan with it. But I still wore my sneakers.

Brunch was at one of Aunt Cassidy's favorite restaurants, and it was amazing. Everything was white, pink, and gold inside, and the food itself looked like art. Afterward, we went and got our nails done, shopped, and visited her favorite coffee shop. Aunt Cassidy bought Maya and I almost anything we asked for. We tried on all sorts of clothes that she picked out for us, most of which Mom objected to, but she bought them for us anyway.

I laughed. Hard. I felt like myself. I felt the warm feeling in my chest you get when you're enjoying *your* people. Your family.

It was at the nail salon where Aunt Cass checked on me. We sat side by side getting pedicures while Mom and Maya were across the salon getting manis.

"How are you holding up, Jordan?" she asked. "Like, really?"

I swallowed the lump that formed in my throat and heaved a sigh. "Not great," I admitted. "Mom's losing it."

She nodded, her eyes widening. "I can tell."

"I don't know how to help her. I think there's something big bothering her, on top of the divorce," I said. "I think Dad tried to figure it out, but he never could."

Aunt Cass eyed me up and down as she ran her freshly manicured fingers through her dark curls. She knew the secret. And she knew I was onto it. "Jordan," she said, almost whispering, "your mom struggles with something from her past. Something she's never been able to get over. She—"

Mom's manicure ended then, and she made her way to the chair next to me for a pedi, making eye contact with us as she crossed the room. And she knew. She knew we'd been chatting about something we shouldn't have.

Aunt Cass gave me a smile and a nod, one that said we'd talk later.

I kept my gaze on the woman painting my toenails for the rest of the pedicure, afraid to look at Mom and give away my guilt. Afraid to look at Aunt Cass and make Mom more suspicious.

That night, we went home with Chinese takeout and ate it in our pajamas while we watched TV. Mom and Aunt Cass made cocktails, while Maya and I made hot chocolate. The one thing Mom always said she hated about Aunt Cass was that once she started drinking, it was hard to get her to stop. But after what I'd witnessed just a few days before, Mom wasn't much better off.

By eleven, Aunt Cassidy had drunk a lot. Mom wasn't far behind, but she seemed a lot more level headed. After Aunt Cassidy made a vulgar joke, Mom tried to send Maya and I to bed. Maya's eyelids had already been drooping, and she stood without hesitation.

"Can't I stay up longer?" I objected. "I'm not a kid anymore. Why do I have to go to bed?"

Mom started to respond, but Aunt Cassidy beat her to the punch. "Let her stay up, Reagan. She's sixteen now. If you hover over her all the time, she's going to go wild behind your back like we did with Mom and Dad."

"Jordan isn't wild," Mom said, then turned to Maya. "Head on up to bed. Your sister will be up in just a bit. I won't let her stay up too much longer."

Maya pouted a little and rolled her eyes at me on her way to the stairs, but she didn't resist.

I went to the kitchen and got a soda out of the fridge. I could hear Mom and Aunt Cass singing along to one of the songs in the movie we were watching. I went back in and plopped down on the floor across from the couch where they sat, feeling a sense of pride that I was getting to stay up with later than Maya. I felt like I deserved to.

"Didn't we watch this at your seventeenth birthday party?" Aunt Cass asked, nudging Mom's shoulder clumsily.

She laughed. "Yes. That was an awful birthday. And it was your fault."

"My fault? Mom would have never caught us if your friends hadn't been so loud. I let the guys up, but it was the girls' fault we got busted."

I thought about what Mom would do to me if she found me having a party at our house with guys. She'd kill me.

"You shouldn't have let them upstairs to begin with," Mom said, and she eyed me a little. "It wasn't right."

Aunt Cass rolled her eyes. "Poor Jordan will be smothered to death by the time high school ends. Think about all the stuff we did. We learned from it, didn't we? It never killed us."

Mom didn't say anything but took another swig of her drink.

"Besides, I was always there to get you out of trouble, and I'll do the same for you, Jordan. You just let me know, and I'll take care of it."

I smiled. "Thanks, Aunt Cass."

"Your mom hasn't even told you all the messes I've gotten *her* out of."

"There's no sense in encouraging her to make the same mistakes I had to learn from."

I rolled *my* eyes this time. What a cop out. She'd only never told me because she never told me anything, not because she was worried I'd follow in her footsteps.

Aunt Cassidy waved a clumsy, dismissive hand her way. "She's young. She'll get into trouble whether you warn her or not. She probably already has, and she's just afraid to tell you because you're so overbearing."

"Jordan's not like we were."

"How would you know? She tells me more stuff than she tells you," Aunt Cass said.

I could tell from the look on Mom's face that the words stung, and I blushed. I wished I didn't care, but I did.

Aunt Cassidy turned to face me. "Life is short, girlfriend. Don't live in fear of what your mom will think of you. Take it from me. I've been there and done that."

"Yeah, and look at all it's cost you. Mom and Dad set boundaries for our protection."

"I don't feel like it's cost much. Sure, you live it up, you're gonna fall and skin your knee a few times. But would you rather play it safe and lose the experience?"

Mom was right. I wasn't really wild like she and Aunt Cass had been at my age. I'd never cared to be. But I wondered then what I might be missing out on in always playing it safe.

"You met any boys since moving here?" Aunt Cass asked, turning the conversation a little.

"Not really," I stuttered, but Evan immediately came to mind.

"Not really isn't no."

Mom's eyebrow lifted, and I felt my face turning red.

"Does he like you, too?"

I shook my head. "He's a senior. And I'm pretty sure he's already got a girlfriend."

A loud laugh erupted from her lips. "I've been with plenty of guys who were older and had girlfriends."

"Cassidy," Mom finally said sternly. I'd been waiting for her to shut it down. She didn't think I could handle these kinds of conversations. And she wondered why I never went to her to talk about them.

"Your mom did, too. Her first real relationship was with a college guy who had a girlfriend."

"Cassidy," Mom hissed through her teeth.

I perked up as I thought about the baby bracelet lying in a box in the attic. Was he the baby's dad?

Aunt Cass eyed me, and I knew she was talking about it. The conversation we'd started at the nail salon. "That's the biggest mess I ever had to get your mom out of, but she survived it."

"What do you mean?" I asked, and my eyes drifted to Mom questioningly. This was it. This was the story.

Mom put off a look of anger, but her eyes told me it was fear.

"How come you never told her?" Aunt Cassidy asked, then turned her gaze to me. "Well, let's just say that your mom got to practice her right to choose. And if you ever need to do the same, you tell me, and I'll take care of it. I've gone through it three times, and I know how to take care of you."

"Cassidy," Mom said again, this time in a plea.

Right to choose? I was still so confused. Abortion? Was she talking about abortion? But there *was* a baby. I saw the bracelet.

"She needs to know, Reagan. It's her right as a woman. And half the reason it's been so hard to keep our rights is because people like you bring so much shame into it. What if you'd had those twins? You'd have never gone to college, never met Mark, never had Jordan and Maya."

"Twins?" I blurted. My mind was reeling.

Mom looked at me, and her face seemed sunken in, her eyes hollow. "It's a right I hope she never has to practice."

Aunt Cass rolled her eyes. "Your mom's dramatic. Like I said, if you can't go to her, come to me. I'll go with you, I'll pay for it, I'll feed you well afterward, and we'll raise a toast to your rights as a woman," she said, and took the final swig of her drink.

Twins? Abortion? This didn't make any sense, and my stomach tied in knots at the thought of having twin siblings that now didn't exist. I had so many questions but didn't have the courage to ask. After all this time of wondering, I wasn't sure I wanted the truth anymore.

I'd summoned the final skeleton from the closet.

Aunt Cassidy was right though, wasn't she? Mom's life would have been so different if she'd had kids so young. But did that make it right?

An uncomfortable silence fell over us with only the TV to fill the void. I glanced over at Mom again, who looked back at me, almost apologetically.

"In your Mom's defense," Aunt Cassidy began again, a little bit gravely, "your Mom did experience something I didn't have to, and that was going through the whole pregnancy and labor, even after the abortion. That would turn me, too, I guess. But that's rare. The fetus doesn't usually survive."

"The baby survived?" I asked, perking up again, but my voice cracked as I spoke.

"One of them did," Mom said, staring absently at the glass in her hand. "They didn't know it was twins when they did the procedure. One of them lived, and they were afraid to try again for risk of infection. I went a few more months before they induced me. They didn't think the baby would make it anyway. But she did, and I placed her for adoption."

"Don't tell your grandparents though," Aunt Cass piped in. "We never told Mom. She's too religious. She'd have a heart attack. Your mom lived with me during the pregnancy until it was all over."

So that was it. My Mom had given birth to the child she'd tried to get rid of. My mind immediately jumped to the thought of Rain's missing hand. I didn't know how abortions were done, but wasn't it possible that it had caused some sort of defect to the second baby? The more I considered it, the more I believed it was her.

And then the thought hit me. If Rain found out that her own birth mother had tried to kill her, she'd be devastated. And I knew then that Aunt Cassidy had to be wrong. She had to be.

I still didn't know if Rain was the surviving twin, but what did it matter? Those twins were people. One of them died and the other was supposed to. Abortion couldn't be right.

"Don't look so scared," Aunt Cassidy said. "Honestly, that was an exception. Abortion is normally pretty easy. Like a bad period." The tone of her voice wasn't the least bit convincing, and she was looking off distantly, like she was remembering something awful. It was a similar look to the one Mom wore the day I found her drinking in hysterics.

"It's still worth avoiding if at all possible. Don't waste your time on the wrong guys, Jordan," Mom said.

I brought my knees to my chest and wrapped my arms around them. "Do you know where the baby is now?"

"DSS took care of it," Aunt Cass said dryly. "Honestly, I feel bad for the little wretch. A life in the system is worse than death. She'd have been better off dead."

I winced at the harshness of her words. I couldn't help but feel bad for a baby that had been so unwanted. So disregarded.

"Is that for us to decide though?" I asked before thinking, and the following look from Aunt Cassidy made my blood curdle.

"Of course it is. It was your mom's body," she sneered. "She has every right to decide if she wants to carry a baby and then birth and raise it."

I didn't answer. There was a fire in her eyes that I didn't have the courage to play with, and it was being fueled by all the alcohol she'd downed.

From where I sat on the floor, I could see the faint red stain that remained in the carpet from the day Mom hit me and I shattered the wine bottle. I remembered her clutching her abdomen as she cried, and I'll bet she was thinking about the baby that died. The baby she killed.

Finally, Aunt Cass spoke again; this time cool and collected, but in an emotionless tone that sent chills up my spine. "Just think of all the reasons we need abortion, Jordan. What if you got pregnant now with your whole life ahead of you? What if the baby had some sort of birth defect? There are tons of reasons we need abortion."

My mind went to Thomas. His life had been at risk simply because he was different and had no say over it.

I started feeling sick to my stomach, and the feeling was rising up my throat.

"I think you've stayed up late enough," Mom butted in.

I resented her for it. She treated me like a kid after she'd just told me all of the things she was doing at my age. She should be thankful I was so mild and obedient. The least she could do was treat me with respect in front of Aunt Cassidy and let me stay up past midnight. But at the same time, I didn't want to stay up any longer. I didn't like this side of Aunt Cass. I'd always admired and respected her, but she was different tonight. So I compromised. I cut my eyes at Mom and made my way upstairs.

That night, I hardly slept as I thought about a woman's right to choose.

It seemed to me that a baby wasn't a woman's body, and even if it was inconvenient, you couldn't kill a person because of inconvenience.

It also seemed to me that, even if it was my Mom's right, practicing it had scarred her deeply.

And I couldn't get over the haunting thought that somewhere in the world there was a wandering girl who wasn't supposed to be alive, probably wondering why she hadn't been good enough to belong.

What I didn't know was if she was right here in my new hometown.

E V A N

> "It's all very well to read about
> sorrows and imagine yourself
> living through them heroically,
> but it's not so nice when you really
> come to have them, is it?"
>
> L.M. Montgomery, *Anne of Green Gables*

I TOOK ANOTHER SIP of my milkshake and read the last few paragraphs for the hundredth time.

I was stuck.

I'd come so far with this story, and here I was, quickly approaching the end without knowing how to end it. How do you close a story that's still very much being fleshed out? I couldn't kick the feeling that something major was missing.

I'd started my writing at the kitchen table, and when that didn't work, I moved to the barn. And now I was at the diner, hoping a brain freeze from my milkshake might scare away the writer's block. I felt straight out of a '50s movie with my typewriter and my milkshake at the small-town diner. All I needed was a dame in a polka dot dress and red lipstick to sit across from me with another straw.

I ran my fingers through my hair. I only had one week left to finish this project, and I hadn't even finished the first draft. There was still so much editing to do.

The bell above the diner door rang, announcing another customer, and I lifted my eyes to follow the sound. Of all people, Jordan walked in, and her eyes immediately locked on mine before she offered a reluctant, halfhearted smile. I smiled back and watched as she made her way to the counter to order.

My dad was always people-watching. He used to say that being able to read what people don't say was way more valuable than listening to what they do and that what they say often hides and protects what they aren't saying. It always confused me, and I had never really needed to take his advice, but I knew that Jordan had become a big part in my story. Maybe even a main character.

Rain told me that one story is never just one story. There are more subplots to most events than we could ever imagine. The more I wrote, the more I understood that.

Rain was a girl whose own mother tried to kill her and then abandon her, but she was my first friend in the small town where I was looking for new beginnings after my dad's death. And she trusted me with a secret about the new girl in town whose family was falling apart and would unravel once the mother realized her own daughter was right under her nose.

We all had our own stories, but in some way or another, they were all connected.

I'd learned that Jordan was quiet in a nervous sort of way. She'd built a wall around herself, and I'd never seen her let anyone in except Thomas. New kid to new kid, I felt bad for her, but I knew I couldn't be the one to tear her walls down. I held too many of Rain's secrets, and I wasn't going to be the one to send this house of cards crashing to pieces. Either Rain would handle it in her own time or the inevitable would happen naturally.

Jordan ordered her chocolate milkshake and waited off to the side while it was being prepared. She glanced back at me again but quickly snapped her head forward and crossed her arms around herself nervously when she saw me staring. My face grew warm at being caught, and I decided that this wasn't the best environment for people-watching.

I let my focus return to the page in front of me, but I didn't get to look at it long because Jordan walked over to me with her milkshake in hand.

"Do you mind if I sit here?"

I blinked at her a few times, my mouth hanging slightly open. Hadn't I just been observing how shy she was?

"If you're busy..."

"No." I motioned to the booth in front of me. "I should be busy, but I can't seem to get anything done today. So yeah, sit."

She lowered into the booth and took a nervous sip of her shake. I could tell she really didn't want to be here, so why was she being so forward?

"What are you working on with that old typewriter?"

I slid it to the side of the table. "A paper for school. I, uh, got a little behind at the beginning of the year, and now I'm trying to make some extra credit by writing a ten-thousand word story."

"That's harsh. What are you writing about?"

My thumb found a nick in the vinyl table and began picking at it. "My life, I guess, since coming to Ivy Hollow. And the people I've met. Stuff like that."

Jordan chuckled. "I don't know how anyone could write that many words about Ivy Hollow."

"At first, I thought that, too, but Rain's been helping me. She's a big reader and is a much better storyteller than me." I'd found the story. Now if I could just find a way to tie up all the loose ends.

"Is that why you two are always hanging out together?" The determined look on Jordan's face had red flags waving wildly in my head.

"Yeah, that's sort of how we became friends, I guess. She offered to help.".

"I assumed you guys were dating."

"Nope. Just friends." In the weeks since starting this paper, I'd imagined Rain thought the same way about me that I did her, but she was so hard to read. Everything about her was so whimsical and poetic, it was hard to know what was intended especially for me and what was just her being herself. But the more I wrote about her, the harder I fell for her. It made me laugh because I'd teased Rain so many times for falling for fictional guys, and here I was, falling for her as she came to life on the page in front of me.

But this was different. She was real, and writing her made me love the real thing even more, because goodness knows my depiction of her fell short.

Jordan ran her finger over the ridges of her milkshake glass. "Rain seems like a nice girl."

The red flags waved harder. Something told me she was only here to talk about her connection to Rain.

"Yeah, she is."

Jordan's grip on her milkshake glass tightened, but her voice remained steady. "She was adopted, right?"

My palms started sweating, but I nodded.

"That's gotta be hard."

"In some ways, sure. But Rain has a way of making the best of things. She loves her life and the family she has."

Jordan nodded slowly, but her eyes were asking more questions.

Now it was my turn to take a nervous sip of my milkshake.

"I think she likes you. At least, she acts like she does. Everyone thinks so."

My face felt really hot.

Jordan brushed her blonde ponytail behind her shoulder and leaned back in the booth. She was avoiding eye contact but kept the questions coming. I had to think of a way to change the subject.

"Come on. You guys are obviously close," she pushed.

I shrugged again, trying to ignore my racing heart. "Kinda. We're great friends, but that's really all there is to it. Sorry to disappoint."

She seemed to pick up on the fact that I was trying to shut down the questions, so she took a different approach. "I found out recently that my mom had a daughter before I was born. I guess it just makes Rain's adoption experience more interesting to me."

"Wow, that must have been a pretty big shock," I said, trying to sound surprised.

Goosebumps rose on her arms from the ice cream, and she rubbed them to get warm. "Yeah, it was. I'm still trying to put all of the pieces together."

"What have you gathered so far?" I asked, hoping to turn the tables a little.

Now she was the reluctant one. "Not much. I just found the baby's hospital bracelet packed away with the date and my mother's name."

"I'd say it's hard to find answers with so little information."

Jordan paused and eyed me like she wanted me to guess her suspicion.

I sighed and leaned back in the booth. She was waiting for me to spill the tea, and I wasn't sure how to get out of it. Rain was never going to forgive me.

"What are you getting at, Jordan?" I asked through a defeated sigh.

Jordan pulled out her cellphone and reached her arm across the table to show me a photo of a woman who looked uncannily like Rain.

There was no room for doubt in my mind that she was Rain's mother.

I glanced up from the photo. "You think Rain Brooks is your sister just because she was adopted?"

Jordan nodded.

"Have you asked Rain?"

"I'm asking you."

I gave a short, dry laugh. "Why me?"

"Because you're close to her. I know you know her story. You have to."

I pushed my straw around in the bottom of my cup, gathering the last bit of my milkshake. "I don't have to. Rain is a super private person, and like I told you, we're just project partners."

"It was a little weird the first day I met her at your house, don't you think? She saw me and spilled your drinks."

I shrugged. "Yeah, it was a little weird, I guess. So ask her."

"I can't."

"Why not?"

Jordan went silent and closed her arms around herself. "Because there's something else, and I don't know what it'd do to her if she found out. So I have to ask you. To protect her."

I knew she had to be referring to the abortion and Rain's twin.

I started fumbling with the stack of papers next to my typewriter. Pages of Rain's story. A story she'd trusted me with. I felt like I was betraying her more and more with every second this conversation continued, but I didn't know what else to do. Jordan was uncovering the plot almost as quickly as I was.

"So let me get this straight," I said, eyeing her sternly. "You want answers for your own personal gain, but aren't willing to give Rain answers about her own story?"

A look of guilt swept over her, and she pushed a piece of hair behind her ear. "Well, putting it that way sounds wrong. But really, if you knew what it was, you'd want her to be protected from it, too. Trust me."

I shook my head and slid the stack of papers into my backpack that sat next to me in the booth. "Protect her from it all you want, but you aren't going to pull me into this and make me the bad guy. If you want answers, you'll have to face her yourself."

Jordan sighed in defeat. "Please, Evan. I have to know the truth. I think this whole thing is what pulled my family apart."

I never had before, but at that moment, I felt truly sorry for her. Before, I guess I felt like she was entitled to the family issues. After all, at least her mom wanted her. But I knew then how wrong I'd been.

Rain's twin was a victim of his or her mother's actions. Rain was a victim of her mom's actions. And so was Jordan. What had one terrible choice done to Maya, too? And their mom's husband? And her ex-boyfriend? And what about her parents who lost a grandchild? Where did the domino effect end?

I ran my fingers through my hair and gave a heavy sigh. "Jordan, I think you do need answers. Truly. But I think Rain needs closure, too. You both need this."

A smirk slowly grew on Jordan's lips, and my heart skipped a beat at the realization of what I'd done. "So you're telling me it is her. That her story lines up with mine."

My face went warm as I tried to backpedal my way out of what I'd confessed. "No, I'm not. I'm saying that hypothetically, *if* your stories add up... There's no way to know for sure unless you two compare them."

She didn't believe me, and I knew I'd dug my grave.

Jordan inched forward in the booth. "Does she know who I am? That we're sisters?"

"I never said she's your sister."

"You didn't have to." Jordan took the last sip of her milkshake and stood to her feet. "I know you're trying to protect her. You're a good friend. But trust me, that's what I want, too. I want her to be happy, and I want my mom to be happy."

I looked up at her uneasily. "And how do you propose to accomplish that?"

"I've got to get us out of Ivy Hollow before their worlds collide."

ell

I loaded Rain's bike into my truck bed outside of the antique store while she worked on closing up. It had rained most of the day, leaving behind a wet blanket in the air that chilled me to the bone. Through the store window, I saw Rain flip the sign to CLOSED, and she walked out with a smile, locking the door behind her.

"Ready?" I asked, opening the passenger door for her to slide in.

She tightened her oversized, cream sweater around her shoulders and looked up at me with a smile before she hopped into the truck. "Ready."

My pulse raced as I made my way to the driver's side. I knew I was going to have to tell her about my encounter with Jordan, but I didn't know how.

"I can't wait to hear about what you've written over the weekend," Rain said as I slid in and closed my own door.

"I didn't write very much." I put the truck in gear and headed in the direction of my house. "I have a new idea, but it would take forever to add it in, and I'm not even sure how to start tying it up and finish it off. I was hoping you would give me some ideas."

"What new idea do you have in mind?"

I held my breath. "Well, I wrote one scene last night. But it feels more like a beginning or the climax than the end. Something's missing."

"Maybe it is."

"I don't have time for it. I've got to get this paper wrapped up."

Rain tilted her head at me with a knowing look. "But you wouldn't even be asking me about it if you didn't feel like it might be worth the effort."

She was right. Ever since yesterday, I felt like I'd found the missing link that was going to tie everything else together. But it still didn't solve my problem of not knowing how to end it.

I cleared my throat. It felt dry.

"Come on," she said, smirking in a way that made her eyes dance with curiosity. "What is it? You're red as a tomato."

I chewed my lip and readjusted my grip on the steering wheel. *Here goes nothing.*

"I think I need to add in Jordan's side of the story."

Rain's brow furrowed. "What do you mean?"

"Last night, I wrote a scene where Jordan cornered me at the diner demanding answers about you," I rubbed the back of my neck nervously. "It definitely added friction to the plot."

Rain's eyes narrowed when she realized it was a part of the story she didn't even know about. A part of the story that tied her sister's story even tighter to her own. "She cornered you?" Her face flushed. "Evan, tell me you didn't say..."

"I didn't say—not exactly. But you were right. She knows, Rain. She suspected it, and she wanted me to confirm it."

Rain covered her face with her palm.

"I tried to get her off your trail, I swear. But she was determined. I don't blame her."

Rain's head whipped up to face me. "What?"

"Wouldn't you want to know? This is a part of her story. You know yours, and you've had your whole life to come to terms with it. She just found out there's a secret destroying her family, and she deserves to have answers."

A look of betrayal slowly appeared. "*Destroying* them? Is that the word she used?" Rain shook her head in anger, but I'm certain I saw a tear run down her cheek. "I'm so sorry that my existence was such a problem for them."

I winced, realizing how harsh my word choice had sounded. "I don't think she meant it like that. I think the abortion is what she meant. You said yourself that you felt bad for your mom, having to meet the child she tried to get rid of. I'm sure she's in a lot of pain."

Pent up anger was finally getting released. I hated to be the one to witness it. I hated to have to see her walk through it. But with the death of Dad so fresh on my mind, I knew it had to come, and I would be here for her while she worked through it.

"Then, why hasn't she found me? If that's how she feels and Jordan knows, why doesn't she tell our mom who I am and let her get the reconciliation she needs?" I knew she wasn't really asking me; she was just asking. Processing. Wondering why things weren't happening the way she thought they should.

I turned my head at an angle to check for oncoming cars before I made a left turn. "Jordan thinks that your mom doesn't need to know. She wants to get her family out of Ivy Hollow before your paths cross." I visibly winced. The answer was blunt, and the minute I said the words, I regretted them.

Rain stared at me, eyes swelling with tears, but the rest of her face looked numb. I'd never seen her so broken before.

I hadn't meant for it to come across so heartless. I just didn't think through how badly the news would affect her. But of course it would, and my heart squeezed in my chest knowing the pain I'd just inflicted.

My mind flashed to my mom, crumpled on the hospital floor with my dad's limp hand in hers. I stood, watching from a distance, feeling lost and out of place, not knowing what to do or what to say to make it better. I felt that way again now.

"Rain," I stuttered. "I should have told you slower. I—"

"Will you take me home?" she interrupted, her voice weak like she was holding back a sob.

"Rain..."

"Please take me home." She was staring forward now, eyes on the road.

Rain had been afraid of facing the inevitable, but deep down, I knew she wanted the happy ending that came with bravely approaching the battle. The issue is that happy endings are only promised in fairytales. Sometimes you fight for the best outcome and something worse comes of it. She didn't believe it was worth the risk. I swallowed hard, searching for something—anything—to say that might help.

"I know you wanted reconciliation, but you knew it might not happen."

Her head fell to the window. "And now I know it won't."

I turned my gaze away from the road long enough to see a tear fall and hit her hand. Her hand was painted that day with a bookshelf full of the spines of different colored books, similar to the very first day I saw her. Her own story was taking a dramatic turn for the worst, and I had to be the one to write it. Maybe after this, she wouldn't even want me to anymore.

"Rain," I said, breaking the tense silence. "Let me take you to get ice cream or something. Jo won't be home until late tonight." I didn't want to leave her to work through this realization alone.

She shook her head.

I slowed the truck a little, trying to buy time in hopes that she'd change her mind. "Jordan thinks she's doing you a favor. She doesn't think you know about the abortion, and she's afraid for you to find out."

Rain gave a dry snicker. "I can't imagine why."

"I tried to tell her that you needed the closure as much as she did."

Rain faced me again. The reaction of betrayal had returned, but this time, it made her look weak and lonely. "So you did tell her. What all did you say about me exactly?"

"No, I said that if her suspicions were true, you'd need it," I said with a sigh, knowing that I'd dug my grave once again. Why was I so bad at this?

"It sounds to me like you're on *her* side."

"I'm *not* on her side," I said sternly. I wanted to grab her by the shoulders and get it into her head. There was no one on this earth I felt more dedicated to than her. I would stand with her 'til the end of this, whatever happened, and then I would fight until every color on her hand pointed to a mind that showed acceptance and even joy because of—or in spite of—the outcome. But I was doing a terrible job of showing her that.

Rain wiped her eyes, smearing mascara all over her face, and I reached into the glove compartment to grab her an old napkin. She took it from me with a sheepish glance and pulled her mirror down to examine the damage and dab her eyes. By her jerky movements I could tell she was still fuming inside. "I wanted closure. I'd be lying if I told you I didn't want an apology. I don't need it. I have a family and friends that I love more than anyone. But my whole life I knew I wasn't wanted by my mom. Of course I wanted her to feel sorry and to want me one day. But I was also afraid that if I had the opportunity of meeting her, she'd just abandon me all over again, and I wasn't sure I could handle it. And here I am."

"Technically, she still doesn't know about you. Maybe Jordan's wrong. Maybe she does need to meet you."

Rain blew her nose into the napkin. "She said it was tearing them apart."

"And maybe it will until she has closure with you. Talk to Jordan so the two of you can figure out what's best. Tell her you know the truth and you want closure as much as she does. Find out for sure where your mom's at in the whole thing."

"And what if she tells me that my mom still wishes I'd never survived that abortion? That she doesn't want to find me?"

I hesitated before I answered. I didn't want to give Rain false hope. "Something tells me she didn't move back so close to the place you were born by accident. She didn't come here, to Ivy Hollow of all places, looking for a new beginning for no reason. I don't know for sure, Rain, but I think that just like you and Jordan want answers—so does she." I pulled into Rain's driveway and put the truck in park. "Whatever you decide to do, I *am* on your side. You know that. But I think it's worth remembering that Jordan has a side to this story, too, and it's worth looking into."

Rain didn't speak, and I wasn't even certain that she'd registered the fact that we were in her driveway.

"Please don't make me leave you here. We won't work on the paper. We'll just hang out and forget it all for a bit."

We sat, listening to the continual drip on the truck roof. It had started pouring again.

"It's fitting," Rain said quietly. "It stormed the week I was born. My existence was the storm that destroyed my mom's world. And now I'm doing it all over again."

"Don't think like that. You know better," I reprimanded. "Don't sink into a pit, weighed down by the pity you feel for yourself. What your mom did was wrong. It *should* be criminal. But don't forget that you were given the chance to live, and there are a lot of babies that don't get that. Including your twin."

Rain looked at me with hurt, but I could tell she knew I was right.

I sighed and softened my voice. "The day we sat in my barn loft and you told me your story, you said that you knew you couldn't get what you wanted. You knew you'd never have your twin back or know why things had happened the way that they did. But you also told me you'd created a new goal to do your best to create a life worth living out of the shattered pieces left behind. You told me you had to trust the Master Storyteller as He penned your story with purpose. You have every right to be upset for a bit, don't get me wrong. But you can't stay there. Don't forget your goal."

She gave a reluctant nod and slipped her fingers over the door handle to get out.

"And, Rain," I said, feeling my face grow warm. She turned to face me, the trails of tears still on her face. "Don't forget what your name can also mean." I thought back to what I'd told her the day she came to help me with the greenhouse. "Rain doesn't always mean ruined plans and wrecking storms. Rain brings life. And from the day I met you, you've been exactly what I needed to bring life back. You, with all your color and optimistic outlook on the world around you. Don't lose that. I need that."

A faint smile appeared, but her bottom lip quivered.

I let out a huff, as if releasing the tension between us. "Now can I please take you out for ice cream?"

She shook her head. "Not today, Ev. But thanks."

I massaged my forehead with my finger and thumb. I didn't like the thought of her being here alone right now, but even with friends and family about her, Rain was a lonely soul. She was like Mom in that respect. I was always looking to busy myself when the grief struck, but Rain had to be alone and face it. I guessed she'd probably lock herself in her room, splashing colors of black and gray on a canvas until she felt better.

"Alright. Have it your way," I said. "But if you change your mind, I'll come back and get you. Even if it's five hours from now or the middle of the night."

"Thanks," she said, attempting in vain to smile as she opened the truck door. "I'll see ya."

yellow

warmth; joy; hope

JORDAN

> "I wish you to know you
> have been the last dream
> of my soul."
>
> Charles Dickens, _A Tale of Two Cities_

I WRUNG MY HANDS nervously as I waited. I could almost hear my heart pounding in my chest.

Evan had ratted me out. Of course he did. He loved her.

When Rain's text came through the night before, I wanted to die. I hated confrontation, and I did _not_ want to be the one to tell her the truth about her mom. About _our_ mom.

Hey, Jordan. It's Rain Brooks from school. I've been talking to Evan a bit, and I think it would be a good idea for us to meet up. Any chance we could talk tomorrow after school? I'll be alone at the antique store in town where I work tomorrow if you want to come by.

What could I say? She was right of course. We did need to talk. She had answers I wanted, and I had answers she wanted. But the thought of facing her made my stomach tie in knots.

hey rain. yeah, ur probably right. I'll come by before I pick up Maya from Evan's house. c ya then.

But there I was, sitting in my car outside the antique store where Rain worked, trying to gather the courage to go in. If I pushed through and got it over with, I would have the answers I'd been wanting. But did I really want them? I was afraid of the truth. Once I had it, what would I do with it? All my life, Mom had hid this secret from me. Was it right to do the same and hide her daughter from her?

Finally, I found myself walking in the door.

Rain sat on the floor organizing some vinyls. She smiled at me reassuringly, calming my nerves a little. "Hey," she said. "Thanks for agreeing to come by."

I sat down across from her with my legs folded in front of me. "Sure."

THE COLORS OF RAIN

Her hand was painted, of course. A blue sky with clouds and a vibrant orange and yellow sun covered half of the back of her hand, while the moon and a sky full of stars and constellations covered the other half. It was stunning.

"Thomas told me you paint your hand with your mouth," I said, pointing to her art.

Rain nodded.

"You're amazing. I couldn't do that with my hand, let alone my mouth."

"You could if you'd done it as much as I have. It's been a part of my daily makeup routine since I was thirteen."

I highly doubted it but didn't say so.

Rain paused to fumble nervously with the vinyls again before jumping right into the topic of interest. "Evan told me you found my baby bracelet in your attic. Was that the first time you knew anything about me?" She glanced up to read my expression and tried to soften the mood with another warm smile.

I swallowed hard.

So she was certain. She was the baby.

I pushed my hair behind my ear and hoped Rain didn't see how much my hand shook. "I... I didn't know it was you at first. I wondered, since you look so much like my mom, but I thought it was too big of a coincidence to really be you." My words came out stuttered.

"It is a little odd," she agreed. "I wondered why your mom moved back so close to the place I was born, but I wasn't born here exactly. It's interesting that we both ended up in Ivy Hollow."

"When I first met you that day at Evan's, I really began thinking it had to be you."

Rain laughed, her eyes closing until they were thin slits. "Why? Because I spilled tea everywhere?"

I laughed, too, and it helped ease the nerves I still felt swarming in my stomach. "It definitely made you look a little more suspicious."

She set the vinyls down and leaned her weight on her hand behind her. She seemed so calm, and I still felt so nervous. "So, your mom never mentioned me at all?"

I shook my head, feeling a pang of guilt. Mom hadn't mentioned it until I'd already found out.

"You must have been pretty shocked."

"Yeah, I was."

Rain paused, searching my face before asking, "Do you know about the abortion?"

My eyes widened. "You know?"

An understanding smile crossed her face, but I could see the broken look in her eyes. "Yeah, I know. I've always known, so I'm recovered from the shock. Don't worry."

How could she stand it? To sit across from me with a kind and welcoming smile on her face? I had all that should have been hers. I had been kept, and she was completely thrown out of our mom's life.

In some ways, I could relate. Maya was Mom's golden child, and I was the ugly duckling. It had always been that way. But Rain was experiencing an entirely different level.

I gathered my blonde ponytail into my fingers and tossed it over my shoulder. "And... your hand? Is that because of the abortion?" I tried not to look down at it—the stub. It would be rude.

Rain nodded.

I started feeling a little queasy, and I tried to carry on the conversation to keep from dwelling on it. "My aunt was the one to tell me. Mom was there when she did, but she didn't say much. I believe Mom regrets it, but Aunt Cass has had three abortions."

Rain winced slightly.

I hadn't thought much of Aunt Cassidy's abortions; I'd been so caught up in Mom's. But I'd lost three cousins to abortion. More, if there'd been twins like Mom. What would our family have been like if I'd had cousins to grow up with? We would have been living so close to them after moving to Ivy Hollow, and I thought now about how fun that might have been.

"Jordan," Rain said seriously, though her eyes wouldn't meet mine, "I've forgiven your mom for the choice she made back then, and I don't hold anything against you or your family." She paused to bring her knees to her chest. "But I'm just as afraid of her finding out as you are—trust me. She left me once, and I'm terrified of going through it again. I'm hoping that I'm worrying about nothing. I'm hoping we can move past this. You and I have both found answers. We both know the truth. But your mom is left wondering. She doesn't know what happened beyond her last day at that hospital in Richmond eighteen years ago. Maybe knowing that it all turned out okay in the end will help her."

I bit my lip. I wasn't sure what to think. They say it's the truth that sets us free. Maybe Mom would find some peace knowing Rain had forgiven her and was happy. But then, I thought about the night she slapped me and felt that gripping fear rising up all over again. Mom was falling to pieces, and this could be the straw that broke the camel's back. I wasn't sure I could handle that.

"You don't have to give me an answer today," Rain went on. "You live with her. You know what's best for her more than I do. But either way..." She paused, and her eyes drifted to the painting on her hand shyly. "Either way, I hope you and I can be friends. Even if I don't meet my mom, I'm glad I got to meet you, and I would really love to know you better." And then her gaze met mine again, full of hope.

I don't think Rain and I could have been more different, even being related. Her hair was dark; mine was light. Her eyes were brown; mine were blue. She wore skirts and dresses almost everyday; I lived in sweatpants. She was an artist; I was an athlete. But there was a bond there—something in me begging to be her friend. Maybe it was the bond between sisters, even if she was only a half-sister.

"I'd like that, too," I said, and she responded with a genuine smile.

"Good," she said, standing to her feet. I did the same. "Then maybe—if you want to—you could come with me to Evan's house tonight. He already asked me to invite you and Maya to stay for dinner since you're going there anyway. He's grilling burgers."

I blushed at the thought of Evan wanting me to come for dinner. It was silly, and it didn't mean anything, but still.

"I'll call my mom," I said.

A few minutes later, Rain was in the passenger seat of my car as we headed to Evan's house. It was the nicest day we'd had all week, and we rode with the windows down, watching the Virginian hills roll by in shades of gold and brown.

We passed the time asking each other questions. Rain wanted to know all about Maya and Mom. We talked about Thomas, too, and I filled her in on the whole situation with Drake. We both nearly died laughing when we talked about the broccoli soup incident. Our laughs sounded similar, and we both noticed, which made us laugh harder.

Toward the end of the ride, I started asking her questions.

"Evan never gave me a very clear answer," I said, half lying. "What's the status on you two? Are you a thing?" Evan had made it pretty clear they were just friends, but I also felt like it was really clear there was something else there, too.

Rain smiled and eyed me suspiciously. "No, we aren't a thing. Unless project-partner-turned-friends is considered a thing."

"But you like him."

She shrugged awkwardly. "He's a really nice guy."

"That isn't what I asked," I said with a laugh.

"I don't think we see each other that way."

A spark of hope lit inside my chest.

"Why do you ask?"

At her question, my grip tightened on the wheel a little.

Noticing, Rain smirked. "I see. Well, he is a great guy, and you're very pretty and sweet. Maybe tonight will give you the chance to get to know each other better."

I turned to face her briefly. "You really don't mind? You're serious about just being his friend?"

Rain hesitated. It was hardly noticeable, but it was there. "Evan and I aren't dating, and I'm not going to hog him to myself. If he wants to date you, he should."

"And if it's you he wants, I'm fine with that, too," I said. "I think you guys would make a cute couple."

An awkward silence followed before Rain chuckled again. "We've been sisters for all of thirty minutes, and we're already fighting over boys."

I grinned. "Well, I'm certain he likes you already, so I don't think there will be much of a fight. I've seen the way he looks at you. And the way he talked about you at the diner the other day."

"He hardly knows you yet. Give it time."

"He'll probably think I'm too young. I like that he's older. He acts grown up and gentlemanly. Not stupid like the boys my age."

"You never know. You're beautiful, and I may not know you very well yet, but I'd venture to say there's a lot about your personality that Evan could fall for. Just get to know each other. The thing about being too young is that time will always fix it."

I turned my blinker on and made a sharp left. The sun was nearly setting now, and the sky held beautiful shades of pink and purple. It was incredible and made me think of the skies on Rain's hand.

"How do you decide what you'll paint on your hand each day?" I asked.

"Most of the time it's based on my mood or what things I have in store for the day." She turned away from the window and smiled at me. "Today, I painted thinking of you."

"Really?" I asked, glancing again at the two separate skies.

"We're pretty different, and our lives don't look alike at all. But we're cut from the same cloth. Just like the sky we're looking at now is the same sky we'll see tonight. Each is completely unique, but it's the same sky."

I liked the thought of being cut from the same cloth. Being the same, yet unique. I wondered if I'd been wrong about Ivy Hollow after all. Maybe this was the new beginning I'd needed all my life.

When the car was parked in the driveway, we made our way to the back of the house where Evan was already firing up the grill. There was a bonfire going, and Maya sat with Ava near it, wrapped in blankets.

"I'm glad you could make it," was the first thing Evan said, and he said it to me.

I felt butterflies swarm around in my stomach, and I wrapped my arms around myself, half afraid one might escape and give me away. "Me too," I said. I was a girl of few words. I always have been. I'd never been able to express the words in my mind. I felt deeply, but I knew I came across as shallow. And somehow, Evan made it a hundred times worse.

"How was work?" he asked, averting his attention to Rain.

"Slow," she said. "I spent a lot of the day reading. Is your mom in the kitchen?"

"I think so. She was working on macaroni and cheese last I went in."

"I'll go see if I can help her."

"I'll come, too," I said, and started to follow Rain.

"I'm sure we can handle it," she replied with a mischievous wink. "Enjoy yourself."

As I watched her disappear into the house, I wondered how in the world she could bear it. I felt certain she was head over heels for Evan, so why did she encourage me?

"So I guess you and Rain had your little talk today," Evan said, bringing me out of my thoughts.

I glanced over at Ava and Maya near the bonfire. They were well out of earshot. "Yeah, we did."

"And?" He cocked his head at me.

I slid my hands into the back pockets of my jeans. "It went well. You were right. I needed to talk to her about it."

"What are you gonna do about your mom?"

I moved a little closer and sat down in a pale yellow patio chair near the grill. "I don't know yet. For Rain's sake, I want to tell Mom, but I've never seen her the way she's been lately. She's really struggling. And when I found out about the abortion, she really didn't even want to talk about it. She wouldn't go into details about Rain or the twin. She looked so... emptyinside." Evan looked at me with concern, and I know I blushed again. I tried to think of something else to say to hide my embarrassment. "She's been drinking a lot since the divorce, and she's always keeping to herself. Maya and I barely spend time with her. She's in such a dark state of mind."

"Were you close before all of this?"

"Not really. She never made much of an effort to be involved in my life, but it was never this bad. And there was always Dad to fill some of the void. At least when he wasn't working."

"That's sad," Evan said, opening the top of the grill and looking inside. "I'm sorry, Jordan."

My throat felt tight. I didn't know what else to do but shrug it off. "I'm used to it."

He smiled at me knowingly. "That's not something you get used to. Maybe you've learned how to deal with it, but you aren't used to it."

"Maybe you're right," I admitted.

Evan closed the grill again and leaned his weight on the patio table next to him. "I've been doing a little research since meeting Rain, and I've found studies on women who've had abortions that experience a lot of trauma and depression for years after."

I thought about Mom's face when Aunt Cass brought up the topic. I thought about the nights she sobbed uncontrollably without telling anyone why. Was that why?

I pushed the emerging memories of Mom's outburst out of my mind. "My aunt seems so proud of the abortions she's had."

"I'd say it's different for everyone, but abortion takes a life—the life of your own child. You know that has to be hard to get over."

Despair left a hollow feeling in my stomach. "I wonder if Mom can ever get over it."

"I think so," Evan said, putting the first few burgers on the grill. "I think it would take a lot of surrender, repentance, and supernatural healing, but I believe God could do it. He's in that kind of business after all," he said, following it with a chuckle.

I gave a snort. "My mom and God are not on good terms."

"Neither are any of us until He saves us. She could be. And maybe one day she will, and she can finally face her past."

I looked him over skeptically. "You're a Christian, then."

He glanced up from the grill briefly with a half smile and a nod. "I am."

"Neither of my parents are Christians. I've only gone to church a few times in my life."

"Well, I've been going to Rain's church. You should come with us sometime."

I wondered what Mom would say if I told her I'd be going to church on Sunday morning. She probably wouldn't know what to say.

"Maybe I will," I told him.

"Awesome. Let me know if you ever need a ride." Evan finished placing the burgers on the grill and closed the lid. His eyes met mine seriously but with compassion, like he wanted me to know that there was hope. "No sin is unforgivable," he said. "God can do it. If she'd go to Him for it, He could break the chains that hold her back. That's the Gospel, and it's the same one that saves anybody else. She isn't a special case. What she did was wrong; it was murder, and now she's facing great consequences. But she can be freed by the same gospel that saved me."

At that moment, Rain appeared at the sliding glass door and tapped it with her foot. Evan went to open it for her, and she walked out carrying a pitcher of iced tea in her hand and a stack of glasses in her arm against her chest to place on the patio table. "Jo's here," she said. "And the sides are all done. If the burgers are almost ready, we'll start bringing everything out."

"It'll be a few minutes," Evan said, then turned to Ava and Maya. "Ava, set up some more lawn chairs, please."

Rain disappeared back inside, leaving me with Evan again.

"Do you talk to your dad a lot since moving?" he asked, flipping the burgers and closing the lid again.

"He's called a few times since we moved in but not much. We probably won't see him again until Christmas."

"That's gotta be hard, too."

I nodded.

"If it makes you feel any better, you fit in perfectly with this crowd. We all have broken families around here, so we've kinda just... made family out of each other."

I watched Rain, Ms. Brooks, and Mrs. Lawson through the glass door as they talked and laughed while they gathered plates and utensils. Ava and Maya were whispering together as they walked out of the barn with extra chairs. And Evan and I sat here chatting. It did feel like a family in a different sort of way. It felt like a family should feel, where everyone got along and wanted to be together.

"I appreciate you letting me be a part, then," I said, fingering a rip in my jeans.

He smiled, and his gaze made me hold my breath.

I tried to hide my shyness with conversation. "And this all came about because you asked Rain to help you with that school paper?"

"Yep. That's how it all began."

"Could I read it?"

His face flushed. "The paper?"

"Well, yeah," I said through a laugh.

He rubbed the back of his neck. "I don't know."

"Didn't you say that it was about Ivy Hollow and the people you've met since coming here?"

"Yeah, it is."

"So... am I in it?" I knew it was a long shot, and I regretted asking the second it escaped my lips.

He paused and gave a short nod. "A little bit, yeah."

I could've swooned. Which is stupid. So stupid. I'd never crushed like this before. Savannah and Molly did, and on the same guy—Justin O'Malley. If I hadn't been the peacemaker in that situation, our friendship wouldn't have survived seventh grade. But I'd never been the swoony, crushing type. Mostly because I only hung around boys. Not, like, real guys. You know... young men. I couldn't bring myself to crush on boys who acted like kids the way Molly and Savannah did. I'd always been too old for my own age.

I smirked at him, trying to keep my eyes from cowering and averting away. The task seemed impossible. "Then, don't I have the right to read it before you go submitting it?"

Evan lifted the grill lid again. And then again. He must be nervous, too. "Alright. Maybe later on tonight."

Rain and the others made their way outside then, bringing the buns and what they called "all the fixin's."

Before we ate, Evan prayed over the food, and I could tell he meant what he said about being a Christian. It was real to him. God was someone he talked to with complete and total conviction.

And then we ate around the campfire, watching the sun disappear behind pink and purple clouds. I laughed stomach-cramping laughs that night. I sat between Evan and Rain, both of them close to either side of me, huddled in blankets by the warmth of the fire. We talked and joked together like we'd been friends our whole lives and were just catching up after a long time away. They asked me about my parents, Aunt Cassidy, and my friends in Florida. Rain talked about her art and her favorite books. Evan showed me his garden and greenhouse and told me about his plans for a bigger garden that summer.

By the end of the night, Rain felt like more of an older sister to me than I could have ever imagined.

I fell in love that night. It wasn't with a person, but with people. With this place—the place I'd wanted to escape only yesterday.

Evan was right; they'd created a family. A group of people who loved to be together. And they were settled in this place, surrounded by what I once thought was nothing, but I began to see it now—the beauty of the empty fields, creaky old barns, campfires, autumn night air, and crickets playing their evening song.

It felt like paradise.

Long after the last burger had been eaten, Evan disappeared into the house, leaving me with Rain. Maya and Ava had gone inside, and all of the adults had retreated to the warm indoors too. It was just Rain and me under a sky of a million stars. You could see them so clearly in Ivy Hollow.

"It's breathtaking, isn't it?" Rain asked, watching me admire them. "I've lived under this same little piece of the sky my whole life, and I've never once grown tired of them. The view of the stars is my favorite thing about the world."

"Really?" I asked.

She nodded. "What's your favorite thing about it?"

I'd never stopped to ask myself what my favorite thing about the world was, but somehow I knew. "The sun. The way it warms your skin and makes life bright. I used to love to watch the sunrise at the beach."

Rain brought her hand close to the fire. The painting was pretty smudged now, but I could still make it out. The sunny sky and the starry one. "Then, I guess we do go well together. And now we know who's who."

Behind us, the door slid open and shut, and Evan sat down beside Rain with a leather folder in his lap.

"Is that your paper?" I asked leaning over Rain a little to see him.

"It is, as promised."

"You're going to let her read it?" Rain asked with shock.

"If that's alright with you," he said.

She nodded, but it seemed reluctant to me.

Evan passed it over to me. "Now remember, this is the rough draft. I haven't done much editing yet. Plus, writing is definitely not my thing."

I opened the folder to find a small stack of pages with type-writer print.

Evan turned to Rain, and they whispered back and forth while I read.

"I haven't even read it yet," I heard Rain whisper to him, and a little spark of pride made me smile behind the quilt I had covering my chin and mouth. I was probably reading into the gesture a little too much, but it felt good to hope.

"Yeah, well, the thought of letting you read it is far more intimidating," Evan whispered back.

Evan had said he was a terrible writer, but he was either wrong or lying. His paper was like reading a novel that introduced Rain as a unique character whose art on her hand spoke more about her than she spoke about herself. The way he described her made me feel certain he liked her. He included so many details about her personality and the little expressions she used that made her unique. He'd observed her so well.

I couldn't help but wonder what he'd observed about me. But I didn't get to find out because Mom called, wanting us home.

"Will you let me finish it? Maybe at lunch on Monday?" I asked Evan, after I hung up with Mom.

He nodded. "Sure. I'll bring it Monday. Maybe by then it'll be finished."

"You're humble, you know," I said, pushing my hair behind my ear. "You're a great writer. It felt so alive to me."

I could tell by the firelight he was blushing. Rain noticed, too.

"Well, not that I disregard your opinion, but I can't say I agree with you," he said.

I drove home with my head in the clouds. Ava came with us to spend the night with Maya, and the whole ride home, I didn't hear a word they said.

I felt certain that this was my home. I just hoped when Mom found out the truth about Rain, she wouldn't try to pull me away from it.

EVAN

> "I keep turning over new leaves,
> and spoiling them, as I used to
> spoil my copybooks; and I make so
> many beginnings there never will
> be an end."
>
> Louisa May Alcott, _Little Women_

AFTER JORDAN LEFT WITH Ava and Maya, Rain and I sat alone by the bonfire, listening to the popping of the wood under the pressure of the flames. Up to this moment, that's how life had felt—a constant pressure under fire. But that night seemed to usher in the results of what I'd been fighting for. Mom had been happy, Ava had been happy, and I had been happy.

Rain had finally gotten a piece of what she'd been hoping for, too. She and Jordan were friends. Sisters.

It was weird watching them together. Eerie even. They didn't grow up together and they'd hardly even met, but there was a similarity I couldn't put my finger on. The way they laughed, the way they both tucked their hair behind their ears when they were nervous... Little things like that.

"Now do I get to read over it?" Rain asked, glancing at the leather folder in my lap. She seemed happier to be sure, but ever since telling her about my encounter with Jordan, there had been an invisible wall between us.

I hated it. I hated the feeling of being the one who put it there. It had all turned out alright in the end, but I knew there was still a level of distrust.

I grimaced. "I guess so."

Rain took the manuscript into her hand and leaned closer to the fire so she could see.

I read her as she read my work.

I watched her eyes squint and the smile that would occasionally tug at the corners of her mouth. I watched as her handless arm went to her lips as though she were in deep thought.

Only a few moments into reading it she exclaimed, "You're writing it in first person. You're writing *me* in first person."

I rubbed the back of my neck as I nodded. "I hope that's okay. I'm doing my best to get in your head, and I might be taking a few liberties, but I wanted it to feel personal to you."

From the first day that I sat down at that black typewriter, I knew I wouldn't be a Dickens. Nor would I be a Barrie. I wouldn't even be my dad. I'm just Evan Lawson—a guy with a project to complete and a story way out of his league.

But with a story as powerful as Rain's, I knew I had to try and capture her as closely as I could, and getting into her head was the best way I knew to do it.

I bent down and grabbed a stick by my feet to poke at the logs in the fire, agitating them, and then watched as the flames grew.

Rain smiled. "It's odd to read myself saying things I didn't write down, but I like it. I like seeing what you think goes on in my mind. You're becoming a real storyteller."

"If you say so."

She paused to look me over, as if examining me one last time before she spoke. "I know so."

My cheeks went warm under her gaze.

"Honestly, I'm shocked at how well you've gotten into my head." She tightened her blanket around her shoulders shyly. "But you make me feel like a heroine, and I'm not sure I live up to your description."

I shifted just a little closer to her. "I think I remember you telling me once that you can become like the books you read." I forced my eyes to lock with hers. "I think you've become like all the heroines you've read about, Rain. And I think you're taking on your own story incredibly."

It was her turn to blush and look away.

She went back to reading, and I let the silence linger between us, taking in the last sounds of summer. The crickets' song, the wind swishing its way through the grass, the eerie creaking of the old barn, and the melodic crackling of the fire.

I knew where the conversation needed to go next. I didn't want to bring it up again, but we had to get over it. I didn't want this barrier between us to stick around any longer than it had to.

"I still think it's missing Jordan's side of the story," I said, turning to read Rain's expression.

Her eyes traveled from the page to her hand as she nodded. "Yeah, maybe you're right."

"Think of everything she told us tonight," I prompted. "About your mom and aunt and her home life. Your mom's one choice changed everything. It hurt a lot of people. I think that's a piece of the story worth telling." I wanted her to see why. It had nothing to do with being on one side or the other. They were the same side—different chapters of the same story. You couldn't have one without the other. In my head, I was laughing at myself. Rain may have been right—she was turning me into a storyteller after all.

In the firelight, I saw a smile grow on Rain's lips. "You're definitely beyond the point of overthinking this paper now. It's just for school, and yet you're giving it your all."

"Yeah, I know," I mumbled.

I was invested, and with every line I typed on that typewriter, it was becoming less of a school project and more of a way to prove something to myself. I was doing what my dad had wanted to do, and I wanted to do it well.

Rain's eyes went back to the page and mine went to the stars overhead.

Stars always took my mind to J.M. Barrie's world of Neverland these days, thanks to Rain. A world full of pirates, mermaids, fairies, and make-believe.

Rain had said at the beginning of our project that she wanted to escape there sometimes. Where you never grow old and things don't change. Each day holds another adventure for you and your family of lost boys, but the problems are far less scary than those of reality. Pirates feel far less intimidating than facing long-lost mothers.

But how far she'd come since that day.

She'd faced her sister and was prepared to reconcile with her mother should the opportunity arise. Not that she wasn't afraid anymore, but she was doing it scared. I admired that.

And now we had something like a band of lost boys—a family of misfits and unlikely members.

Rain stacked the papers neatly in the leather folder and closed it, swiftly tying it shut—despite her single hand—with the leather bands that wrapped around it.

I couldn't help but hold my breath as I waited to hear her thoughts.

"Evan Lawson," she said, her voice quiet yet full of emotion. I could feel the wall between us crumbling. She was coming back to me. "I believe you've found your love for words. You can't tell me after I've read this that you didn't pour your entire heart and soul into it."

I shifted in my seat nervously. "I have poured a lot into it, but I think it's because it means something to me. This isn't just a paper anymore. I feel like I have to do you justice."

"You've exceeded my expectations in every way, Evan. This is incredible. Your dad would be beyond proud."

The thought of my dad reading my writing made me want to cringe. I'm not sure I would have let him. His talent left me in the dust.

"I just wonder..." In the glow of the flames I could see a suspicious look in her eyes. "Exactly how much is fact and fiction?"

"What do you mean?" I asked, even though I was sure I knew exactly what she was asking. My palms started sweating, and I rubbed them on my jeans.

"You seem to be the love interest in my story. And I like it. It was a needed component." She searched my expression and then asked, "But is that fact or fiction?"

I cleared my throat. It felt dry all of a sudden. I'd like to blame it on the smoke from the fire, but who would I be fooling? "Well, of course all of your thoughts are things I've either heard you say, I make up, or I assume. So I really can't speak for you."

"But what about you? What about your thoughts?"

I hesitated. My finger found a groove in the plastic of my chair's armrest and began tracing it up and down. "I'd say mine are all pretty true to life."

Her lips lifted at the corners, but before she could respond, the glass door behind us slid open.

Just my luck.

"Rain, are you ready to head home? It's pretty late," Jo called.

Rain turned in her chair to look behind us. "I'll be right in."

Once the door had closed, she stood, and I did the same.

"You're doing a great job with it, and I can't wait to see it completed," she said, as if nothing had happened.

She passed the folder to me, and I rubbed rough circles into the leather with my thumbs. I know my face fell, and I wondered if she could see it in the firelight.

"Thanks," I finally muttered. "You'll have to fill me in on your whole conversation with Jordan at the store today so I can write all of that in."

"I'll tell you Monday."

"Great."

Rain pushed a piece of her dark hair behind her ear and looked up at me. It was down today, not in her usual bun or braid, and it fell over her shoulders in dark waves. Behind her glasses, I noticed for the first time that her eyes weren't entirely brown, just mostly brown. Like the water she dipped her paint brushes in to clean them. There were hints of other colors, too, like a cloudy hazel and gray.

"You've gotten into my head a lot better than I imagined you would," she said.

"There are still things I don't know for certain. Things I'd like to hear you say for yourself." I slid my hands into my back pockets. Standing farther away from the fire made the outside air seem frigid.

She paused, and I thought I saw sadness or maybe guilt in her eyes. "Well," she said finally, "let's just see how things go."

What was that supposed to mean? What was there to see? I couldn't help but think she still saw me on Jordan's side.

Rain must have seen the questions in my eyes, but she only offered a look of sympathy as an answer. We heard her ancient truck's engine roar in the driveway. "Jo's waiting, so I guess I'll see ya."

I wanted to object, to ask more questions, but I didn't. I knew Rain. She would tell me what she wanted me to know when she was ready.

I watched her disappear into the night. And I was left alone under the stars.

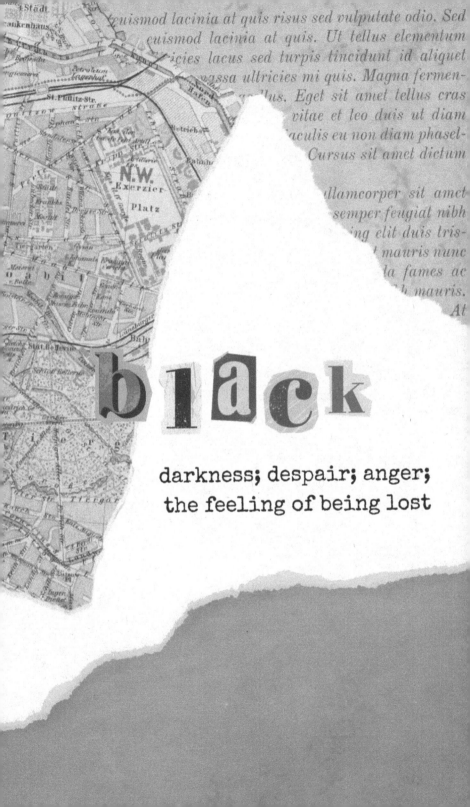

black

darkness; despair; anger;
the feeling of being lost

RAIN

"I wish you to know you
have been the last dream
of my soul."

Charles Dickens, A Tale of Two Cities

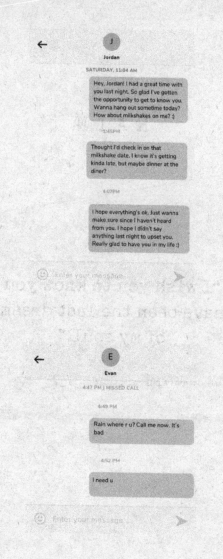

← **J** Jordan

SATURDAY, 11:04 AM

Hey, Jordan! I had a great time with you last night. So glad I've gotten the opportunity to get to know you. Wanna hang out sometime today? How about milkshakes on me? :)

12:45PM

Thought I'd check in on that milkshake date. I know it's getting kinda late, but maybe dinner at the diner?

4:07PM

I hope everything's ok. Just wanna make sure since I haven't heard from you. I hope I didn't say anything last night to upset you. Really glad to have you in my life :)

Enter your message...

← **E** Evan

4:47 PM | MISSED CALL

4:49 PM

Rain where r u? Call me now. It's bad

4:52 PM

I need u

Enter your message...

JORDAN

> "Perhaps it has sometimes happened to you in a dream that someone says something which you don't understand but in the dream it feels as if it has some enormous meaning—either a terrifying one which turns the whole dream into a nightmare or else a lovely meaning too lovely to put into words, which makes the dream so beautiful that you remember it all your life and are always wishing you could get into that dream again."
>
> C.S. Lewis, <u>The Lion, the Witch and the Wardrobe</u>

THE NIGHT OF THE bonfire, I laid in bed, but sleep didn't come. There was a restlessness inside me I couldn't describe. I wondered at first if it came from the excitement I'd felt with Evan and Rain, but it was something else. Something deeper. It wasn't a joy in my heart—it was a sorrow in my soul.

After thinking on it a while, I decided it must be guilt. The hollow look in Mom's eyes the night she talked about the abortion with Aunt Cass still haunted me. Evan was right. She deserved answers and healing, and I might be the one keeping it from her. But Evan had also said that it would have to come from God.

God. I'd never even given Him much thought until that night. Thinking of Him then made me shudder. And maybe that's what was causing the restlessness.

Evan had written about Him in the little bit of his paper I'd been able to read that night. He talked about his garden and how it taught him about who God is. But I didn't know Him at all. I never had.

But He knows me. The eerie thought went through my head as I lay there, staring into the darkness. He had to know me if He was God. He had to know everything about me. Suddenly, I felt exposed, like I was laying underneath a giant magnifying glass, being observed.

He knew the anger and hate that boiled in my heart toward my parents. He knew I'd never once acknowledged Him or even cared to. He knew the terrible thoughts I'd had about Molly and Savannah since they'd forgotten about me. Everything.

He knows. He knows it all.

The thought repeated itself in my head over and over, making my palms clammy, but it gradually turned from a cry of fear to a whisper of peace.

He knows.

He knew the burden I've carried since the divorce. He knew my anxiety. He knew the longing in my heart to be loved—truly loved—by my parents. He knew my fear of my mother. He knew.

He's in the business of forgiveness and redemption. That's what Evan said.

And something in me knew that the sorrow in my soul wasn't going to leave until I surrendered. Until I was forgiven.

I'd been thinking about the hollow look in Mom's eyes, but it was a mirror of my own. In our own ways, both of us were empty. Lost.

"I don't know how to do this," I whispered, thinking about how Evan prayed over our meal so confidently, like God was waiting to hear from us. "I'm not sure what to say. But I need to be forgiven."

ell

I woke up late the next morning, and the sorrow in my soul wasn't there.

I think maybe I expected to find a halo floating over my head when I looked in the bathroom mirror to brush my teeth, but there was nothing new. Nothing visibly different. But the invisible burden I'd carried for so long now seemed to be lighter. Or maybe it was just a different kind of weight.

← E
Evan
SATURDAY, 10:45 AM

I think I found it last night. The forgiveness u told me about. Do u really think mom could find it 2 after all this?

I had to tell Mom about Rain. I didn't want her healing hinging on me. This time, being the peacemaker would mean stirring the pot. I just hoped it would pay off and actually bring peace in the end.

I could hear Maya and Ava chatting as I passed by Maya's bedroom door to head downstairs. I glanced down at my phone in my hand as my feet tapped down the stairs; it was nearly eleven o'clock. I'd slept the day away.

As if to confirm my conviction to tell Mom the truth, there was a text message from Rain asking me if I wanted to hang out and get milkshakes.

The thought of getting to spend more time with Rain excited me and filled me with dread at the same time. Mom would have to know who she was, and I would have to be the one to tell her. I'd kept the peace between our family my whole life, and now I would hopefully be able to create peace between her and Rain.

Mom was sitting at the dining room table when I entered the kitchen, and she glanced up at me with a small smile.

I exhaled. She seemed to be in a good mood.

"I thought you'd never wake up," she said, sending her eyes back down to the laptop in front of her. "I made the girls waffles this morning. There's a few in the freezer if you want to pop them in the toaster."

I slipped into the kitchen behind her. We were separated only by the short island countertop, and her back was to me as she sat at the kitchen table.

"I guess I was just tired from hanging out with Evan and Rain last night," I said, trying to ease into the conversation. But I'd apparently plummeted into it, because Mom's head shot up.

"Rain?" she repeated.

My chest tightened. I'd just assumed that Jo had named Rain after Mom abandoned her. Did Mom know her name?

A forced, dry chuckle quickly followed as Mom tried to recover. "An awfully strange name, isn't it?" Her head was still tilted in my direction. I couldn't see her face.

"Yeah," I stuttered. My fingers tightened on the icy plastic the waffles were wrapped in. "A little odd, I guess."

"I thought Ava only had a brother."

"She does. Evan. But he's friends with Rain. She and her mom were there for dinner last night."

Mom paused. When she spoke again, I heard her voice shake. "I wonder if I've met her mom around here yet. What's her name?"

I didn't answer. I put the box of waffles back in the freezer and walked over to stand at the table across from her. I couldn't sit; my nerves were too on edge.

"Mom," I said, my own voice shaking now. "It's her. It's the baby you left. I wondered, but I wasn't sure. Not until last night."

Mom stared at me with eyes wider than I'd ever seen. Horror clouded over her face like she'd seen a ghost.

"She knows who we are," I blurted, the silence making me eager to fill it with something—anything. "But she's okay. She wants to be friends—"

Mom stood with a jolt, causing me to jump backward a step. Her palms covered her face for a moment then fell to her side, her hands clenched into fists. She looked on at me with anger—far more than the night she'd slapped me. She hadn't been in her right mind then. Now she was. "What did you tell her?" she demanded, her voice cracking.

I shook my head. "Nothing. She already knew. She knew before I did."

Mom looked at me doubtfully. "How? How could she have known?" She walked around the table toward me, closing the distance between us. "You're lying to me. You want to be treated like an adult, and you like how Cass makes you feel grown, but you're not, Jordan. You can't even keep your mouth shut. This is *huge*. This isn't just something you go spilling around town. This is *my* secret. You have no right." The words were flying from her mouth in a low tone, cautious of the girls upstairs.

"I swear, Mom," I said, my eyes filling with tears. "She knew. She's always known. Jo told her."

Her eyes squinted as if she were trying to remember. "Jo?"

"Her adoptive mom. She worked at the hospital in Richmond."

The lightbulb seemed to go off in Mom's mind, and a look of shock replaced the anger. Her body slowly turned until she leaned against the wall, her back to me again. I wished I could hear her thoughts.

Was there any openness to reconciliation? Was there even a chance?

I cleared my wet cheeks with the back of my hands. They were shaking like leaves. "I know it's hard," I whispered. "But Rain isn't mad at you. Neither is Jo."

Mom shot around again and pointed a finger at me, moving in until it pressed against my chest. "I don't want you talking to her anymore. Do you hear me? We're leaving."

"Mom," I mumbled, so quietly I could hardly hear myself. "Mom, just think it over."

Her finger rose in front of my face. "I don't have to see her. I don't have to apologize. I'm not the villain." She was scolding me, but I knew she was fighting the voices in her own head. The guilt. And again, I would be the one who would have to carry it as though it were my problem. As if it were my fault.

Oh, God, I prayed in my head, *help me carry it.*

"You could never understand the weight of this. You're a child," Mom sneered. "If I find out you have any more conversations with her before we get out of this town... I swear, Jordan, I'll never forgive you. And you'll lose your phone, your laptop... everything. I will make your life miserable."

I swallowed hard. I wanted to burst into tears. I'd finally found a home in Rain and Evan, and now she was going to pull me away. Was this payment for trying to help her heal?

"You've always had a rebellious streak," she jeered, her eyes digging into mine. "You've always been so numb and unfeeling toward people. You could never understand my pain."

"I haven't done anything wrong. I just told you—"

"You run to Cassidy, not me. You've never respected me or cared for me."

"I've tried, but you never—"

Mom interrupted. "You just won't have it. You're unfeeling and ungrateful, and you've gone and stabbed me to top it all off."

I did burst into tears then. I collapsed on the floor with my knees at my chest as I cried into my arms. There was no use in trying to make her listen. She wasn't going to. She'd decided it was my fault.

All my life I had tried so hard to make her proud of me. I'd tried to carry things so she wouldn't have to. And all I'd ever gotten was a cold shoulder. She'd been civil, she'd say nice things, but it always felt fake. What had I done? Why did she target me?

I could feel her looking down at me, but I kept my head buried in my arms.

"I bet it'll make you love your Aunt Cassidy so much more to hear that she wanted me to abort you, too. I'd just gotten through an unwanted pregnancy, and there I was, in the same mess. She told me to do it again and get through college. Lucky for you, I was traumatized by the whole bloody thing. And still, you're ungrateful. Still you love her more."

I felt like a thousand arrows had punctured my heart.

My own mother. My aunt.

I couldn't even think straight. I felt like I was falling deeper and deeper into a dark hole. I never wanted to crawl out. I wanted to die there.

Mom's voice had remained low throughout our conversation, but it had a wild tone. Now, it softened into a controlled, icy pitch that felt like thunder. "Take Ava home. Tell her to pack her things, and take her home. I don't want her here right now."

I still sobbed into my arms, but I heard her walk up the stairs and then close her bedroom door.

How had Rain borne it, knowing her very existence was despised? I wasn't sure that I could.

I'm not sure how long I sat there crying. It felt like forever. But I finally lifted my head and wiped my eyes with the hem of my pajama shirt. The moment I stood on my feet, I wanted to collapse again. I felt dizzy and shaky as I crept up the stairs and tapped on Maya's door.

Their voices went quiet, and I did my best to speak without giving away the tears in my voice.

"Have Ava pack her things," I said. "I've gotta take her home soon." My voice didn't hide the tears at all, but Maya seemed not to care.

"But she was supposed to stay all day," she whined.

"She's gotta go, Maya," I said weakly before walking to my room. I didn't have the strength to fight with her.

I washed my face in the bathroom, trying to clear away the evidence, but it was no use. The splotchy redness was there to stay. I stumbled into my bedroom and grabbed the outfit I'd worn yesterday off my floor. It still smelled like a campfire. The tears threatened to fall again.

Maybe she would change her mind. Maybe she just needed time to process it.

Regardless, the words that passed between us could never be taken back. They could never be unsaid. They would hover between us forever, filling the gap every time I faced her from now on.

But Rain had forgiven her. Maybe in time, I could, too. After all, just last night I was begging God to forgive me.

Once I'd changed out of my pajamas, I waited in the car for Maya and Ava, my head resting on the steering wheel.

As they slid into the back seats, Maya's eyes met mine through the rear view mirror. Concern shaped her expression, and she opened her mouth to speak, but she stopped short. A look of understanding passed between us in the few short seconds our eyes met. She knew. She knew it was Mom.

I put the car in reverse and pulled out of the driveway.

Maybe I was wrong to tell her. I'd wanted her to find healing, but instead we were both left with gaping wounds that hadn't been there before.

I'd always wondered where the disconnect was and why she never cared for me. It sounded like I was as unwanted as Rain and her twin; Mom just hadn't been brave enough to go through the procedure again.

I didn't want to know anymore. I wished I didn't know.

Tears began to fall down my cheeks again as I turned left onto a back road. I didn't fight them. It was no use.

And Aunt Cassidy. How could she treat me that way? How could she seem to love me so much when she'd been the one to suggest getting rid of me? Didn't my existence remind her of her own babies whose lives she'd taken? Couldn't she see that if my mom had listened to her, I wouldn't be here? How could she be so proud of her own abortions? She'd been the one family member I felt I could still trust and rely on.

Maybe it will be worth it, I thought. If Mom could eventually process it all and be able to move on, this pain would be worth it.

"Is your sister okay?" I heard Ava whisper after I sniffed a little too loudly. I'd forgotten all about them.

I wanted to yell that I wasn't. I wasn't okay. How could I be okay?

So I did.

I vented my guts out. Not to them really, just trying to get it off my chest and release some of the pressure I felt. I'd been on the other end so many times—dealing with Mom, Dad, and Maya. For once, I would be the one to fall apart.

I spilled it all, all my questions and doubts. All that I'd learned but couldn't understand. And I didn't stop until I glanced in my rear view mirror again to find Maya bawling—broken-hearted sobs escaped her lips without a sound.

My heart squeezed in my chest as I realized what I'd done. The burden I'd now passed to her.

Tears clouded my vision. My entire body was still shaking. I brought a hand to clear away the tears so I could see where I was going.

That's when Maya screamed, making my blood curdle.

By the time my hand left my eyes, all I could see was the massive tree trunk flying toward my windshield. And there wasn't even time for the scream to leave my throat.

E V A N

"May it be a light to you
in dark places, when all
other lights go out."

J.R.R. Tolkien, The Fellowship of the Ring

NO ANSWER.

I swore under my breath and sent Rain a desperate text message to call me back, all while jogging to the truck with Mom on my heels.

She was in hysterics, and I was almost there myself. But I'd stay strong enough for both of us.

Thunder rumbled and lightning struck in the distance as I opened the driver's side door. The sky looked like all hell would break loose at any moment, but something inside me knew it already had a few winding country roads away.

In the driver's seat with my soil-covered hands gripping the steering wheel for dear life, I willed Ava to be okay. To be alive and breathing when I got to her.

"Hours, they told me," Mom said, almost in a moan. "They've been on the side of the road for hours!" She removed the sweaty bandana from her hair and wiped her forehead and neck with it. We had been pulling weeds from the flower beds when we got the call.

I swallowed hard, trying not to let the scene of Ava stranded in a crumpled car—injured or worse—take over my imagination. I just needed to drive. Safely and fast.

"She's okay, Mom," I said, just like she assured me the day Dad died. That he would be okay. That we all would be.

Mom turned her head to face me, and from the corner of my eye, I saw her look at me with doubt laced in her expression.

We'd been here before, and it definitely hadn't turned out okay.

That's when we passed it—the wreck site. Tow trucks had lifted Jordan's SUV from the steep bank, and now it sat on the side of the road, totaled.

A sob escaped Mom's lips.

I fixed my attention on the road. I couldn't look at her and lie to her at the same time.

Maybe Ava would be okay, but I didn't believe it. Something in my gut told me otherwise. Something in me knew bad news waited for us at that hospital.

R A I N

> "To die will be an
> awfully big
> adventure."
>
> J.M. Barrie, Peter Pan

MY HEART POUNDED IN my chest as I tried for the third time to crank the truck.

Again, it stalled.

I cursed and tore my fingers through my hair.

I'd talked to Evan moments before as he ran into the hospital. Ava had been in an accident. He didn't give details, he just repeated the phrase, "I can't lose anyone else, Rain. I can't lose her," over and over again.

I took a deep breath and listened to the rain pattering on my windshield. I was getting to that hospital if I had to ride my bike there. I mumbled a prayer before giving the truck one last crank. The engine roared. I lifted a brief word of thanks before putting the truck in reverse.

My phone rang when I was halfway there, Jo calling me from the hospital. "Rain, I just saw Evan and his mom run into the hospital. Something isn't right. Where are you? Are you in the truck?"

"Yeah, I'm heading there now. Ava's there. Do you know anything about her? She was in a car accident."

I heard Jo gasp on the other end, and I could feel my already-racing-heart pick up speed. "Three girls were brought in from a car accident. I've heard it isn't good, Rain. I heard one of them didn't make it."

"Oh, God, no. Please, God."

"Rain, calm down. I don't want you in an accident next. Focus on driving. I'll find out what I can. Is it raining out there?"

"Yeah, it's raining." Actually, it was pouring, and my mind felt as blurry as my view of the road in front of me. I could hardly carry on the conversation.

Who would Ava have been with except Maya? She had spent last night at their house. And who was driving? Jordan or my mom?

"Did you say it was three girls or was one a woman?"

Jo hesitated. "I'm not sure. Rain, I know what you're thinking, and don't. Just get here, and we'll figure it out then. Where are you? Are you almost here?"

"I think so."

"Please focus. Worrying right now won't help her any. Just focus."

Jo stayed on the phone with me, and after a few minutes, I knew I was close. I was coming up to the diner which was just around the corner from the hospital.

That's when my check engine light came on and the truck started sputtering a weird noise.

"Come on!" I screamed.

"What was that? That doesn't sound good. I told you the engine didn't sound right this morning."

I pulled over into the restaurant parking lot and jumped out of the truck. Smoke was seeping out from under the hood.

"I'm running the rest of the way. I don't have time for this," I yelled through the rain and into my phone. "I'll be there soon." I locked the truck and slid the keys in my pocket. I was already soaked all the way through.

Then, I ran. I was glad to run. It gave me something more to do than sitting in a car, anxiously waiting. I counted the times my sneakers hit the pavement to busy my mind. The rain was practically ice. I felt each individual drop hit my skin.

Everything felt like it was in slow motion, like a bad dream where you want to scream but you can't, except I felt like I was moving toward the hospital where life was moving on but I was running in place and would never actually get there.

Was it true? And if it was, who had died?

I wanted to hope it wasn't Ava, but I didn't want to hope it was Maya, or Jordan, or my mom.

"Let it be a lie," I cried into the raging storm. "Let it not be true!"

I felt bile rising in my throat. I didn't have time to throw up. I had to keep running.

I could see the hospital now. My skin was frozen, but my lungs and legs were on fire.

It seemed like an eternity had passed, but I finally reached the hospital lobby, nearly slipping on the floors in my own puddle. "Ava Lawson," I breathed to the receptionist. "Where is the family of Ava Lawson?"

She looked over me with a mixture of heartbreak and fear.

I knew her, of course. I knew almost all of the hospital staff with Jo working there.

She pushed her purple glasses higher on her nose. "I'm sorry, Rain. They can't have visitors."

I brought my hand to my abdomen still trying to catch my breath. I was gonna be so sore the next day. "They asked me to come. Please, Anna. I've got to see Evan," I pleaded.

She looked reluctant but told me the room number. "They probably aren't allowed in right now. They're probably in the waiting room on the third floor."

I nodded and darted toward the elevator, actually slipping that time and landing hard on my left wrist. Pain shot up my forearm and a moan escaped my lips.

Behind me, Anna gasped at the front desk.

I sat up and tried to wiggle my fingers and shake it off, which only made it worse. I struggled to my feet. I would have to worry about it later.

My eyes landed on the elevator again where a nurse was walking out. I sprinted to slide in before the doors shut, this time a little more cautious of my wet sneakers. I just barely squeezed through in time.

The ride up to the third floor seemed to take longer than running here did. Absently, I massaged my wrist with the stub on my right arm. I didn't acknowledge the pain very much then, but I knew I would later.

When the doors finally opened, my gaze locked on Evan who sat across the room from me, hunched over his knees in a chair. His mom sat beside him with one hand on his back and the other covering her face.

Please, God. I didn't know what I was asking for. I wasn't sure what to ask except that it all be a lie or a misunderstanding. But by Evan's disposition, I knew it wasn't.

Someone was dead.

For the first time since he called me, I moved slowly, afraid of the news I'd get when I reached him. No matter what the news was, it would be terrible.

Soaking wet and still breathing heavily, I kneeled in front of him.

Evan's head rose, and shock immediately covered his face at my appearance. He'd been crying. Hard. His green eyes were surrounded with a deep, bloodshot red. They were puffy and swollen. My own eyes pleaded with him, begging him to tell me quickly.

His shaking hands grabbed my shoulders, and his forehead met mine. In a cracked whisper he said, "Rain... I am so, so sorry."

And I knew.

I knew it wasn't Ava.

Relief began to flood over me, but it immediately replaced itself with a gripping fear.

"Which one, Evan?" I whispered back, pulling my head away from his, a sob building in my throat. "Tell me who it was."

His mouth opened slowly, but he didn't get to speak. Behind me, I heard the elevator open again, and Evan's eyes landed on the person who got off. His grip on my shoulders tightened.

"Where are they?" a shrill voice cried out, and I knew before I turned around that it belonged to my mother.

I never imagined this being the way that I'd meet her. Why did it have to be like this?

My hand was on Evan's knee, and I dug my fingernails into his skin, but he didn't flinch. When I turned to look, I saw a reflection of myself.

Older. Years of stress and pain were written in the lines of her makeup-less face. Gray sprinkled her hair at the roots. But my reflection was there. Would she see it, too?

I jerked back around to face Evan again, hoping she'd been too focused on seeing her daughters to notice me—her first daughter. The one dripping in a puddle on the floor.

"She can't do this now," I whispered to Evan. "I can't do this now."

He nodded, understanding. His eyes began searching the room, like he was looking for a way to get me out.

"Mrs. Carson," said a collected voice, and even with my back to her, I knew from all the time I'd spent at this hospital with Jo that it belonged to Dr. Patterson. "I know you're worried, but I really need you to calm down."

"Where are they?" Reagan yelled again. Her tone sent tingles up my spine. She was going to break.

"Why don't you make your way back to my office, and I'll tell you everything that's going on."

"Tell me now! Are they alive? I need to know now!"

Dr. Patterson heaved a sigh that sounded like it carried the weight of the whole world's sorrow. "Mrs. Carson, I'm a mother as well. I know you're worried, but I really need you to get a hold of yourself."

The suspense was tying my stomach in knots, but I didn't want to find out this way. My eyes welled with tears, and I covered my face with my hand, holding back a sob. I wanted to go to her, to wrap my arms around her, and tell her it was going to be okay.

My mother's tone went low and firm. It was controlled, and yet it was threatening. "*Tell me.*"

There was a pause from Dr. Patterson, and you could have heard a pin drop.

For the first time since I knelt at Evan's feet, I glanced over at Mrs. Lawson. Tears streamed down her cheeks as she watched my mom with deep pity.

"Mrs. Carson..." Dr. Patterson finally sighed. "Your youngest daughter has a few moderate injuries, including a few broken ribs and a concussion, but she'll be okay."

Again, acid burned my throat as I prepared for the final verdict. But my soul knew. It felt the void forming before the words of death were even uttered.

Even Dr. Patterson's voice cracked as she spoke. "I'm afraid your oldest didn't survive the crash. She passed before anyone reached the scene of the accident."

"No," I moaned, and my head fell to Evan's knee. His grip on me tightened.

"What?" I heard Reagan whisper.

Mrs. Lawson stood and made her way over to Reagan. "Have a seat," I heard her say, but her voice was like an echo. My ears were ringing.

"*What?*" she repeated as she took Mrs. Lawson's arm and lowered down into the chair. Two chairs to my left. So close I could smell her perfume.

It was too much. All of it.

For the first time since I was born, my mother and I were under the same roof, mere inches apart. Two people bound by blood, whose lives had been lived out so intentionally far apart, finally coming together. It was inevitable, but I'd expected to bump into her at the grocery store. Not this. Not here.

Instead, our worlds collided violently. My mother still dealt with the trauma of the last time she saw me in a hospital. And here we were again, coming full circle.

It made my head spin and my palms sweat.

I turned to catch another glance.

She wore sweatpants and an oversized t-shirt with a coffee stain on the front. Her face was covered in her hands which shook. My hand looked like hers—those long, slender, bony fingers.

She sobbed over her daughter. My sister.

A few doors down, my sister is...

I fought the gag.

Oh, God, why? Why Jordan?

Behind me, I heard the elevator door slide open again, and I turned to see Jo, who was staring at me, dumbstruck. I knew Mom wasn't paying me or anyone else any attention, so I stood quickly and hopped on the elevator beside Jo, holding her arm and shaking my head to keep her from getting off.

Evan followed and punched the button to the first floor.

The elevator door slid shut, putting a welcome barrier between me and Reagan. But also between me and Jordan.

"I guess you figured it out yourself," Jo said, tucking a sopping wet strand of hair behind my ear. "I found out just after I got off the phone with you. I wanted to warn you before you got up there, but I guess I was too late."

"She didn't see me," I said, and my voice still tremored. "She can't know I'm here. Now isn't the time." The elevator began moving downward, and I had to grab the bar behind me to steady myself.

Jo nodded her agreement, her face full of concern.

I turned to Evan. "How's Ava?"

His Adam's apple rose and fell as he swallowed. "She's gonna be okay. She's been in surgery nearly an hour now. They're repairing a bone in her leg that punctured through her skin, but she's gonna be okay."

"That's good," I said.

Our eyes stayed locked on each other. His seemed to ask mine if I meant it. After all, what about this was *good*?

His jaw flexed a few times. He was fighting tears. I knew I would lose it if I saw him break down. His eyes suddenly squinted as they fell to observe my green dress and wool sweater that were dripping with enough water to drown us in this elevator.

"Did you walk here?"

I noticed for the first time that my entire body was shaking. I couldn't tell if it was from the adrenaline or the cold. Likely a little of both.

I wrapped my arms around myself. "Ran is more like it. But only part of the way. The truck broke down, and it's sitting at the diner."

He pulled his gray sweatshirt off and handed it to me. "Go put that on instead."

The elevator door opened to the front lobby, where the janitor was cleaning up my trail of water. His tired expression deepened as he realized I was about to create another mess he would have to deal with.

Evan sat in the lobby, and Jo went to locate me a pair of her scrubs to change into. She always had an extra pair at work. I went to wait for her in the bathroom.

The first thing I did was puke my guts out.

When I finally had the strength to lift my shaking body away from the toilet, I stood over the sink and wrung out my dripping hair, pain shooting up my wrist with every movement. When the pain became too intense, I gave up. I shrunk to the floor in sobs. It wasn't the pain in my wrist that overcame me. It was the pain in my chest. It was a steady ache and an emptiness I couldn't bear.

"Why?" The sound barely escaped through my lips. "First my twin, and now her. I don't understand." I could hardly breathe as my cries grew deeper and deeper inside of me. My throat burned.

A storm cloud seems to follow me through life. Maybe my name was a curse.

I gasped for a breath and opened my eyes slightly. Through the tears, I could make out my blue and purple swollen wrist. Just a few hours ago, I'd painted the rolling hills and the sunrise on that hand. A sign of new beginnings and that things were looking up. I'd painted them with her in mind, as though she was the sun in my story. There had been a brightness and warmth I'd never expected to get from her.

But the sun had hardly made an effort to rise that morning. I never saw it through the inky black rain clouds. Now, the storm had long since washed off my painting, and all that remained were colors that showed pain and brokenness. It was fitting.

Jo came in with the scrubs and crouched on the bathroom floor beside me, wrapping her arms around me and burying her face in my wet hair.

I felt my mind go back to the day when she told me the story behind my name. The brokenness I felt.

Jo was my world. I would be lost without her. And a few stories above me, my mother's world was falling to pieces. But it had been falling apart since the day she found out about my existence.

And now, this.

"We were friends," I finally muttered. "She was so... so..." I couldn't finish.

Jo rubbed my back as I paused to gather my words.

"She was beautiful," I sputtered, thinking of her soul that longed for home, just like mine. Thinking of her heart where Thomas found a place to belong. Thinking of her pain that took me far too long to notice. "She was so young. She was hurting, and she wanted answers." The words that escaped my mouth were only the Cliffsnotes of what went through my mind. "She was my sister."

The thought hardly registered in my mind that the girl I sat with by a bonfire last night—just mere hours ago—was gone from this world forever.

How will we heal?

"Poor Reagan," Jo whispered into my hair. "That woman has been through so much. Granted, she put herself through a lot of it, but it's sad to watch."

I nodded and pulled away to wipe the tears from my cheeks with my burning wrist.

Jo cupped my face in her hands and looked into my eyes the way she had so many times before. "Rain, I'm so sorry. Sometimes it seems like life prefers to kick us while we're down—all the bad things seem to happen at once." Jo knew all about that. Her time in the foster care system had been nothing but one bad event and placement after another. "But you and I know better than anyone that God is at work in these nitty-gritty parts of our lives. While we're crying on bathroom floors, He's busy doing great things." She offered a half smile. "That doesn't make this suck any less. It hurts. But He hasn't left you, Rain. He's still here. And He's busy making something out of this we can't understand."

I nodded my agreement, unable to say the words that came to my mind. In fact, words didn't come. My mind felt jumbled and empty all at once.

Jo stood, towering over me. "Now, change before you freeze to death. I'm going to go see what I can learn about Reagan without going up there. I don't want her recognizing either one of us right now. Insult to injury is the last thing she needs."

I obeyed and changed into the fuchsia pink scrubs, which felt too happy a color. I pulled Evan's gray hoodie over me, balancing out the happy hues with a dull one, bringing immediate warmth and comfort. It smelled like he did, a mixture of pine and earth.

I found him waiting for me out in the lobby in the same position I'd found him in earlier, leaning over with his elbows planted on his knees and his face buried in his hands. I wondered if he was praying. I wondered if his mind was replaying the memories of the last time he sat in a hospital lobby on the night that he lost his dad.

I lowered onto the couch beside him, and he glanced up at me. "You look a little warmer."

"Much warmer. Thank you."

For the first time, he noticed my hand and instinctively took it into his own fingers to examine it. "What happened?"

"I slipped and fell on my way to the elevator."

"Do you think it's broken?"

"I don't think so. Sprained maybe."

His thumb gently ran over my knuckles as he looked. "How will you function with it being your only hand?"

"I'll manage. It'll suck, but I'll be alright."

Evan set my hand down on the couch between us.

And then came the silence.

Neither one of us knew what to say. I had the urge to burst into tears again, but I wanted to be strong in front of him.

I felt anything but strong as yesterday's memories played through my mind on repeat. When she arrived at the antique store, she'd been so reserved and on guard. By the end of the night though, her personality had fought to reach the surface. I had watched her closely and listened for the things she didn't say. I'd be lying if I told you I wasn't on guard myself. Presumptions I'd created over the years in my imagination where she was the evil stepsister in my story creeped at the back of my mind, trying to taint what was actually in front of me. My imagination could be beautiful, but it could be a weapon used against me and others just as easily.

Jordan was no evil stepsister. By the end of the night, I'd seen the ocean she called home alive in her blue eyes and the sun in her blonde hair that glowed when the firelight reflected on it.

Again, tears began to fall.

"She had a crush on you," I found myself mumbling to Evan when I couldn't take the quiet any longer. "She asked me all about you and our relationship when we met up. She thought you were a real gentleman, and grown up, and she liked that."

Evan was half smiling, like he was flattered but didn't have the heart to really smile under the circumstances. "Is that why you wouldn't give me a solid answer last night? You were giving her a fair shot?"

I blushed under the tears.

He nodded as though that were all the answer he needed. "I'm not sure how to feel about girls fighting over me."

I sniffed and wiped my moist cheeks with my sleeve, Evan's soft hoodie brushing the tears off my face. "Don't let it get to your head," I said with a forced smile. "I never admitted to anything."

Evan snickered and lightly knocked my shoulder with his, mixing the sorrow in my stomach with butterflies.

The silence came again. It followed after every sentence, every thought. It tagged close behind each word, as if one wrong thing said could shatter everything to pieces in the fragility of the moment.

Finally, Evan rubbed his jaw thoughtfully. "Your mom has burned a lot of bridges. If only she'd seen that before it was too late."

I hated the thought, but for some people, this is what it took. It took learning far too late. All I could do was hope that Maya's life would be better for it.

"The night Dad died," Evan said, a slight quiver in his voice, "I felt the world close in around me. The grief felt larger than life itself. It suffocated me. I thought it was too much to bear, that I wouldn't be able to live through it. But that night, I went home and I read a letter that Dad handed to me before he died. He gave each of us one—Mom, Ava, and me.

"In my letter, he gave me purpose. He told me that he needed me to fill his shoes now that he was gone. He wanted me to be the glue that held our family together. That seemed impossible at the moment—I couldn't even hold *myself* together. But as time went by, and the funeral was behind us, and the reality of our new life set in, I was thankful for a purpose. Something to strive for. A tangible goal to reach for." Evan paused to face me for the first time since beginning his story. "Ivy Hollow was my way of doing that. I wanted to fight for the dream that we'd had as a family. I got my mom on board and made it happen. And I still believe it's what we needed. Ava needed Maya, my mom needed Jo, and I needed you."

My stomach fluttered again, and my bruised fingers gripped the scratchy couch, despite the pain that shot through them.

Evan noticed me tensing up, and he fought to hide a smirk, but he leaned back in his seat and kept going. "Now that Jordan's gone, your mom is going to need a purpose. And I think it's you, Rain. Maybe not yet, but I don't think God arranged all of these pieces by accident. She has a lot of holes to fill, and He's the only one who can fill them, but I wouldn't be surprised if He's going to use you to start the process."

Moments ago, my heart had broken at the gut-wrenching sound of my mother's cries. I'd wanted to go to her and wrap my arms around her. But when it really came down to it, could I actually be the one to help her recover when she had been the one to cause my pain? She'd tried to take my life, and she robbed me of my twin. Could I be the one to comfort her after the death of the child she'd wanted?

I knew I could. Because I'd been forgiven of much, I could forgive her, too. And I had. A long time ago. But I'd learned forgiveness wasn't always a one-time event. It was a daily choice to love someone and put behind you what was in the past. And sometimes, you had to forgive even when you never got the apology.

My mom didn't deserve my forgiveness or my love. But I didn't deserve God's forgiveness and love either. And I didn't deserve Jo's love or Evan's friendship. The truth is, none of us are entitled to anything. All of it is freely given. And if we could just grasp that, how much more would we give? How much more beautiful would life be?

I still wasn't sure that Mom would let me into her life, but if she would, I would be ready for her. Ready to open my arms to her, and tell her I loved her, and that I couldn't wait for her to be my mom.

I shifted in my seat on the couch before smiling at Evan. "I can't think where I'd be right now if I hadn't told you all of this. If I hadn't trusted you," I said, using my stubbed arm to massage my hand. The throbbing was getting worse, and the pressure seemed to help.

Evan grabbed my hand again and began gently massaging it with his fingers. Jordan had been right. He was a gentleman.

My eyes welled with tears again.

So many terrible things had occurred at the beginning of my life, and yet God somehow redeemed each part of it. My biological family had hurt and abandoned me, and yet He surrounded me with the most incredible group of people I could have ever asked for.

Jordan hadn't gotten that the way that I had.

There was a time that I'd been jealous of her and ached to be wanted the way she had been, yet she would have given everything for our mom to love her the way Jo loved me. To be accepted by her the way that the Clarks had accepted Jo and me. To have a friend like I had in Evan.

"Well," Evan said, his eyes still on my hand, "I'm glad you know I'm on your side. I always have been."

I thought back to my outburst in his truck after Jordan cornered him at the diner. I'd lost it on him in my fear.

I released a heavy sigh. "I know you have. It wasn't you I doubted or was upset with, but I took it out on you. I shouldn't have, Ev."

He waved a dismissive hand. "It's alright. I knew what you were going through. You can take it out on me any time. That's what friends are for."

"Nothing about how I blamed you made me a good friend."

"Hindsight is twenty-twenty. Sometimes, though, you just act. Trust me, I get it. And it's okay."

"Yeah, but I had a temper tantrum worse than Ava."

A doubtful laugh escaped him, and he shook his head. "Oh no, Ava still has you beat. You'll have to try harder next time if that's what you're aiming for."

I made eye contact with Jo across the lobby as she approached us, and I felt Evan's hand slide off of mine awkwardly, but she definitely saw, and I couldn't keep from smirking at him as he blushed.

"Reagan is with Maya now," she said, sitting on the coffee table in front of us. "And they're wrapping up Ava's surgery. They should let you in to see her within the next hour or so."

"That's good," Evan said. "Is my mom alright?"

"She's still waiting upstairs. I talked to her for a bit. She's doing fine." Jo faced me and looked me over like she was trying to see how I was holding up. "I got permission to leave early. I think we should head home to avoid bumping into Reagan. The rain has slowed down a lot. We ought to go take a look at the truck."

"Let me take you home," Evan butted in. "We'll get the truck towed and worry about it later. I'll take you home tonight."

"No, stay with Ava. We'll be fine," I said.

"It'll be a bit before I can see her anyway. It's cold and wet. Let me do it."

Jo nodded at me, and I agreed.

As Evan took us home, me in the passenger seat and Jo in the back, I watched the world outside roll by. It was dark, and the clouds hid the stars in the sky, making it feel even darker. My throat began to feel tight again, and a few tears slipped from my eyes, masked by the dark. Yet Evan seemed to sense my strength failing me.

He turned his head to glance at me briefly. "Tonight will be the hardest," he said. "Get some rest. Tomorrow will be better." His pinky tapped my hand resting on the center console between us. "And put some ice on that hand before bed. Let Jo get a good look at it."

I snickered. "My hand is fine, Ev."

"It's the only one you've got," he teased. "We gotta make sure it's taken care of. What if you can't paint anymore?"

"I can paint with my mouth."

"I guess that's true."

Once home, Evan opened Jo's door, and then he walked over to open mine.

After I slid out of the passenger seat, he stood in front of me, eyes searching mine in the dim light coming from his headlights. "Call me when you wake up tomorrow," he said.

"I will."

"Are you going to be okay?"

I smiled and gave him a steady nod. "I'll be fine."

"I know you will. I'll make sure of it."

I watched his truck disappear from the living room window while Jo looked at my hand.

"It's just a sprain," she confirmed.

"That's what I thought."

"He's a good guy, isn't he, Rain?" she said.

I offered up a reluctant nod.

Jo smiled and planted a kiss on my forehead. "You'll never know how thankful I am that you came into my life, Rain Brooks. Your past is hard, but I'm selfishly so thankful. Remember that always."

I wrapped my arms around her, and she held me tightly. I felt her tears hit my neck. "My past is hard, but I wouldn't change it for the world if it meant I wouldn't have you as my mom."

She paused, and when she spoke, her voice was laced with tears. "I'm glad you feel that way. A lot of people would be resentful," she said. "But you've always had a fire in you, Rain. A zeal for life and a determination to love it, no matter what. I've learned so much from you."

"Well, I probably learned it from you first. Your life hasn't exactly been easy either."

"We've learned from each other, then," she agreed. "Now try and rest. We can face this tomorrow with clear heads. Tonight, we sleep."

I did try, and it eventually came. But not for a long time. I lay in bed thinking about my sister for hours, well into the morning, wishing I'd met her sooner. Wishing I'd known her better. Wishing

I'd been brave enough to face her and welcome her that first day she walked into my life.

And the weighty thought of her lifeless body at the hospital, our mom crying over her, threatened to smother me.

EVAN

"Never say goodbye because goodbye means going away and going away means forgetting."

J.M. Barrie, Peter Pan

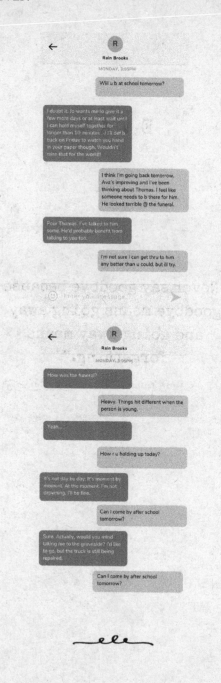

I went through the motions.

Without Rain there, school felt sort of lifeless and empty. The day seemed to drag on forever.

I'd never really spent time with Jordan at school before, but I'd at least known she was there. I'd felt her presence enter the room when Rain would tense up upon seeing her. I'd snuck glances across the cafeteria, looking for a resemblance between them. I'd watched her, trying to decide if I thought she was skeptical of Rain or not.

And now I felt her absence.

Her funeral was heavy.

We went, of course, mostly so that Ava could be there for Maya. Her leg was still in bad shape, but she insisted on being there. It made me proud of her.

I couldn't help but have flashbacks of the last funeral I'd been to. I was much more alert and observant at this one. At Dad's, I had been in a complete daze. But I'd promised Rain I would pay close attention and tell her everything after it was over.

She and Jo decided not to go. They knew that for Reagan to recognize them was the last thing she needed. It killed Rain not to be there, but she knew it was best.

So I watched everything. I watched the faces of Jordan's family—her mom, dad, sister, and aunt—as the casket was lowered into the earth. I watched as they threw a few roses onto the casket as a final farewell. I watched the heartbroken faces of the few friends who'd traveled to Ivy Hollow for the event, and the faces of strangers from Ivy Hollow who came to show their support. You didn't have to know her to be struck by the loss of her. There's something about losing the life of a youth that stirs something in all of us. It awakens a fresh fear of our own fragile mortality.

Her two friends were there—the girls Jordan told Rain and me about at the bonfire. The ones who slowly let the distance pull them apart until they eventually abandoned her. They were here for her now, hardly able to hold themselves together.

After it ended, Ava hugged Maya as she cried. Mom grabbed Reagan's hand and told her how sorry she was for her loss. She didn't seem to hear Mom, and I thought she must feel the way that I did at Dad's funeral.

Oblivious. Numb.

Watching her parents, I couldn't help but think about what Jordan had told me about them. How absent they'd been in her life. They'd missed out on so much. And they'd never get it back.

Maybe the face that broke me most was Thomas's. He was there with his mom, and though he didn't appear to move a muscle the entire service, tears continually streaked down his cheeks.

Which is why I knew I had to go back to school. Someone had to check in on him. I didn't know if he'd even listen to me—he hardly knew me. But it was worth the effort.

When the bell finally rang for lunch, I drifted along with the swarm of other kids to the cafeteria. Thomas was already seated at his usual table when I got there. Alone. I took a deep breath and started making my way across the room to him, reciting in my mind the different things I thought I might say—things that maybe I would have found helpful when Dad died. I hoped that walking through Dad's death had prepared me for being what Rain and Thomas needed now. Grief and mourning were recent and familiar to me.

I took a seat across from him, and he didn't even seem to notice. He'd withdrawn inside of himself. There was no lunch in front of him, just an old, pulled apart rotary telephone and a set of tools. By the frustration on his face and his jerky movements, I could tell it wasn't coming together the way he wanted it to.

"How've you been holding up?" No fluff. No beating around the bush. There was nothing I hated more than that when Dad died. We all knew what happened, and none of us wanted to talk about it, but we all needed to talk about it. People tiptoed around the subject, trying to decide which side to err on. There was no right way to go about it. There's no perfect protocol to approaching grief. You just have to get through it.

"I'm fine," Thomas mumbled, his eyes lifting to glare at me while his head remained angled down over his work.

I snorted. "Yeah, right."

He lifted his head in shock at first, and then anger and rage shadowed over his eyes. He didn't say anything, even though he looked like he wanted to yell at me.

"You're not gonna figure out why it happened," I said. "You're not gonna feel better any time soon."

He released a short puff between his lips. "Aren't you a ray of hope."

"I'm just telling you the truth. You know I'm right."

He glanced at me for the briefest second before surrendering a short nod as he focused in on his telephone again.

"I guess what I wanna say is this: don't fight it. Let it come. Cry. Throw things. Maybe stop fixing things for once and break something instead. It's gonna happen whether you want it to or not. No use in fighting it." In time, I knew he would get back to his tinkering the way that I went to my garden and Rain went to her art, and it would give him purpose and motivation again. But as I watched him now, it was only an outlet for anger. Another thing that wasn't going his way.

He ignored me, but his features softened, which told me he was processing what I said.

I leaned in a little closer with my chest pressed against the edge of the table. "And then you get to decide what happens from there. You get to decide if you want to stay there or if you want to move on, even when it still sucks."

He looked over me with an impatient glare. "Why are you telling me all this? We're not even friends."

"I'd like to be. Don't let losing one friend make you push out all the people who are here for you. Rain is here for you, and I'm here for you."

Thomas leaned back in his wheelchair, letting his arms rest in his lap, still gripping a screwdriver. "She called me last night. She said your dad died. She said you wanted to talk to me."

I laced my fingers together on the table in front of me. "Yeah, he did."

"And it still sucks?"

"Yeah, it still sucks," I told him. "It always will. You won't learn how to make it go away, but you'll learn how to live in spite of it. You'll learn to let it drive you to live differently because of it, I guess. Will it make you better, or will it leave you worse?"

Thomas's gaze was exploring the cafeteria. It buzzed with life around us. There were over a hundred souls in this room, and each one had their own life. They entered this building each day like we did. Some had one parent; some had two. Some were fighting grief; some had never known it. Some looked forward to the weekend; some hated their home life.

The things that shatter us, most people around us didn't even notice. Life went on even when we feel like it should come to a screeching halt.

I had experienced that when Dad died. I felt like the world should have to stop after something so terminal shook my world at the foundation and sent it tumbling around me. But it did go on, and I ended up wanting it to. I wanted the pain to go away. I wanted some form of normalcy again, even when I knew it would never be the way it used to be. But wanting to get back to normal had made me feel a sort of guilt deeper than I'd ever known before. It didn't feel right to try and move forward, leaving Dad in the grave and carrying on with my life.

But his letter gave me his permission to. He wanted me to fight for his family—for our family—and fight for their recovery after the blow of his loss.

It was just that moving on can feel like forgetting. And I was so afraid of forgetting.

"You'll stay here a while," I said, opening my lunch bag. "You'll grieve a while. But don't get left behind. Don't be determined to stay here forever. Remember her and miss her, but don't miss out on the rest of your life just because she isn't here to do it with you."

His Adam's apple rose and fell, and I wondered if he was fighting tears. "Rain said that God has a plan in this."

"He does."

"I'm not sure I agree yet."

I rubbed at a notch in the table with my thumb, thinking about what God taught me through those blasted strawberry seeds. "Well, that's where our faith goes through the refining fire, isn't it? To see just how genuine it is. Are you only going to trust His plan when He gives you what you want, or do you trust that He's far bigger than this whole thing and good in all of it?" I took a bite of my sandwich while he chewed on my words. "God is bigger than our perception, Thomas. You're good at figuring things out. You pull things apart and find what makes them tick, what makes them run. You're good at understanding why things work the way that they do. God isn't always like that. He doesn't tell us why things happen the way they do. He tells us who He is, that He's trustworthy, that He's good, and then He tells us to have faith in His character when we can't understand."

Thomas blinked at me a few times, and that was it. He didn't say anything else, but I hoped something I had said resonated with him.

Later that day, I knew at least one thing did, because I saw him during carpool, waiting for his mom. The old rotary phone laid in pieces on his lap. He'd shattered it.

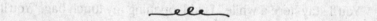

"Hey, Ev," Jo said, opening the door wider to welcome me in. Her smile seemed disingenuous, only there to aid in fulfilling her role of southern hospitality. Not that she didn't seem glad to see me, just that she seemed utterly exhausted behind it, and it worried me.

How bad off was Rain?

The smile livened slightly when she noticed the two milkshakes in my hand that I'd picked up from the diner on my way over. Cookies and cream for me, moose tracks for Rain. She opened the door wider, motioning me to enter with a nod of her head. "How's Ava?"

"She's doing okay." I crossed the threshold.

More mental pain than physical remained for Ava. She didn't remember much of the accident. She had blacked out for a lot of it, and for that, I was thankful. But what she did remember woke her up with nightmares. Each night since coming home from the hospital, Mom and I went running to her bedroom at hearing her screams. Mom crawled into bed with her and held her, while I sat outside the door, my head against the wall as I prayed she'd be able to forget.

"How's Rain?" I asked Jo, the look in my eyes begging her to be brutally honest. I'd talked to Rain a ton since it happened of course, but I wasn't sure how transparent she was being with me.

Jo released a heavy sigh wrapped her arms around herself. "I think she's okay. She's cried a lot. She spends a lot of time alone. You know how she is."

I nodded. I knew she would try to hide herself away in her grief, but I wouldn't let her. I'd give her the space she needed, but I wouldn't let her stay there long.

"I'll take you up to see her. I'm pretty sure she's painting." She made her way upstairs, with me close at her heels, and brought her ear close to Rain's bedroom door before she gave it a few taps. "Rain? Evan's here, and he comes bearing comfort food."

Her voice answered in a muffled tone. "Comfort food? In that case, I suppose you can send him in."

Jo opened the door, revealing Rain on her knees with a paintbrush between her teeth and her hand close to her face. At seeing us, she grabbed the brush from her mouth and dropped it into a glass of water alongside a variety of other brushes.

"Don't stop on my account," I said, walking in and sitting down on the floor across from her. "I've always wanted to watch you do that."

Her head nodded toward the ice cream. "How am I supposed to drink that milkshake with a paintbrush in my mouth? Priorities."

Jo announced her departure. "Keep the door open," she said, swinging it wide and shooting a playful warning glance in both of our directions.

Rain and I responded with an in-sync, "Yes, ma'am."

A silence followed, disturbed only by the echo of the creaking steps as Jo made her way downstairs again.

Rain's eyes locked on mine as an understanding rose between us that there was so much to say that couldn't actually be said.

"I figured anything is easier to face if you have ice cream beforehand." I handed her the Styrofoam cup; it squeaked as it passed from my fingers to hers.

"Not a bad rule of thumb to live by. Thanks, Ev."

I took a sip of my own milkshake and absorbed my surroundings. This was only my second time in her room, and a lot of the art on the walls seemed to be new. Aside from those, there were canvases all over the floor, and we sat on stained drop cloth. Most of the paintings were unfinished or looked like they'd been nearly finished before having a bucket of paint splattered over them in frustration.

"I've tried to paint the past few days, and I can't," Rain said when she noticed me looking. She had a wet rag on top of her hand and was using her right arm to scrub the paint off. I hadn't even gotten the chance to see what she'd been attempting. "Everything I do, I hate and destroy. Normally, when emotion is high, the colors come easy. But now, I feel empty. Colorless." Her eyes seemed desolate. She looked afraid and lost.

Her attention rose from her task, and she met my stare of concern with an apologetic smile. "I don't expect you to understand. It sounds crazy, I know. But it's strange for me. I don't even understand."

"I think I understand a little," I said, thinking about Thomas's rotary phone and my strawberry seeds again. Just another thing that wouldn't go our way.

I noticed a box of tissues next to two empty tea cups on the nightstand by Rain's rod iron bed. A small trash can overflowing with used tissues sat nearby, and another pile had accumulated next to her pillow.

"Been crying much?" I asked, nodding my head in the direction of the bed.

Her cheeks flushed, and she shrugged shyly. "Everything makes me want to cry. Like, everything. And I'm tired of crying. But the minute I stop, I feel like something's wrong with me for not crying about it more."

I remembered that feeling. I still experienced the guilt.

"And I feel out of place," she went on, pulling her straw up and down in her cup absently. "I was actually *supposed* to die, but I lived. Jordan had everything in her favor, and she's the one who's gone. It feels backward."

I stiffened. "You can't control that, Rain," I said. How could she even say something like that? She knew better. I wouldn't let her wallow in a dark hole like that. What good would it do?

She sank back, a blush washing over her cheeks as she wrapped her right arm around herself. She was cowering. From me. "I know I can't. But that doesn't keep me from thinking about it." Of course she thought about it. Who wouldn't?

I exhaled and popped my knuckles, regaining my composure. At least she was being honest with me.

My eyes lifted to one of the paintings I saw the very first time I came to her room—the girl with one hand, holding the umbrella. The one that was black and white, except for the colorful drops of rain. I leaned back on my hands and rested my head on my shoulder while I looked it over. It was bright, and yet there was a melancholiness about it. The colors made me feel excited, and yet there was a dampening sorrow brought by the wildness of the storm and the darkness of the rest of the scene. But the storm brought life, filling the painting with the much-needed hues. It was complicated.

"That one's my favorite, you know," I said, pointing at it. "It's my favorite painting you've ever done."

Rain strained her neck behind her to look where it hung on the wall. "Really? Mine too."

I stood to my feet and walked over to it, mostly because I felt my face going warm and couldn't meet her eyes. "This whole story is complex, and things didn't fall into place in a way that creates a nice ending and ties all the loose ends in perfect bows," I said, and traced my finger along the lines of the storm clouds. "I don't pretend to know the mind of God and why He does things the way that He does, but I know for certain that your life was never ever an accident."

I turned around to catch Rain's expression. Her eyes brimmed with tears, but she chuckled in an effort to fight them off. "Gosh, Ev. I just told you I cry at everything these days. Why would you do that to me?"

I laughed, too, no doubt turning beet red. But if it meant she'd cry over me being sentimental instead of crying over wishing she'd been the one to die, I'd do my best to make her sob her eyes out.

Rain sniffed and wiped her eyes with her paint-stained rag. "I think I've decided to write my mom a letter."

My eyebrows lifted. This was news to me.

"I'll wait and let her get though all of this a bit more before I send it. But I want to give her the truth, in case she's looking for it. Then, she can decide what she wants to do with it. All I know is that I can't keep waiting around to be thrown together by accident. Either we face it, or she runs again."

A smile began growing across my face. She was finding her bravery.

"I was wrong about Jordan," she said, her voice cracking. She held her nose high, staring at the ceiling as she fought the urge to cry. "I should've faced my fear, but I didn't. I succumbed to it. And now I've lost her, and I can't get the time back. I won't make the same mistake with Mom." She looked to her left where those three portraits hung in vintage frames that probably came from Mr. Clark's antique store. I hadn't been able to figure out who they were when I first saw them, except for the one of Rain. I could tell now that the other two were Jordan and Maya. Below them, she'd added two more. Reagan and Jo.

Five girls, with five very different stories, all tied together in a complex way.

"If we never meet, it won't be because I was playing it safe," Rain said.

I think in Rain's favorite books, bravery seemed to come a lot more naturally to the heroes and heroines. It seemed to be a one-time resolve—a quick change in their personality. For Rain, it didn't happen that way. It took time and loss to force her to move forward. She wanted things to stay as they were, but I think she realized the hard way life was moving on, with or without her.

It sucks, but in real life, we learn things the hard way.

I had to give it to her though—fictional heroes give us something to look up to. Something to aspire to be. Because even when they overcome their fears easier or faster than we do, they struggle first, and we empathize with that. Seeing them overcome makes us believe that we can, too.

Rain slurped the last bit of her milkshake before standing to her feet. She gathered her wavy hair into her hand to twist it and lay it over her shoulder. It was loose today. "Well, if there was ever a time to write a paper like this, now was the time to do it. You didn't end up having to wrack your brain for something to write about after all. It was handed to you on a silver platter."

"I wish some of it hadn't been."

Writing what had happened over the past several days had been the hardest easy thing ever. I had plenty of momentum to add drive to the story, but it was heavy. It felt too soon to process what had happened. But the emotion was still fresh on my mind, so it came easily. I had plenty to write but spent half the time cradling my head in my hands wishing I didn't have to.

Rain swallowed hard. "So do I. But, I also know that these events all add up to create a masterpiece much bigger than ourselves. Our lives are just the small strokes of something larger and more complex. We don't have to understand it, we just have to trust the Artist."

"It's easier said than written though," I said, ruffling my fingers through my hair. "I still don't know how to tie this story up before Friday when I feel like we've only just hit the climax."

Rain walked over to her bed to grab her crossbody bag that hung from the rod iron bed frame. "Sometimes, the best endings are the ones that leave scope for the imagination. The reader doesn't necessarily have to know how the story ends, they just have to believe that the characters will be okay, no matter what happens after they close the book."

The wheels in my head began turning, thinking of how I could wrap it all up without knowing the end myself.

"I just wish Jordan could have read it," Rain said, brushing invisible wrinkles out of her black, floral skirt.

Along with catching up on the recent events, I'd spent time typing like mad to add Jordan's perspective in. After the bonfire, I felt sure the story wasn't complete without her side. After the accident, I knew. When I got her text just shortly before it happened saying that she'd found the forgiveness I'd told her about, and once Ava and Maya told us all that she'd said in the car just before the crash, I knew our story wouldn't be complete without her final chapter. Because as much as it hurt, it was the chapter of her story that mattered most. It ended sooner than it should have, but she found the new beginning she was looking for, and I couldn't leave that out. Maybe it's weird, but I felt I owed it to her. No one else in Jordan's life seemed to listen to her or care to see her—really see her. But I did. I saw through her mask of indifference. I saw through her carefree display. I listened to her every word at the bonfire that night—and heard the ones she never said—and I hadn't been able to stop thinking about her story since.

Rain's eyes lifted, and she smiled at me. "Writing preserves a person and who they are, and you've given all of us that. In a way, you gave us a sort of Neverland. Thanks to you, there's a piece of us that'll never die or grow old."

The wind outside blew, shaking the shutters outside Rain's bedroom window, and I watched autumn leaves ride by through the air.

I thought about her words. All of them. The quirky little things she'd said to me since our very first conversation at Mr. Clark's antique shop.

"You told me one time that you'd tried your hand at poetry. I bet you're pretty good at it. Everything you say sounds like poetry to me," I said.

She laughed and eyed her bookshelf. "I have journals stuffed full of poetry from my middle school days. I still write it every once in a while, but I don't practice enough to be great."

"Will you let me read some? Now that you've read my work, I think it's only fair."

Rain hesitated in thought but eventually nodded. "Not the middle school stuff. I ought to burn that," she said with a laugh. "But I guess I can come up with something for you." Her laugh faded as her eyes landed on the open door behind me, and dread fell over her face as she remembered what was coming next.

"You ready for this?" I asked, fumbling with my truck keys in my pocket.

She shook her head slowly and gripped her bag tighter. "Not really, but I have to do it."

I just wished I could do it for her.

blue

surrender; clarity; peace & rest

RAIN

> "She was a lovely lady, with a romantic mind and such a sweet mocking mouth. Her romantic mind was like the tiny boxes, one within the other, that come from the puzzling East, however many you discover there is always one more; and her sweet mocking mouth had one kiss on it that Wendy could never get, though there it was, perfectly conspicuous in the right-hand corner. The way that Mr. Darling won her was this: the many gentlemen who had been boys when she was a girl discovered simultaneously that they loved her and ran to propose to her except Mr. Darling, who took a cab and nipped in first, and so he got her. He got all of her except the innermost box and the kiss."
>
> J.M. Barrie, *Peter Pan*

"I'LL GIVE YOU A minute and then come back," Evan said, his hand landing on my shoulder. I tensed at his gesture without meaning to.

Jordan had been laid to rest in the earth beneath me. The only indication of her former existence was the gray tombstone with a few words and dates. That's all.

I nodded, and Evan walked away.

From my purse, I pulled out a painting on a little, palm-sized square of watercolor paper. It depicted a bursting sunset in bright, passionate colors over an ocean—an ocean full of stars. I'd painted it the night of the bonfire after I'd gotten home. My heart had been full. The colors were uncontainable.

I sniffed in an effort to keep my nose—bit by the chill in the air and encouraged by the tears rising in my throat—from running.

"I was so, so wrong about you," I whispered, laying the paper down on the grave and tucking it into a small bouquet of daisies someone had left. Someone had been here recently, because they were alive and well. I couldn't keep from smiling even as the first tear escaped and tumbled down my cheek, because, thanks to Jo's flower addiction, I knew that daisies were the perfect flower for Jordan; they're symbolic for both innocence and new beginnings.

"If I could go back, I'd welcome you to our school and to our town. Even if I never told you who I was. Even if you never knew we were sisters." A frigid wind blew, and I wrapped my sweater tighter around myself as my shoulders shook in shivers.

Over the past few days, I'd sat alone in my room thinking through the "what-ifs." What if I'd been brave and selfless? What if I'd been less afraid of the unknown and more concerned about being the friend my younger sister needed in a new place? I'd have known how much she was hurting. I'd have seen how much she needed me.

"I wanted Mom to find me and let me into her life, but I wasn't even willing to take the chance for myself and welcome you. I'm your older sister, and I failed you." The wind bit at my nose, but it was nothing compared to the steady ache of guilt in my chest. "I'm so sorry, Jordan."

My numb fingers brushed the daisy petals. If I could help it, I wouldn't make the same mistake twice. I'd be there for Mom if she'd let me. And for Maya.

Reagan,

It's been a while, and I don't know if you ever expected to hear from me. I'm not sure if you want to hear from me. But maybe you do.

Almost eighteen years ago, you left me behind at a hospital in Richmond. While you were there, you met a nurse in the NICU who helped care for me. Her name was Joanne. Maybe you remember. I want you to know she adopted me.

She never hid the truth about who I am, and I've always known the circumstances of my birth. I've always known about you and your family. About my twin. About your two daughters.

For a while, I struggled with my past. I wondered why things had to happen the way they did. But then, I came to realize I wouldn't change my story for the world. The family God gave me through the most painful parts of my story have been a blessing and pure grace.

It also convinced me of what I believe about the value of human life. It has made me the person I am today.

I want you to know I forgave you years ago. I always pitied you more than I resented you.

After Jo adopted me, we moved to Ivy Hollow and have built our life here.

I know the panic you're experiencing, because I felt it myself when I realized who the new girl at my school was. I had the opportunity to get to know Jordan shortly before she passed. The short time I knew her was enough to make my life brighter. It was enough to make it feel darker when she left.

You're going through so much right now, but I want you to know I would love an opportunity to get to know you the way I got to know Jordan. I would love the opportunity to reconcile, put the past behind us, and move forward together. I would love to meet you and Maya and get the chance to make up for lost time.

I've had so much regret since Jordan passed for not having met her sooner. I want to avoid making the same mistake again.

If not, I hope you know that regardless of the past, I love you. I forgive you. I'm praying for you. And I hope you're able to find healing.

I hope you know I'm here, for you and for Maya, whenever you're ready. No matter how much time passes.

Love,

Rain Olivia Brooks

I held the letter to my chest after reading it for the one-hundredth time.

"I have to do it," I whispered. My courage was failing me.

But I knew I had to do it.

All of my life I'd wondered if I would be rejected again or accepted by my mother, and now it all hinged on this piece of notebook paper and ink.

I looked at the clock. It was seven minutes until midnight, but I still had one letter left to write and a promise to keep. My hand was still sore from my fall, and writing the first letter to Mom had it aching. So I kept Evan's letter short.

Evan,

Not long ago, you asked me how much truth there was to the fictional thoughts you penned for me. You told me there were things you wanted me to say for myself. You also told me you wanted a poem.

So, I've decided to kill two birds with one stone, and I'm attaching both with this letter.

Yours,

Rain

Blue.

That's all.

It was a soft blue. It told of calm waters, summer skies, and peace. Sweet peace.

My hand was covered in it before I left for school; my first day back since it happened. My first day painting my hand since it happened without immediately wiping it off.

The peace came in refreshing waves. It didn't stay; it ebbed and flowed like the tide on the beach. It fell like a summer rainstorm on a hot, sunny day. It didn't stay, but it kept coming.

Jo's hand wrapped around mine as the truck rolled to a stop at school. She shot me a knowing look. One that told me I could do it. It would be fine.

Fine and nothing more, but fine nonetheless.

I smiled back and slid out of the truck, immediately spotting Evan in the parking lot.

"Today's the big day," I said, falling into step with him. "Did you get it all wrapped up?" He had his typewriter case in hand which led me to think he had not.

"I'm going to finish it over lunch," he said, which was a little risky if you ask me. "How did the letter to your mom turn out?"

I readjusted my backpack. I'd brought the letter with me so he could look over it later, and I swear I could feel the weight of it on my shoulders. "Good, I think. Either way, it is what it is. The ball will be in her court. I've said my piece, and I'm at peace. Whatever happens, I'm okay."

Evan turned his head to face me and he looked as though he were trying to decide if he believed me. "Even if you never find out why your name is Rain?"

"It's funny; I haven't cared about the meaning of my name since the day you gave it your meaning," I said, fixing my gaze on my shoes. "The day you told me that it was rain that brought life to your garden, and it was me who brought your life back." I reluctantly glanced up to find his green eyes staring at me, and the softest smile tugging at the right corner of his lips. His look gave me a feeling that was abstract and wild. Uncontrolled splashes of red, orange, pink, and yellow.

Passion. Love. Joy. Excitement. Happiness. Warmth.

The most color I'd felt since Jordan left.

Evan stopped walking and set down his typewriter. I turned to face him and watched as he took my hand into his own to examine it. "Blue must be the color for new beginnings," he said. "Starting fresh."

I nodded, because in a way, he was right. I wasn't going to fight the future any longer. I was ready, come what may. A peace that far surpassed all understanding had settled in my heart. I trusted my Storyteller.

"All this writing about me has you knowing me better than I know myself."

He shook his head slowly, still looking down at it. "I could spend the rest of my life getting to know you, Rain Brooks, and I wouldn't even scratch the surface."

"I'm not sure about all that."

He raised his head. "I am."

I hoped he couldn't see the bright red I could feel washing over my face.

We were nearly to the front of the school building, just standing there, my hand in his and a typewriter at our feet. Kids swarmed around us as they entered, eyebrows lifting, nudging each other and whispering as they passed. I knew without a shadow of a doubt we'd be the gossip of Ivy Hollow by lunch time. But Evan didn't seem to notice them or care if he did.

"You want to know what I thought to be one of the most interesting quotes in *Peter Pan*?" he asked.

"Which one?"

"It talks about Mrs. Darling's romantic mind being like boxes stacked in one another and a kiss on her lips. And of Mr. Darling it says, 'He got all of her except the innermost box and the kiss.'"

I smirked. Barrie's writing was brilliant, and I would never grow tired of it. "Yes, I've always quite liked that quote myself."

"I'll bet you do."

I narrowed my eyes. "What does that mean?"

"It's how you are. It resonates with you."

"You think so?"

He nodded, and his gaze was searching. "There's always one more little box in your mind to open, and a kiss in your smile that I've never quite gotten."

My throat tightened, but I wouldn't walk away this time. It was time to grow up. Wendy knew when it was time, and she embraced the beauties of adulthood with grace. I would, too.

"Well, don't ask me for it now." I tightened my hand around his. His fingers were rough and calloused from the hard work he'd put them through over the summer. "Because I'm afraid I haven't got a thimble with me to give you."

Evan laughed, and his evergreen eyes sparkled with amusement. Fall was here and winter was coming, but his eyes would suffice for all the green I lacked until summer. "I wouldn't dare ask it from you now," he said. "Just like I had to earn your trust to get your story, I have a lot to prove before I get the kiss. I know that. I'm ready for that."

My eyes met his, steady and sure, and I imagine they sparkled just as much as his. "One day," I said, "I think I will give you that kiss."

Evan ran his thumb over my painted fingertips. "Until then, a thimble will do."

"Then, I will be sure to get you one. I do have one thing for you now though," I said, and removed my hand from his to reach into my back pocket. It was at rare times like this I wished I had my second hand. I never wanted to have to slip mine away from his again. "I believe I promised you a poem. Read it later."

He put it into his own pocket with a nod and a gleam of anticipation.

We walked into homeroom and sat toward the back like we always did. Yet today was entirely different. Her seat was empty, and it appeared that no one had the heart to fill it.

Evan noticed me staring at it, and he leaned over in his chair to tug gently on one of my braids to get my attention. "You gonna be okay?" he whispered.

I nodded, but I could feel tears welling up.

How interesting it is that it isn't the amount of time you know a person that determines how much of an impact they have on your life; it's something else. A sort of connection. It's how much you know them and how determined you are to know them better.

The final bell rang, and the class settled down to a hush.

And like it or not, life went on.

I knew that from here, all I could do is what I've always done, or at least tried to do well.

Never resent my past, because it has been perfectly plotted by the Master Storyteller.

Never forget the people who left their mark on me and the things they taught me. People are added to our lives at different times with great purpose.

Move forward, determined to make today worth living.

And then always remember that the One who carried me through it all goes ahead.

Peter Pan fought growing up, but I fought growing. Because the scary parts of our stories and the parts that sting are storms. But it's the rain that causes growth, brings life, and creates color.

It's messy now, but when you zoom out, you begin to see the masterpiece He's been working on all along.

Jo called it a fire, but it's really just faith.

God redeemed my story before, and despite the storm I find myself in now, I know I can trust Him with the end.

EVAN

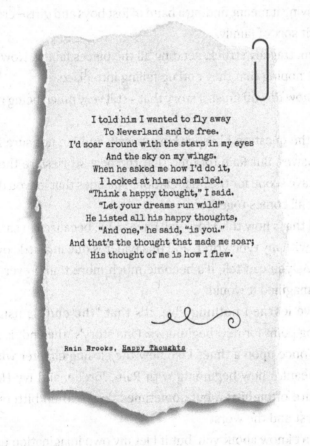

I told him I wanted to fly away
To Neverland and be free.
I'd soar around with the stars in my eyes
And the sky on my wings.
When he asked me how I'd do it,
I looked at him and smiled.
"Think a happy thought," I said.
"Let your dreams run wild!"
He listed all his happy thoughts,
"And one," he said, "is you."
And that's the thought that made me soar;
His thought of me is how I flew.

Rain Brooks, *Happy Thoughts*

"IT WAS THE BEST of times, it was the worst of times," Dickens began, in his iconic classic, *A Tale of Two Cities*. Ironic that the very first

ABIGAIL HAYVEN

line of that confounded book turned out to be some sort of weird prophecy or something, because in a lot of ways, this school year was just that for each of us. The best and the worst.

Summer grief led to chasing dreams, and the loneliness faded into smoke over an autumn bonfire, lifting up to a starry sky that told of Neverland. Neverland was the way to escape change, and yet leaving it meant finding a band of lost boys and girls—creating a misfit sort of family.

Then, tragedy struck, sending all the pieces falling. Now we're all just hoping that they end up falling into place.

So, how do you finish a story that's still very much being played out?

It's the question I keep asking myself, and I'm not sure I have the answer. But Rain told me that the best stories are the ones that leave scope for the imagination. The ones that let you decide how it all comes together.

And that's how this story will have to be, because I'm sitting at lunch with my typewriter, and this paper is due in a little over an hour. As you can tell, it's become much more than I ever could have imagined it would.

If I've learned nothing else, it's that "the end" is usually a starting point for new beginnings. One story's "the end" is a new one's "once upon a time." Like how the closing chapter with my dad meant a new beginning with Rain, Jordan, and Ivy Hollow. Ends are often bitter, but sometimes they end up bittersweet. The best and the worst.

I don't know about you, but if I let my own imagination tell the end of this story, there's a "happily ever after" after all.

Rain's mom finds the healing and reconciliation she needs and becomes a part of a real family, like Jordan was able to.

My own family embraces the new beginning I came to Ivy Hollow looking for, and the empty space that remains gives us room to draw even closer to each other than before.

Rain keeps on being Rain. Looking for the best in life and making everything she touches her own kind of colorful.

And me? Well, I like to think we get a good crop this spring. And I like to think that I end up with a kiss that means even more than a thimble.

But until then, I'll keep going through the boxes of the girl who wears her heart in colors at the end of her sleeve.

So here it is. Do with it what you will.

The End.

A NOTE FROM THE AUTHOR

LIKE RAIN, MY OWN story was never a shock to me, and I never gasped upon hearing it told. Well, at least not the first part. It's hard not to ask questions when you still have the scar.

I grew up listening to every family member's different retelling of the story, and while every retelling is suspiciously unique, almost everyone agrees upon the shock of the doctors and nurses as I scooted across the table after birth. Some family members make it sound like I was practically crawling, though I'd take it with a grain of salt, knowing that tales always get taller as the years go by.

All of them remember how I proved the doctors wrong, eventually taking my first steps and countless ones after, and excelling in all the things they said I wouldn't do.

God proved the doctors wrong.

I grew up knowing the story by heart and telling it. I remember praying as a small child that He would use my miraculous healing to bring Him glory somehow.

In middle school, I was told by a teacher to write out a true story, much like our friend Evan had to—one that, if it hadn't happened, would have altered my life forever. Unlike Evan, however, I had no trouble finding something to write about. I was literally *born* with that story.

That evening, I went home to separate the facts from the fiction. Instead of combining all the tales I'd heard over the years, I went to my parents to ask about the exact circumstances of my birth.

I wasn't at all expecting the plot twist that came with it.

I was diagnosed with one of the most severe forms of Spina Bifida a few months into my mom's pregnancy—that much I knew. But I never knew how hard the doctor pressured my parents to abort me. I never knew that he tried to keep them from taking home any ultrasound photos of me so they wouldn't get attached. I never realized how disabled babies were deemed unfit and unworthy of life based on someone else's opinion that their quality of life would be less than.

As a kid, I knew about abortion; my parents were pro-life after all. But I always imagined it to be something that was done secretly and illegally in back alleys somewhere, and only by really mean, evil people. Because most people were too good to even fathom killing babies.

I never imagined it happened in hospitals, where doctors whose jobs were to improve quality of life, would be suggesting murder when there was a lack of it. I never imagined the numbness of our society to something that could have deemed me unworthy of life without even asking me if I wanted to give it a chance.

My eyes were opened to the reality of abortion that night and the reality of God's grace to me—that I'd been born to pro-life parents when so many had not been.

As I grew older, my heart continued to grow softer and more passionate for the pro-life cause, and shortly after graduating high school, I found myself in a development position at my local

Pregnancy Resource Center. The way God worked that out is another wonderful story for another time.

During my nearly three years of volunteering and then working there, I learned so much truth about abortion. I met women who'd had one. I sat across from women considering it. I cried through memorials for the lives lost to it.

I saw the darkness touch so many places. It brought damage and despair to babies, women, couples, men, grandparents, friends, communities, and our nation.

Creatures made in God's image are not easily disposable. The voluntary taking of a life comes with consequences that can be present for generations.

After moving away from my hometown to a new state, I sat down to write *The Colors of Rain*, wanting to get across the reality of the domino effect. I wanted to show the pain and the loss that abortion leaves in its wake in a world that glorifies it as empowering and merciful.

I want us to consider the truth, and the stories within *The Colors of Rain* are meant to illuminate it.

Abortion harms women. Chances of suicide go up dramatically after having an abortion. It enables rapists and traffickers to hide their abuse for the right price. It can leave lasting effects of depression and even symptoms similar to PTSD, like you saw in Reagan.

It affects future children when their mothers fail to connect with them out of guilt for their missing child, like you saw in Jordan's story.

It causes abortion survivors like Rain, and those who are disabled like Thomas, to question their worth because someone else deemed them unfit to live.

This is truth. This is the reality of "women's empowerment."

But there is a greater truth I want us to walk away with.

Our God is in the redemption business.

He lives and brings life.

He overcomes darkness with light.

He forgives and He cleans.

He makes all things new and redeems.

He's a Master Storyteller, bringing His children from backgrounds of despair to stories of victory.

He's the Master Artist, using the dark shades to highlight His glory.

He never condones sin, but He isn't confined.

He'll take it and remake it until it's refined.

I have seen women redeemed from past abortions. I've seen God use survivors to be voices for those without one. I've seen families heal and thrive.

Because the reality of abortion is great, but the sacrifice of Christ for sin was far greater.

The Colors of Rain is a story of truth. One of darkness, yet much more so of redemption.

I can't help but wonder whose eyes will skim these pages and how your own story has unfolded. I wonder who you relate to most—Evan who mourned a life lost too soon, Rain who feared facing the next chapter, or Jordan who just wanted a place her soul could call home. Perhaps you're Reagan, or see yourself in Thomas.

Regardless, I hope you take away a little something from each of their stories.

God is the Gardener, bringing about a kingdom harvest greater than our own perception of success.

God is the Artist, creating a masterpiece where we are but tiny strokes that collect to produce an image of His glory.

God is Home, a New Beginning, the place of all true and lasting satisfaction where we can find rest for our weary souls—no matter our past rebellion.

My friend, as you close this story, I pray you've found bits of hope to help you trek through your own. I pray you've found truth and reflections of glory.

It's why I write.

That His story may be told through me.

Until next time,

Abigail Hayven

ACKNOWLEDGEMENTS

THE COLORS OF RAIN has been a long time coming. While I'm only mentioning a handful of individuals here, over the past eight years as I've written and rewritten, abandoned and returned to this story, so many different people have impacted my life and have helped this book get where it needs to be.

I think I must first thank McKenna--my "writer friend," and *The Colors of Rain's* very first beta reader. M, thank you for listening to my rants as I worked through plot holes, for helping me navigate this story while it was at its messiest, and for encouraging me throughout the whole process. TCOR is a better book because of you, and my life has more color because of your friendship!

I also want to thank my parents for instilling a love for both reading and entrepreneurship that eventually led me to pursuing professional writing. Their decision to homeschool me and their encouragement to pursue my talents has been monumental in getting me where I am today.

I have to commend Victoria and the entire Glory Writers Press team. I don't think I could have chosen a better press for this story, and the way they've brought my humble little book to life has been beyond satisfactory! Working with them has been a true joy and has created lasting friendships. Thank you for all that you've invested in *The Colors of Rain*, and for creating a press with a mission as valuable as its stories.

I must also include Mrs. Mandy, who played an incredible role behind the scenes to make my dream of publishing *The Colors of Rain* a reality. Thank you for always supporting me. I'm so incredibly grateful that I've had you in my life all these years. You are more of a blessing to me than you will ever know!

And of course I cannot close without acknowledging my beloved husband. John, you've been my voice of reason on the days I wanted to give up, motivating and encouraging me as I juggled publishing this book, planning our wedding, and settling into our new life together. You surpass all the fictional crushes my hopeless-romantic-heart ever had (yes, even Gilbert Blythe), and you love and pursue me harder than any romance novel love-interest could ever compete with. I could fill these pages with words of adoration, and still never fully express how much I love and adore you!

MEET THE AUTHOR

Abigail Hayven is a wife and entrepreneur, but she was once a girl who couldn't get enough books to read. So she began writing to fill the void.

Now with a background in pro-life ministry and a continuing passion for storytelling, Abigail has decided to write about the issues she's most passionate about. Her prayer is that young, hungry readers like herself would find compelling plots, relatable characters, and an abundance of thought-provoking truth in the books that she writes. Abigail's greatest passion in life is to glorify her King and hopes to point others to His story through all that she creates.

When she isn't penning novels, you might find her playing the role of barista at the coffee shop she co-owns, baking something scrumptious, or spending time with her husband and best friend, John.